I0594400

Send Me Crazy

T. GEPHART

Published by T Gephart
Copyright 2019 T Gephart
ISBN: 978-0-6483959-8-0

Discover other titles by T Gephart at the retailer of your choice or on Facebook (https://www.facebook.com/pages/T-Gephart/412456528830732), Twitter (https://twitter.com/tinagephart), Goodreads, or tgephart.com.

This book is a work of fiction. The names, characters, places and scenarios are products of the writer's imagination or have been used fictitiously and are not to be construed as real. Any resemblance to persons, living or dead, actual events, locales or organizations is entirely coincidental.

Cover by Hang Le
Editing by Insight Editing Services
Formatting by Elaine York Allusion Graphics LLC, www.allusiongraphics.com

Send Me Crazy

To Kelly,

You've not only been an amazing friend but a fantastic wingwoman to my crazy. Here's your book.
#DeleteTheMessages #WhatPackage

QUINN- Hey Babe-a-licious, I'm back! Also, don't hate me. But I sent Brad a package guaranteeing he'd meet you for a date! I know, I know none of my business . . . but seriously, he needed a push and it was easier to do while I was out of the country. You can yell at me for it later. Clearly, you're no longer mad. #Winning.

KARLI - Quinn! Girlfriend, I've missed you. Um . . . what package and note? I'm not meeting Brad for a date, what are you talking about?

QUINN- Maybe he didn't get it yet? How long does USPS take to send a red racy G-string? I included coordinates for Beans or Bust. You're welcome.

KARLI - I'm going to kill you! Where did you send it?

QUINN - Ummmm to his apartment, sweet cheeks...where else? 264 Hudson

KARLI - QUINN! He's 246 not 264!!! Hopefully whoever got it returned it to sender.

QUINN- Well, then. No return details included and addressed it to Hot Stuff—in keeping with the theme. This just got a whole lot more interesting. Feel like an adventure? ;-)

KARLI - Lord, I already know I'm going to regret this.

Chapter 1

Quinn

GETTING INVOLVED IN people's business was literally my job.

Not as in *literally* when most people mean metaphorically, I mean literally like the word was intended to be used.

I was what you'd call a life documentarian. Sure, it's not what's on my business card but that is essentially what I do. Birthdays, deaths, marriages—I've got you. Proposals, proms, pranks—also covered. I will photograph, video or a combination of both, all your special—and sometimes private—memories so you can keep them for all time.

It's tricky too, trying to capture the moment and keep my intrusion to a minimum. But I'd made a name for myself in the business, flying all over the country—and like last week, the world—catering to clients who loved my particular brand of *life capture*. So getting tangled in a situation that didn't really involve me was an occupational hazard. And often spilled into my personal life.

"Panties, Quinn? Really? Who even does that anymore? It's not an 80's rock video." Karli blew out a breath of apparent frustration, but her smile told me different.

I rolled my eyes, glancing over the menu she was using as a prop. The coffee shop was busy enough no one was paying us any attention, not that I could convince Karli to keep her cool. And I loved my best friend but she wouldn't last thirty seconds in my line of work. Grinning, I eased back into my seat, "It's unexpected. Elicits a response. That's the *reason* I sent them."

Granted, when I sent the scarlet red lace G-string and the accompanying suggestive note, its intentions had been very clear.

Light a fire under Brad Getty's ass.

And see if he would *rise* to the occasion.

See, life was too short to sit on the sidelines playing it safe, and nothing great ever came from inaction. Better to ask forgiveness than permission. And all great journeys started with a single step. And not willing to continue sounding like one of those books in the self-help department, I preferred to get my inspiration from experience rather than between the pages.

Karli couldn't be more different.

Short, with brown eyes and corkscrew brown curls, she was the embodiment of cute-as-a-button. Add in that adorable Texan accent and manners for days, she was the polar opposite to the five-foot-eleven, blonde hair and blue-eyed Yankee that I was. I looked like a towering Amazonian when I stood next to her, our differences almost comical when we went out together. But it wasn't just looks that had us at opposite sides of the spectrum. Karli liked rules, recycled, and made homemade protein balls with vegan choc chips. While I made life choices by flipping a coin and couldn't remember the name of the last guy I'd slept with.

But to be fair, I'd been traveling through foreign countries, so it was more a pronunciation thing. Not that I cared if people raised their eyebrows at my *questionable morality*, I just wanted to make sure the facts were right.

For all our differences—Karli's heart-of-gold goodness and my fly-by-the-seat-of-my-pants madness—we were as close as sisters.

"But Brad would have known they weren't from me. Not to mention they were postmarked Paris instead of New York. Honestly, Quinn." She shook her head, her disappointment being an easy read. "I'm almost relieved you got his address wrong."

"Sure, like you enjoy being his *friend* and don't want to move this along to the next level. Wasn't it you who said that he'd missed every subtle hint? Newsflash, girlfriend, time to be less subtle."

In all honesty, Karli hadn't had a lot of opportunity. Both her and Brad worked in the restoration section of a high-end bookstore and spent their days very gently and quietly handling books older than dirt. Not like she could peel off her dust-resistant coveralls and go at it on a first edition *Pride and Prejudice*. Although, I'm fairly sure Jane Austen would have probably approved. Still, given what we were working with, I had to intervene.

Except.

Accidentally transposing the numbers in Brad's address meant I'd sent the scandalous underwear, saucy note and the playful coordinates to someone else. And while some people might have sighed, and bemoaned the lost opportunity, I decided it was the perfect chance to have a little fun. Maybe the little slip up was the universe's way for *me* to meet a new guy? Have a fling? Or at the very least make a new friend. Either way, we were staying the course and seeing if our mystery addressee turned up.

"What if it's an old lady?" Karli asked, forcing the grin as she stirred her decaf coffee.

"Honey, if it's an old lady and she still shows up, I'm shaking her hand and hanging out with her." I laughed, fairly serious about my intentions of befriending whoever walked through the door. "Come on, clearly they'd have to have a sense of humor or they wouldn't bother. And I've got nothing booked for the rest of the day. In fact, I'm going to make a promise right now." I didn't blink, putting every ounce of conviction behind my words. "Whoever shows up as a result of my little scavenger hunt, I will embrace and make an effort to get to know. It will be like a social experiment."

Sure, I'd prefer if some tall—when you're a female giant, you want someone who is taller than you—good-looking Adonis strolled through the door and made my toes curl. *Who wouldn't?* But the last few months had me questioning my purpose, with my life "documenting" making me a little cynical.

Yes, I loved my job, and the excitement that came with it. It enabled me to travel and experience so many new things. But it was always from the other side of my lens, watching vicariously while "other" people found love, happiness, and adventure. Meanwhile I was on the sidelines with their hair and makeup team making their extremely scripted proposal, complete with stenciled message in the sand, seem candid and impromptu. We'd been so caught up in documenting literally *everything*, we were missing out on living the actual moments. And for the person who was capturing those memories for everyone else, I'd missed more than my fair share.

Karli laughed, amused by my sudden and probably rash declaration. "Well, that's one hell of a promise, but if there's one person who's capable, it's you. And hell, someone just walked in." Karli's eyes widened, her head not so discreetly tipping toward the door. "Oh my God, it's a guy. He's super hot."

It wasn't that I didn't trust her judgment, but our tastes in men were markedly different. She liked guys who were cute in that farm boy kind of way. Wrangler jeans and cowboy boots—the soft strains of the anthem and the unfurling of Old Glory accompanying him as he walked. My palate ran a little more diverse and I wanted someone a little less genteel and a lot more dirty.

Carefully—I was so used to being invisible it was almost second nature to me—I turned to see the *hot guy* who'd just walked in.

And wow.

She was not wrong.

Lord, was he tall.

Not just the average *I could probably wear flats and his hairline would be above mine* either. No I'm talking TALL, as in I could break out the highest heels in my closet and he'd still be taller. He had to be six-four, six-five? Maybe even six-six, with not a single inch of him wasted. Sculpted, muscled—his clothes were doing a poor job at hiding what had to be spectacular underneath.

Dressed casually in a pair of jeans and a black Tee, he didn't look like a guy who'd work in an office. Not sure if it was his rippling muscles or his sun-kissed skin but he for sure had a job that worked with his hands. And his hands were just as impressive as the rest of him.

Strong, agile, flexing as he pulled off a pair of mirrored Aviators, they unmasked a breathtaking pair of chocolate-brown eyes that played off perfectly against his masculine chiseled jaw.

He was a Super Bowl advertisement for beer, cologne and deodorant, and I was buying whatever he was selling.

Please be him, please be him, I prayed to a nameless deity as I watched him stroll into the coffee shop and look around. I wasn't sure if he was casing the joint, checking his exits so if he robbed the place he could make a quick getaway or if he was looking for the sassy panty bandit. But either way, I was taking it as a sign and rose to my feet.

It wasn't just his body—while currently it was winning as my favorite attribute—it was a weird kind of aura that had followed him in. He didn't slouch, stumble, or try and fade into the landscape. He was casual while radiating self-confidence, every step and flick of his eyes deliberate with intent.

Jesus.

In my head I was thinking up something plausible to say. Whether I came clean about the panties or pretended to be just some random woman he'd meet in the coffee shop. I didn't have much time, the sight of his spectacular front stolen from me as he ordered his coffee. Lucky for me, my view of his amazing ass more than made up for it.

"Karli?" A gruff voice coughed from behind me as I took a step closer to the counter, interrupting my mental mapping of future dialogue. "Are you the lady who sent the panties?"

The *new guy* wasn't quiet about it either, the entire coffee shop silenced as they turned to look at me. The gorgeous mystery man was no exception.

"Excuse me?" I turned around, both confused and annoyed. "What did you say?"

"I said," new guy pulled out the scant fabric from his pocket and dangled it off his fingers, "are you the lady who sent these?"

There they were, my *panties*, like the Zapruder film shot from the grassy knoll.

While he wasn't unattractive, he was not what I'd been hoping for. Tall, and fit, and had I been about twenty years older, I would have been totally into him. Maybe. His face was weathered, deep lines marking the skin like a testimony to his years on the planet. And while I knew nothing about him, I'd been pretty good at reading people and this guy had probably seen more than most.

Not sure if it was my face or the gasp from Karli that betrayed us but a smile broke across the older man's face. He looked pleased, making no attempt to be discreet as his thick Brooklyn accent was louder than it needed to be. "Did you want them back? Or should I hold on to them for a souvenir?"

The mystery hot guy who I'd hoped had received my panties had yet to divert his attention. His interest unabashedly alternating between me and the fire engine red lace dangling from the other guy's fingers.

"Errrrr . . . it wouldn't be much of a gift if I took them back." I tried to recover, pretending that talking to strange men about my underwear was an everyday occurrence. "So they're yours. Congrats!"

Karli coughed trying to stifle her laughter as she watched with renewed purpose, from her seat at our table giving her the perfect view of all the action.

The panty thief—fine, technically not a thief since I'd sent them to him—stuffed them back into his pocket and held out his hand. "I'm Mack."

Well didn't I have a choice to make?

I could lie, pretend to be Karli—risk her tiny wrath—and leave as soon as possible.

Or come clean somewhat, tell him it was all some big misunderstanding and leave as soon as possible.

But . . . I had promised I was going to be friends with whoever turned up. And I wasn't going to renege even if my chances of talking to the hot guy with the sensational body and gorgeous face were slipping away by the second.

"Quinn," I answered without thinking, shaking his hand. "You can all go about your business." I turned to our attentive coffee shop audience. "Nothing more to see here."

He chuckled, amused by my attempt. "Not sure it works like that, Blondie. And I thought the letter said your name was Karli?"

I was just about to launch into my explanation when Karli stood. "Why don't y'all have a seat? I mean, no point everyone standing around."

Mack folded his arms across his substantial chest as he seemed to consider Karli's offer. He sure was muscular for an older guy. No middle age spread on him. "Is that what you want?" he asked, directing his question to me.

My eyes flicked to the hot dude who'd originally caught my attention, his equally hot eyebrow lifted as he waited for me to make my decision. "Sure, let's all take a seat."

I turned, internally weeping at the loss of what would have been a perfect meet cute. We'd laugh about my silly brazen attempts to get my friend and her nerd man out of the platonic zone, and then make sweet, sweet love like animals in heat. Then he'd go bench press a Chevy with his shirt off while I documented it for the good of all womankind. I mean, I said I was cynical, but some shit just *needed* to be recorded.

But alas, that wasn't what happened. Instead, I forced the grin, trying to not be any ruder as I gave Mack the attention he deserved.

"So, interesting story. I accidentally transposed the numbers on the address and sent you my panties. But I guess it all worked out, because look at us making new friends!" My hands waved with enthusiasm, not really telling poor Mack a whole lot of anything.

Although, I had to hand it to him. Not only did he sit down casually like it was no big fucking deal, but he showed complete lack of surprise. Like walking around with a stranger's panties in his pocket was totally normal, and then sitting down to have a chat was the next normal progression. "Well, that is interesting. Not only are you not Karli, but I'm not the *Hot Stuff* you were looking for. Kind of disappointing, Quinn."

Yeah, for you and me both, buddy.

"I'm Karli, and she was interfering." Karli leaned across the table, throwing out her hand. "But I had no idea she'd done any of it until after the fact."

"I interfered, sue me," I volunteered without much resistance.

"So why did you turn up? If you knew the package hadn't reached its intended destination."

It was a fair question and one I'd expected from Mack. After all, it was logical. If you accidentally dialed the wrong phone number, you didn't redial the same number. No, you cough out something inaudible or apologize and got the hell off the line. But I hadn't been running my life lately with logic high on the agenda so I saw no reason to start.

"Because, why not? If we hadn't, we wouldn't have met you." *Or seen the hot guy who'd surely left by now.* A quick glance to the counter unfortunately didn't reveal him standing there like he had been moments before. Of course he'd gone. Why would he stick around? Most of the coffee shop was back to ignoring us, especially since the lacy underwear had been stuffed back into Mack's pocket. Plus, it was New York—*weird* was just another Tuesday. Except it was Saturday, which meant the weird was even more expected.

Mack's eyes floated over me like he was doing a mental stocktake. Probably trying to decipher whether I was sincere or if Karli and I were working some elaborate plot to steal his wallet. Which ironically would also be like another day in New York.

"We should get coffee," I decided, standing up to head to the counter. "I'm buying. Karli, you want another?" I looked at her mostly untouched decaf—yeah, I wouldn't be drinking that either, girlfriend—and then to our new friend. "Mack, what are you having? Let me guess." I tapped my finger against my lip for dramatic effect. "Hmmm, soy, non-fat, two pump caramel Frappuccino, hold the foam... Just kidding, you want an Americano."

His eyes widened, my ability to *guess* his coffee order impressing him on what I thought was an obvious choice. "Um, yeah. But I think I should pay." He reached for his wallet.

"It's fine, I've got it. And while I'm gone Karli can tell you all about me and my interfering." Without giving either of them a chance to respond, I strolled to the barista hoping some caffeine might improve the situation. I mean, it could be worse. From what I could tell, Mack seemed like a decent guy and wasn't sizing us up for a black market sex ring. Not to say we were going to be launching into a long lasting friendship, but he was hot in that I-have-daddy-issues kind of way. See, it definitely could have been worse, it was just a shame that—

"You're still here." I hadn't intended to say it out loud but I was so genuinely surprised that I couldn't stop myself.

Wow.

Not sure where he'd been or why he was back but none of it was important. I'd been given a gift, a second chance, and I wasn't about to toss it away without at least talking to the man.

And Lord, what a man he was.

If he'd been impressive from across the room, up close and personal was almost cruel. He wasn't just good looking; he was breathtaking.

He was a tower.

An architectural wonder so genetically perfect I fought the urge to pull out my phone and tag myself at his location. I'd sure as hell love to *check in*, that was a certainty.

Hard lines fought against the cotton of his shirt as a halleluiah affirmation that he probably worked out. "Hi." A pair of warm chocolate eyes more sinful than a decadent fudge lava cake gave me their full attention. And I was never any good at saying no to dessert.

"So red lace, huh?" He grinned, clearly not making any attempt to ignore the earlier spectacle. "A bit stereotypical isn't it?"

Not sure if his smile was unintentionally smug or he was just cocky by nature. But I didn't know if he was trying to lighten the situation or make me blush, and not being able to read a person's motivations unnerved me.

I knew people.

I could see their manufactured smiles and fake sincerity a mile away. It was innate, an internal gauge that called bullshit whenever someone wasn't being on the level. But for some reason, I couldn't get a fix on his—flying completely blind as to whether the hot guy was flirting or calling me a fake.

Not a good place to be.

Which was why I got defensive.

"Of course it is, that was kind of the point. Not like I was going to send a pair of cotton high-waisted granny panties, that would have served zero purpose. But if you must know I do wear lace and look sensational in red." My smile edged wider as I turned to the bewildered barista, "And I'm ready to place my order."

Chapter 2

Quinn

SURE, I COULD have giggled, batted my eyelashes and flirted shamelessly with the hot dude. Because really, what did I have to lose? But he'd already accused me of one stereotype, and I wasn't going to give him just cause for a second.

So without taking a full breath I rattled off my coffee order—including Mack's boring Americano—and whipped out my credit card like I wasn't secretly intrigued by what the hot guy would do next.

He could walk—bored or offended—and take those delicious chocolate eyes and the rest of him right out the door. It was a big city, and chances of us running into each other weren't great. Especially since I'd moved here five years ago from New Jersey and it was the first time I'd seen him.

Or he could stay, and see where it took us.

"Cotton panties get such a bad rap."

So option two it was, and I couldn't get any more excited as I turned to face him. If his arms folded across his chest where anything to go by, he wasn't in any hurry to leave either. "I've seen some pretty sexy ones."

He wasn't wrong, and probably would've been interested to know that was exactly what I was wearing.

Information I'd have shared if I were flirting.

Which I wasn't.

I grinned, pretending to write on an invisible note pad. "Good feedback, I'll tell you what. I'll take that little piece of information and put it in the suggestion box for next time." I folded the invisible note and tucked it into my invisible pocket.

"Riley. Double shot cappuccino."

My eyes widened as he turned to collect his order.

"Riley," I repeated, unable to resist using the new intel I'd received. I ignored his drink choice as I watched him wrap his hand around it and bring the cup to his lips.

He took a deliberate swallow before lowering his cup and smiling. "That would be me."

"Quinn," the barista called out, three cups placed on the counter. "Americano, decaf soy latte and double shot cappuccino."

"Quinn." Riley rolled my name around in his mouth before nodding toward the coffees waiting for me. "Double shot cappuccino? Interesting."

Interesting was one choice of words, or freakishly coincidental was another. But there we were, two caffeine addicts who'd just learned each other's names and apparently shared an appreciation for underrated female cotton panties.

We were clearly meant to be.

"How do you know I'm not the one drinking the decaf?" I raised my eyebrow, wondering if he was a people reader like me. We were a rare breed, the skill diminishing with society's preoccupation with perception rather than fact.

"A woman who sends underwear in the mail isn't the decaf drinking type." He smirked, his eyes shifting from me—where I liked them—to the table where Karli was having an animated conversation while Mack looked on slightly confused. "I should let you get back."

The urge to yell, no, that Karli was more than capable of entertaining Mack while I mentally categorized every part of his body, was overwhelming. But I swallowed the urge—to speak, the categorizing was still happening—and instead nodded as I tried to juggle three cups of coffee and not end up in a burns unit.

"Yep, Mack is probably already regretting his morning. I'll go put him out of his misery," I chuckled as I winked.

I freaking winked.

Who even does that anymore unless it's an emoji? Still my attempt to leave casually had been a bust so trying to salvage it was just going to make it look worse. And I was just about to commit to my shady, awkward departure when I noticed Mack had come up beside me.

"You were going to let her carry all of these by herself? What the hell is wrong with you?" He shot Riley an angry look.

Not sure what surprised me more. That Mack felt the need to be chivalrous, and save me from the weight of carrying three coffees. Or that he accosted Riley with such vehemence, especially since Mack was at least two inches shorter, a few pounds lighter and at least fifteen years older.

Trying to ignore I was both impressed and horrified, I straightened my shoulders. "Umm Mack, I'm fine. More than capable of carrying three coffees. You should see what I can manage at a bar—six beers, two hands—without even breaking a sweat."

There were a lot of things I could use a man for, and being my drink porter didn't even make the top ten.

"See, she was fine." Riley smirked as Mack insisted on taking both his Americano and Karli's latte out of my hands.

Mack's eyes narrowed, an inappropriate amount of hostility thrown at Riley. "I didn't ask if she was fine."

Whoa.

Maybe my assessment of Mack being a nice older guy had been premature, and he was really some crazy psycho with anger management issues. It wasn't like I hadn't experienced more than my fair share of those. Especially from men who liked the gym, the steroid use was usually responsible. Well for that, and the shrunken testicles.

"Okay," I waved my free hand, the second time today calling more attention to myself than I would have liked. "Not sure what's going on here but I think we can safely assume it has nothing to do with coffee. Which is such a shame because this is a nice place and the drinks are great." My cup lifted to my lips as I took a tentative sip. "Mmmm, so good."

The effort to diffuse whatever the hell was going on wasn't my best, but it got both their attention. And as long as no one was threatening to take it outside, I think we were fairly safe. I glanced over at Karli who was on her feet, wide eyed and open mouthed, unsure of whether to get involved. She might look like a sweetheart, but her daddy taught her how to shoot a gun and hogtie a steer, so her ability to do damage was a little more than blessing-your-heart.

There was a brief game of eyeball ping-pong before Mack took a much needed breath. "This was a shitty idea."

"Now, I wouldn't say that," Riley responded, an alternate conversation apparently happening both wordlessly and without my involvement.

"You guys know each other." It should have been a question, but it wasn't. Because unless there was a serious man rage flu happening in the tri-state area, these two had at the very least a passing acquaintance.

"We've met," Riley answered, offering as little information as possible.

Mack raised an eyebrow, seeming to be surprised by Riley's admission. "We work together," he clarified.

Well that just made it a whole lot more interesting.

Karli—who had largely been spectating from the table—decided she'd stayed idle long enough and wandered over. "Y'all just happened to be at the same place?"

God love her, she was ever the optimist, assuming the chances of them being there had been some random coincidence. But I knew better. Or was more jaded. Take your pick.

"No, they're here together." I shook my head, annoyed that I'd been so distracted by the hot guy I hadn't seen it right away.

His lack of hurry, lingering at the counter—he could have ordered, collected his double shot goodness, and been out the door before Mack had even pulled out the panties. But he didn't. And I was secretly not so mad about it.

"I think it's sweet of you." My lips edged into a smile. "You came here to make sure we didn't kidnap Mack or take advantage of him."

Mack didn't share the sentiment, raising his hands to protest awkwardly while hindered by the coffees he was still holding. "That's not exactly what this is about."

Riley laughed, amused by his friend's need to set the record straight. "Oh come on, Mack. I think we should come clean and tell them how I'm here to make sure you didn't get into any trouble. And it looks like you had the same idea," he nodded to Karli.

Oh, so not the same. Not that I was angry at the development, oh hell no. I was ecstatic Mack had needed a wingman or Riley was being overly concerned. I didn't even care which of them was responsible, glad it had somehow worked out in my favor.

"Not really the same, but sure whatever. Since you've been discovered and no longer have to lurk in the shadows, why don't you come join us?"

Another wordless exchange passed between them, Riley not waiting for Mack's answer—verbally or telepathically—and shot me a smile. "I'd love to, lead the way."

The four of us walked back to the table and took a seat. Mack handed Karli her decaf—to match the one she already had sitting on the table unconsumed—and took a swallow from his cup, stretching out the silence.

"This is Karli, Karli, Riley." I offered introductions, my bright and bubbly friend presenting her hand a little too eagerly. "But the panties were mine, I was just trying to get her laid."

"Quinn!" Karli's eyes widened as she shook Riley's hand. "I'd like to tell you that she's not usually like this, but she is. Keeping up with her is almost like a fulltime job."

"Well, not sure what *Hot Stuff*'s problem is," he winked at Karli, dazzling her a little before smirking back at me. "but it was definitely his loss."

She swooned.

Right there in her chair in the Beans or Bust coffee shop, her chestnut-colored eyes got all glassy as a huge smile broke out across her face.

"Awww, you're just the sweetest." A blush crept up her cheeks as she waved her hand.

Riley shook his head, discounting Karli's assessment. "Trust me when I tell you that I'm not being sweet. You're beautiful."

His eyes momentarily swung back to me, a secretive grin playing on his lips as he surveyed his handiwork. He knew *exactly* what he was doing.

Cue Karli melting into a puddle of goo. And it wasn't just her. Every woman within hearing distance—one hot older guy and one scorching, ridiculously gorgeous twenty-something dude were bound to get attention—was heart-eyeing him with intent.

Man, he was good.

Not sure if charming was his baseline or he was just putting some extra effort in for us, but Riley could do nothing but grin and half the female population would volunteer to crawl through enemy territory just to please him.

Not me, though. Because as good looking as he was, I couldn't be dazzled by a sexy smile or enthralled by a few choice words. No, I'd seen the game too many times, usually staring down the barrel of my lens as I captured it for the masses.

That didn't mean I didn't want to smash my mouth against his, and rub myself against that body of sin. Oh hell, given half a chance I'd leap into his lap and unashamedly purr like a kitten. But falling under his spell wasn't on my agenda.

Karli managed to put her swooning on the backburner and filled Riley in on my *diabolical* plan to capture poor Brad's attention. And failing that, how we'd—i.e. me—decided to friend the random underwear recipient—Mack.

"Well buddy, sounds like you won the jackpot." Riley clapped his friend on the back. "And ladies, in case you're wondering, he is single."

Mack shook his head, coughing asshole into his hand before adding, "Thanks."

I couldn't quite work out their dynamic but it was obvious they were more than just colleagues. Sure, they worked together, but there was some sort of brotherly connection that needed to be explored.

While his buddy squirmed under the scrutiny, Riley seemed to be enjoying himself, leaning back into his chair and grinning. The fabric of his T-shirt pulled against his torso, caressing his chest and giving me a better hint at what was hiding underneath. Sure didn't need a full reveal to know I would very much like it. Yum.

Careful not to let my eyes linger too long—or convey any indecent thoughts that were rolling through my mind—I met his gaze to find he had his own ocular exploration happening. He wasn't even trying to be subtle, checking me out like I was a danish on the menu, and giving me an unapologetic cheeky smirk when it was obvious he'd been caught.

He didn't even bother to look away, raising a brow like an unspoken challenge for me to say something because he knew I'd been doing the exact same thing.

"So you haven't told us what you guys do?" I purposely avoided his telepathic dare and went for gathering more information. After all, if we were going to be *friends*, I should at least confirm they weren't shady partners in an illegal drug gang or worse—parking inspectors.

"We're firefighters, in Hell's Kitchen," he answered, giving me as little as possible. "Mack's the chief."

Holy.

Freaking.

Shit.

Great, because I didn't have enough trouble keeping my hormones in check, he needed to pour gasoline on the fire. And never had a metaphor been so freaking accurate, his commitment to extinguish blazes admirable considering he was probably responsible for starting most of them.

God I hoped they had one of those calendars for charity, standing half naked, brandishing hoses. I was going to Google it the minute the conversation ended.

"Wow, what a great job. So noble and heroic," I mumbled out, pretending I wasn't entertaining dirty thoughts. After all, it was kind of wrong to be objectifying him when he ran into burning buildings and saved people like a smoking hot Medal of Honor recipient. I was still going to get the calendar if it existed, because I might be polite but I didn't have any saint like qualities.

"It's not as glamorous as it sounds," Mack interjected, thumbing in Riley's direction. "And keeping these guys in line is more time consuming than the call outs."

From the look of Riley's grin, he wasn't wrong, and I imagined it was one hell of a job. I couldn't help but picture Riley all dirty and sweaty after responding to a fire, that image alone was probably going to feature as my fantasy for the next year, or two.

If Karli had been impressed before, the new intel had elevated the level up by about twenty. Her doe eyes were filled with such adoration as she sighed. "Still, y'all put your life on the line, you both must be so brave."

Poor Brad.

Not only did he miss out on a fantastic package, but he was going to have to up his game after Karli finished talking to those two. Fireman trumped antique book restorer every day of the week, and was five times hotter.

Mack coughed, clearly uncomfortable with the hero worship. Or maybe he didn't get out a lot and conversation with relatively strange women wasn't his thing. His buddy sure didn't have the same problem, lapping up the reverence as he smugly sipped his coffee.

"And what is it that you do, Quinn, when you're not sending your panties in the mail and meeting random men in coffee shops?" His smolder hit me with the full weight of its intent, making me swallow a few times as I tried to drink my own coffee and not choke.

Through the course of hearing about Karli, and Brad—and his tendency to make her heart flutter—what Karli did to earn a paycheck had been revealed. Mine had remained a mystery so it was natural for him to ask.

"I'm a photo and videographer. I record and edit people's life moments for them," I offered, curious to see if he rolled his eyes or faked enthusiasm.

Look, I wasn't ashamed of my job. Sure, there was no danger of me winning a Pulitzer, but it was honest work and it paid for my apartment in Brooklyn. But I could see how it looked to a man who had a "real" job.

Curiously, there was no eye roll. No sarcastic smirk or condescending tone. "Sounds interesting. You know, most of the time when someone's house is burning down it's the photos and videos that they're most devastated to lose. Lucky most people save to a cloud now, but the older generation," he glanced over at Mack, "like this guy, they would risk life and limb rather than watch it all burn."

Mack clipped him over the back of his head, chuckling. "Hey, I'm not *that* old."

It was weird that it wasn't more awkward.

Hopefully neither he nor Mack could tell that my heartbeat was somewhere south of normal and my hormones were on spring break. But other than that, I'd have assumed it would have been stranger.

I used the opening to talk a little bit more about my work, mentioning I'd just come back from a shoot in Paris—newlyweds, who wanted their Instagram followers to be a part of their honeymoon—and how crazy busy I was. But other than Mack being confused by the idea people paid me to stage what was supposed to be candid shots, it was like I'd known them for months.

While I tried to ignore the logic that potentially I'd never see either one of them again, we fell into an easy conversation. Riley had just started to tell us about their station when Mack looked down at his wrist and tapped his watch. "Ladies, while this has been great, Riley and I are both on shift in an hour. We need to get to the stationhouse."

Damn Mack, his damn watch and his damn need to be responsible. Even though it was ridiculous, I wasn't ready for it to end. Not sure what would have been accomplished, Riley had said Mack was single, but hadn't made any bold claims regarding his own relationship status. And honestly—I think he'd flirt with a park bench if that was all that was around—the attention he gave me not that different to that he was giving Karli.

"Sure, of course. Well, it was great meeting you." I stood, sticking out my hand and offering it. Not that shaking his hand was what I wanted, but burying myself in his amazing chest and forcing him to wrap his arms around me probably would have been too much. Social conventions being what they were and all that, and I was determined to not make it weird.

Riley's eyes lowered to my still waiting hand, a smile I couldn't interpret edging across his lips. "Yeah, it's been great." His fingers wrapped around mine, and held it.

Interesting.

I wasn't going to ask him to let go, so we could be there awhile.

"Riley," Mack coughed. "You ready?"

"Sure thing, Chief." He released my hand and turned his attention to Karli. With her he didn't hesitate, giving her a quick shake and saying goodbye. "Hope it works out for you and your guy."

"Awww thanks," a blush covered her cheeks, "it was so wonderful meeting you both."

Mack shifted on his feet uncomfortably, sinking his hands into his pocket. "Well, Quinn, thanks for the coffee." His eyes moved up to mine. "See ya."

See ya?

Unless one of them gave me their phone number—I had a preference, but getting Mack's would mean I'd still have a connection—the chances of seeing me were remote. Unless I started a fire in Midtown, and hoped Riley showed up to put it out. And as ridiculous as it sounded, the thought had crossed my mind.

I was cycling through what other emergencies would warrant a 9-1-1 call—cats up trees weren't really a thing were they?—when I felt Riley's eyes on mine. Like me, he was ignoring Mack and Karli as they said goodbye to each other.

Go on, he taunted, *say what's really on your mind.*

Why don't you, I countered, willing to bet he had other things to say too.

There wasn't a lot of time, the window to have the last word slipping away as Mack looked at the two of us, his hands back in his pockets.

"Sure, that sounds great."

What the hell was I saying?

It had come out of my mouth before I'd been able to properly give it some thought. Because firstly, what the hell was I agreeing to? And why the hell was it so great? Nothing. Nothing in my sentence was great other than it finishing before I volunteered even more random declarations that didn't make sense.

Ironically, Riley seemed to be the only one not confused, biting his lip as he settled back onto his heels. Whatever game we'd apparently been playing, he'd won the first round.

"To see you that is." I did my best to recover, turning to Mack. "You said see you, and I think that would be great. When is your next evening off, maybe we could have dinner?"

Asking Mack out was not part of the plan.

Apart from the fact that we had absolutely nothing in common—and he looked like he'd rather spit fire than date me—I had a serious attraction to his friend. The same friend who'd in no way made any moves to show that attraction was reciprocated, unless you counted the serious eye fucking and sexy smirks.

So of course it made perfect sense that while Riley would be happy for us to go our separate ways, never to see each other again—save the fire I might light and he forced to respond to—I wasn't.

But I wasn't desperate either, so asking for his number like an awkward rookie and giving him a chance to shoot me down wasn't happening either.

Oh hell, no.

Which was why I shifted my attention to Mack, taking his inconsequential parting words *literally*. Because that made sense.

"You're asking me out?" Mack's brows shot up into his hairline, unable to contain his shock.

I chuckled, fully committing to the path I'd apparently decided to travel. "Yes, Mack, women do that these days. We do all kinds of crazy stuff, and asking out a man on a date is just one of them. So what do you say? You want to be a part of the madness?"

Honestly, if he said no, I wouldn't have been devastated or surprised. In fact, it was pretty much what I was expecting. An awkward cough while he shifted uncomfortably on his feet, and then tell me that he'd sampled enough of my crazy. No need to see it again up close and personal, and especially not alone. But it was an option and I was taking it—to hell with the consequences.

"You want to go out with *me*?" he asked again, his sideward glance to Riley in no way discreet. Yeah, he wasn't an idiot, not buying my sudden interest. It remained to be seen if he was going to be chivalrous—play along with my game, or rat me out in front of my friend and his.

Tough call.

"Well, not if you're going to have that attitude." I laughed, pretending like I had everything under control. Spoiler alert, I had nothing under control. "But Riley did mention you were single. And I'm single. So why not?"

"I agree, why not?" Riley folded his arms across his chest, anteing up and putting some skin in the game. He was calling my bluff, but I wasn't going to be the first to blink. "It's been, what? A year since your divorce? Sounds like the perfect time to get back on the market, right Quinn? Besides, I'm sure she'll be gentle."

There was no going back, and if someone wanted the shit show to end, they were going to have to do it their damn selves.

He padded his pockets for a pen, nodding as he responded. "Okay. I guess I'll give you my number."

It was clear that while Mack might not know where Riley and I were going with the charade, he wasn't going to hang me out to dry. What a great guy, and I was totally going to set him up with a decent woman who wasn't me when this was over.

"Here, just add it to my contacts." I held out my phone, my eyes floating over to Riley as I smiled. *Not what you expected, is it?* I'd wanted to say, but I kept my mouth shut and my game face on as Mack added his digits.

Mack handed me back my phone, his eyes shifting between me and his buddy. "Well, I guess we'll head out."

"Yep, see you soon. I'll give you a call and you can check your schedule." I waved as I watched them move to the door. "Oh, and you take care, Riley."

He tipped his chin as he slid on his sunglasses, his ever-present smile getting wider. "Likewise, Quinn."

Why did I get the feeling that my win hadn't been as spectacular as I'd first thought?

Chapter 3

Quinn

"WHAT THE HELL was that!?" Karli grabbed my arm, pulling me back down to sit. "You asked Mack out?"

"Sure, I said I wanted to make friends didn't I? Unless I totally misread it and you were interested." I tried not to laugh, pretending to look suitably sorry. "The idea was to get you laid so if you want me to step aside, I will totally do that."

Karli rolled her eyes, her finger poking me hard in the ribs. "You know full well that I'm holding out for Brad. Although, maybe if he saw me with someone else, it might give him a shove that I'm not going to wait around forever."

"There's the spirit, maybe Mack has a friend," I suggested, positive that Karli wasn't serious.

She pursed her lips, shaking her head. "Yeah, we've already met his *friend*. And let me tell you, I'm not dumb enough to get between the two of you. Maybe Mack couldn't feel the zap in the air, but I sure as hell could."

"What zap, there was no zap," I tried to argue, refusing to acknowledge out loud what I knew to be true. There was definitely something between us. A charge. A connection. And enough sexual tension to make a prostitute blush.

It had to be because he was hot, that body of sin working up suggestive thoughts that I had no hope of controlling. Or perhaps it was his job, his courageous, honorable and heroic pursuits enhancing the fantasy on an emotional level. Who didn't love a guy who looked danger in the face and put himself on the line for the betterment of all mankind? No one. It was like female catnip, hitting right between your thighs and making your ovaries clench. I bet he was a demon in bed. A man built like that had to know what to do with it surely.

Plus he was hot, not sure if I mentioned that.

"Let me ask you something, Quinn." She turned, ignoring my bullshit denial. "What exactly are you hoping to achieve by dating Mack? Because I know you aren't the kind of woman who's gonna mess with that man's feelings."

She had a point there.

I was fierce and strong and didn't allow myself to be a doormat. But being vindictive or cruel in relationships weren't my thing.

"No, I'm not going to mess with his feelings. And I'm sure Mack knows a little more than you think." He wasn't a moron. And I doubted he harbored delusions of us building a lasting relationship.

Karli let the silence settle between us, giving me a look that was too introspective for that time of the morning on a Saturday. "Quinn, just don't do something you'll regret later."

"Come on, Karli. You know I don't do regrets." And that wasn't just rhetoric, I meant every word of it. Not to say I hadn't made some bad decisions. But there was always a reason, a purpose, a lesson. Everything I'd done had shaped me into the person I was, living the life I had, and trust me when I say I had a really good life.

My parents had been cookie cutter awesome, supportive and loving in every way. Sadly, my dad had been taken from us a few years before I moved from Jersey to New York. But I'd have rather spent those twenty amazing years with him, than a lifetime with a dad who didn't care. And my mom, well she still checked in with me every Sunday morning regardless of where I was in the world. Didn't care I was twenty-eight and old enough to know better. Every Sunday without fail, I got that call. We didn't see each other as much as we should, but I was grateful my sister, brother-in-law and three nieces kept her busy enough she didn't miss me too much.

Karli arched her brow but saved me the sermon, mostly because she knew it wouldn't do much good.

We'd been friends for over five years. She'd moved into the apartment right next to mine, living there with the boyfriend she'd had since college. Not Brad, of course, he was some other guy who was hot as hell but not all that bright. He was a man-child, who paid too much attention to my boobs and they'd only been in the city a few months when he cheated on her. So she kicked his ass to the curb and took over the lease. BOOM! One minute she was coupon cutting in their kitchen and the next she was threatening to castrate him with a pair of blunt scissors. And she had grown up on a farm so I didn't doubt she was capable.

After the showy break up in the hall, I invited her in to my place for celebratory cocktails and we became instant friends. Her younger sister moved in about a month or two later and we've shared a wall ever since.

But while Karli has a tendency to have a crazy moment or two, her general default was sweet. She overlooked my shenanigans, even if she found herself in the middle of them like the current one. But she didn't try to change me, even if it would probably make her life a little easier.

"You want to head back to the apartment?" I offered, thinking after our eventful morning, I should probably do some work. It was early, our seven a.m. rendezvous catering to Brad's tendency to run in the mornings. "I have some photos that need editing but if I get them done, I'll have my whole evening free. We can sit and watch trashy television. There's a new vegan place we could try."

She tapped her lips, stalling like she wasn't going to agree. "Well, I suppose I don't have anything planned and Josie is going out."

Going out was a euphemism for going to her boyfriend's place and having sex. Karli knew it, and I knew it, but for some reason we kept up the pretense that her little sister wasn't getting screwed seven ways to Sunday. At least one of the Kelly girls was getting some.

"Sounds like it's settled. I'll let you know when I'm done."

We left the coffee shop with me pretending like my mind wasn't on the hot fireman who we'd met not an hour before. No, not the guy I was apparently going to go out with, but his uber-hot friend. Images of his gorgeous smile and sexy-as-sin body had taken up residence in my temporal lobe on a permanent loop. And most of those thoughts weren't fit for company.

Karli chatted as we walked back to our apartment, the sun of the late spring warming me from the outside in. Of course there was another reason I was feeling heat and it had nothing to do with the calendar.

"Are you listening to me?" Karli tapped her foot impatiently when we reached our respective doors. While walking and talking, I'd been participating with appropriate nods and well-placed responses, keeping my flirty thoughts to myself. But clearly my half-hearted effort hadn't been enough.

I didn't even try to lie, sighing as I grinned. "Sorry, no. I wasn't listening."

"I said, when are you going to call Mack?" She was wearing a grin of her own and had probably guessed why I wasn't paying attention.

My shoulder lifted, giving her a hint of a shrug as I attempted to be nonchalant. "A few days, we'll see."

"Yeah, like I believe that," she laughed, opening her front door. "Buzz me when you're done. And don't think for a second I'm not going to want to hear all about your plans for poor Mack tonight."

She didn't close her door till I agreed, my plans for Mack not even really formed in my head yet. What I did know was that letting Riley disappear out of my life wasn't going to happen.

Maybe it was some weird fantasy, an infatuation where the attraction only lasted until I'd had him in some way. I'd had those before, the thrill of the chase more interesting than the man himself and probably the reason why I hadn't had a steady boyfriend in the last seven months. And unlike Karli, I wasn't holding out for some cute but mostly clueless guy who made my heart flutter.

Determined to keep my mind off Riley and all things tall, dark and handsome, I sat at my desk and turned on my computer. My suitcase was on the floor where I'd left it when I had gotten back from my trip, still mostly packed save for a few necessities.

Honestly, the travel wasn't as glamorous as it sounded. Sure, it was exciting and I'd seen a lot of cool places, but lately I'd been looking forward to coming back home. Maybe I was finally growing up, or maybe I was just getting weary. Either way, I was glad I didn't have to leave anytime soon and was seriously considering sticking to local work for a little while. Who knows, I might stay home long enough to finally get a dog. I'd wanted one for so long but it hadn't seemed practical.

No, when I finally gave my heart—to a dog or a man—it would be with the promise that I'd stick around. Which was probably the reason why I didn't have either.

Throwing myself into work, I sat at my computer for hours while I edited photos. It wasn't my favorite thing to do, but was required to turn out the product everyone wanted. It didn't matter if the image's integrity was lost, or that it had been filtered so much that it no longer looked real. Perfection is what was wanted, even if I had to wave a magic wand—or in my case Photoshop—to get it.

I was glad when I was finally done, mailing off proofs to some clients before heading into my bedroom to change. Take out and trashy television with Karli called for yoga pants and an oversized sweatshirt, and I didn't want to let the team down by turning up in the jeans and cute top I'd worn to the coffee shop. Not that it had done me any good, because as much as I felt there was a mutual attraction between me and Riley, he hadn't acted on it.

Not sure if it was some game—which secretly excited me—or I'd been reading it wrong, he'd happily let me walk out the door with his buddy's number in my pocket. It was strange, and yet tantalizing, the riddle still playing out in my head as I walked over to my neighbor's apartment and knocked on her door.

"I thought you were going to buzz me?" Karli peered into the hall, her hair twisted into a messy knot on her head while her face was covered in a paper beauty mask. "I need to leave this on for another five minutes."

I chuckled, making my way inside without waiting for the invitation. "So leave it on and I'll start flicking through the menu. Though I have to tell you, our Saturday nights are getting kind of tragic."

At twenty-eight, I'd had my share of going out on the town and partying until morning. There were more than a few Saturday nights where I didn't even make it home, crawling back to my apartment sometime after breakfast. It had been fun, and reckless, and I couldn't remember when it had all stopped. But lately my crazy nights out had consisted of sitting on my couch—or Karli's—eating junk food and watching questionable television.

Jesus.

I used to be the person everyone turned to for adventure, the one who not only found the trouble but jumped headfirst into it. And my latest escapade had been what? To send a lacy thong to my bestie's crush and then turn up to a coffee shop for some pseudo blind date?

Oh.

Hell.

No.

"Hey!" My ass had barely hit the couch when I leapt back up. "Change of plans, we're going out."

Karli hadn't even made it to the bathroom yet, her mask still requiring a few more minutes before she could peel it off. "What are you talking about? I'm already in my comfy clothes and took off my makeup. Hello, can you not see I'm cleansing?"

"So? We're twenty-eight, not eighty-eight, and we'll have plenty of time to sit inside under crocheted blankets, judging people's silly life choices when we're older. Until then, we should be making some questionable ones of our own."

It was a fine speech, and if I hadn't already been convinced, that would have definitely done it. But since Karli was looking at me like a deer in headlights, I could tell I was going to have to go the extra mile for her. "We are young, successful, talented, and beautiful. We have our *whole* lives ahead of us. We need to be out there," I pointed to the door with a dramatic flourish, "not cloistered like medieval virgins."

Karli opened her mouth ready to protest, but my arched brow hinted it wouldn't be a good idea. I wasn't easily swayed when I made up my mind, and it was locked in. "We're going out. Go back into your room, put on some clothes that do not have an elastic waist and I'll be back ready for action."

"Fine, but only because I love you." Karli disappeared into her room under protest while I slipped back into the hall and into my apartment.

It was the first Saturday in a long time where I was actually excited to go out. Not because I wanted to go sit in some random bar so some random men could leer at me like a slab of meat, but because I knew exactly where we were heading.

Like my apartment was on fire, I dressed in a sexy black dress that left little to the imagination. Makeup and hair were also achieved in record time, my transformation from *homely* to *happening* in less than forty-five minutes flat.

Then I was back in Karli's apartment, waiting while she deliberated which shoes to wear and how much she was willing to punish her feet for the evening.

"Come on, I'll pay for a cab. Just put any on," I moaned as I shimmied impatiently by her bedroom doorway.

Her look was murderous as she pulled on a pair of heels that matched with her cute skirt and top. Clearly we hadn't coordinated our outfits, with her looking a little good-girl-on-the-town while I was flying the flag for naughty-to-the-core. The irony wasn't lost on me, our wardrobe choices in perfect harmony with our personas.

Grumbling that we still hadn't eaten dinner, she locked her door behind us and we took the elevator down to the street. It was still early evening, which made me look slightly ridiculous in my sexy dress. Not that I cared, strutting to the curb and hailing a cab like it was my life's mission.

"Hell's Kitchen please," I said, as I shuffled into the backseat, Karli right behind me.

"Somewhere in particular in Midtown?" the driver asked, looking annoyed and probably hoping I'd narrow it down. "You want me to drop you off at Forty Second and you take it from there?"

"Hell's Kitchen?" Karli's eyes flared, the location more than a little coincidental. "Quinn, please tell me we're not going to go look for firehouses?"

"Please, what are we sixteen? We are absolutely not going to cruise firehouses like we're stalking an ex boyfriend." I dismissed her concerns with a wave of my hand before I turned my attention to the driver. "Just take us to *Gino's* on Tenth."

Gino's was a pizza/Italian place that had been serving Manhattan-ites since the Rat Pack was running through town. Complete with its kitschy red and white checked tablecloths, straw-wrapped Chianti bottles and Dean Martin and Frank Sinatra playlist, it attracted a local crowd of regulars and tourists looking for a cheap and easy place to eat. Not the kind of establishment that was fitting of our fancy threads.

Karli looked horrified, probably regretting getting out of her sweats and leaving her apartment. "*Gino's*? Quinn, can't we go somewhere else? Why don't we go to *Nude* in Chelsea, you know I've always wanted to go there."

Mention of Nude got the driver's attention with the smirk over his shoulder hinting he didn't know it was a restaurant.

"It's a raw food place, dude. Just drive to Gino's." I rolled my eyes, pointing to the road.

He shrugged, no longer interested since finding out Nude wasn't a strip club or something equally as salacious. Can't say that I blamed him, a raw food place didn't enthuse me either. Karli grumbled under her breath as we traveled through traffic. She was too polite to flat out complain, but she was less than impressed with my choice. Not that I blamed her, the menu wasn't going to win any Zagat awards but there was a method to my madness.

"We should invite Brad," I half joked, wondering how interesting I could make the evening. "The man has to eat."

"Yeah, not sure it's a good idea when you're being so unpredictable. You still haven't told me why we're going to eat in a mediocre Italian place when the city is literally brimming with amazing restaurants," Karli chuckled.

"Just trust me, okay."

She shook her head as she relaxed against the seat. "Famous last words."

We arrived at Gino's without any more protests or eye rolls, stepping out of the cab and onto the sidewalk. It didn't matter what day of the week or time it was, Manhattan was always bustling and tonight was no exception.

After paying the driver, we made our way into the noise. Like we expected, Gino's was filled with families and tourists. Everyone was happily chatting, enjoying their baked ziti while "That's Amore" piped through the speakers.

"Two?" The hostess wearing a *Vera* nametag didn't bother with the greeting, eyeing us up with suspicion.

"Yes, please." I smiled brightly, hoping my sunny disposition would improve our chances of avoiding the table right by the kitchen. It was bad enough I'd take Karli to somewhere she was going to have limited food choices, if she was pushed up against a wall and a swinging door, she might rethink her trust in me.

Vera grabbed a couple of laminated menus and shoved them under her arm. "Follow me, I'll show you to your table."

We followed her into the fray, avoiding a screaming five-year-old who didn't want his Bolognese and two older guys who were complaining the servings were getting smaller. And like my yet-to-be-displayed good intentions were being rewarded, she led us to a small table right in the center of the room.

Perfect.

Not like anyone could miss us there.

We both took a seat, Vera handing us our menus and letting us know someone would be around soon to take our order. Then with no interest in waiting to see if we'd actually heard her, she disappeared back to the front where there was a group of five waiting to be seated.

"Okay, now are you going to tell me why we're here?" Karli perused the offerings, pulling a face as she turned it over to see if she had any better luck on the back. "Because it hasn't escaped my attention that we're right in the area of Mack and Riley's firehouse."

"Ahhh, but which one?" I tapped my finger against my lip playfully, pretending I hadn't Google searched it while I was working.

My investigations had revealed there were three in the immediate area. But that didn't account for the half dozen or more if you pushed that boundary out a little. Did they mean Hell's Kitchen proper, or *around* Hell's Kitchen? They mightn't even be firefighters, they could be sanitation workers with mob ties, they sure as hell had the physical attributes to be enforcers.

Karli looked around, her eyes scanning the room like it might yield answers. "Please tell me you're not going to pull the fire alarm and hope he turns up."

I laughed.

Actually giggled because the thought had crossed my mind. But apart from being a chargeable offense and an extremely reckless waste of resources—not to mention attract bad juju—it was sloppy. First, how would I know which of the three would respond? It wasn't like I could pull the alarm three times and hope at least one of those times he showed up. And how many trucks were there? Did everyone respond or did they just send one? I had no idea of the operational requirements of the NYFD, nor did I have the time to find out. So instead of being a menace, I decided I'd try a novel approach. Throw out a net, and hope I caught something.

"Hi, I'm Gino, you guys ready?"

The short, pimply waiter was maybe—and that was being generous—twenty-one. Both of us blinking back in surprise as he placed two red plastic tumblers full of ice water on the table.

"Wow, as in *the* Gino? I thought you'd be older, and not as handsome." I smiled at the kid, unable to help myself.

I wasn't flirting, or at least I wasn't trying to. But like earlier with Vera, I was going to need the good people of *Gino's* assistance, and trying to be charming never hurt anyone's cause.

Pink traveled up his neck and spilled across his cheeks. "Yeah, yeah. He was my great grandpa, but there's been a few Ginos since. Every one of the kids, grandkids, and great grandkids has to put in time. It's the way it works in a family-run business. A blessing and a curse, really," he sighed wistfully. "So, if you ladies are ready, I'll take your order."

"Um . . ." Karli frowned, no longer interested in Gino as she stared at her menu. "I guess I'll have the roasted vegetables and the garden salad. The vinaigrette dressing on the side."

He scribbled down her order and asked if she wanted something else to drink. She ordered a wine—probably needing a little extra help to get through dinner—before he smiled down at me. "And for you?"

"I'll take twelve large pizzas but I'm going to need them delivered." I sat down the menu and batted my eyelashes.

"You want twelve pies to go?" he questioned, a confused look on his face.

He wasn't the only one bewildered, Karli shooting me a look like I was crazy.

"No, not to go. *Delivered.* You guys do that, right?" My eyes dropped back down to my menu. "And I'll take the mushroom risotto as well."

"Quinn?" Karli asked, kicking me under the table. "What the hell are you going to do with twelve pizzas?"

"Me? Nothing." I handed my menu back to Gino. "But I do feel that buying some firemen their dinner would be the charitable thing to do. After all, they're out there working on a Saturday evening, away from their friends and family. They do so much for the city. It's the least we can do. Oh, and I'm going to need to split them up between three firehouses, if that's okay, I'll scribble down their addresses if you like."

Gino looked up at the kitchen and then back to me. "Yeah, we can do that, but I'm going to need you to pay up front. If you take off without settling your check for twelve pizzas, my dad will kill me."

"No problem at all, Gino." I fished out my credit card and waved it at him. "Make sure you take an extra fifty for being so helpful. Also, if it's not too much trouble, can I include a note?"

He scratched his neck, nervously. "Um, we don't really have stationery laying around."

"Your order pad will do. It won't be long, I promise." I pointed to the notepad he'd been using to take our orders and the stubby pencil still between his fingers.

Like he'd forgotten he was holding them, he smiled down at his hands. "Sure, here you go. Write down the addresses and the notes, and I'll go put in the order with the kitchen. Any preference as to what toppings?"

"Surprise them, Gino." I waved my hand like I was declaring it a national holiday. "Whatever your crowd favorites are. Who's going to complain about free pizza?"

"True. Okay, I'll go ring this up and be back." He dutifully jogged to the kitchen, leaving his order pad and pencil for me.

Karli had the decency to wait until he'd left, grabbing me by the arm and keeping her voice low as not to make a scene. "What are you doing, Quinn?"

"Isn't it, obvious? My good deed for the day." I grinned, shaking off her hand, reaching into my handbag and pulling out my phone. Then neatly, I wrote down the address of the three closest firehouses. Lord, I hoped he belonged to one of them. If not, I prayed that my efforts would at least be appreciated and it earned me some credit for the afterlife.

"Please, this has nothing to do with good deeds and everything to do with the tall, good-looking guy who happens to be called Riley." She laughed to herself as she glanced down at my note. "You're certifiable, you know that?"

"Awww, you trying to sweet talk me? I already bought your dinner." I tore off three separate pages, repeating the note two more times.

Thought I'd send you something other than underwear.
Enjoy dinner on me,
Quinn x

In truth, even if my pizzas and note *did* find their mark, there was no guaranteeing it would elicit a response. They could take my charitable donation, enjoy their dinner and go about their business. And wasn't that what I was telling them to do anyway? But something told me Riley wouldn't be able to help himself, not sure if he had a sick need to get involved or if he was looking for a little adventure himself.

Gino returned with a big smile on his face and my abused credit card in his hand. Not that I cared, the larger-than-average check worth every single penny considering the excitement I'd felt.

Real excitement.

My excitement.

Just for me.

I couldn't remember the last time I did something totally frivolous just to make myself happy. It had been too long.

So with the multiple pizzas cooking, soon to make their journey, Karli and I relaxed in our seats. We sipped wine, made small talk, pretending like we weren't watching the door to see when my packages would depart. It was a charade for everyone else's benefit, the two of us trading stupid smirks while we waited for our probably ordinary dinner. I'd called Gino back and ordered a few extra sides for us, I figured it would add a little more time so we could sit inside without arousing suspicion.

"You look mighty pleased with yourself." Karli bit her lip as she twirled the stem of the wineglass between her fingers.

"Yes," I smiled back, "I'm very pleased."

Chapter 4

Riley

I GUESS I should be thankful it was a slow night.

Only an asshole with serious issues would want it to be any other way. But asshole or not, I got a serious hard-on when the bell rang and I got to pull on my turnouts. Not because I wanted someone to be hurt or in danger, but because I was ready to go do what needed to be done so they weren't.

It would probably surprise most people that we'd had three calls since my shift started and none of them were actual fires. For some reason—I blamed Hollywood—there was an idea that we hung around the stationhouse playing checkers or watching television. Then someone would call 9-1-1 and we'd go out all sirens blazing to a fire where we burst through the door like a scene out of a movie. But more times than not, we got to intervene in other things—bar fights, ODs, domestic disputes just to name a few—and fires were the last of them.

And as for all that spare time, sitting around catching up on *The Real Housewives of New Jersey*, that shit didn't happen either. There were drills we needed to run, paperwork needing to be filed and shit that needed cleaning.

A lot of shit.

Like the engine for instance, which was what I was busting my ass doing.

It was a warm May night so it was kind of nice to have the bay doors open and the hose running. It also gave me a chance to let my mind wander, which gave me a hard-on of a different kind.

Quinn was unexpected.

Fuck, she was beautiful. That blonde hair and blue eyes had probably launched a million wet dreams.

And her body, every inch of it was fucking perfect.

Legs for days too, which was nice considering most of the girls I'd dated were skating on the bottom half of five-five. My hands were itching to rest on her hips and see if she knew how to use that pouty mouth for things other than talking. The idea that she wouldn't need a stepladder to reach mine made it even sexier.

She radiated heat, and if there was a person who knew temperature, it was me. It wasn't just because of the way she looked either. Women with pretty faces and hot bodies weren't exactly uncommon in Manhattan, and I'd probably dabbled with the "type" more than I should. But the flames I was feeling were more than just surface beauty, it was something in her eyes that made my balls tingle—a blast cap just waiting for the explosion.

Still, I knew nothing about her other than what she'd volunteered over coffee. And I was more than a little tempted to ask her out right then and there. But I had a hunch that was not the way to go, and I'd learned a long time ago to not ignore my gut.

"Pretty boy, you done on the chrome? We could've got a rookie to help you." Leighton called from the doorway, his hand holding a slice. "Some good Samaritan sent us some pizza, you might want to get in here before Tibbs polishes off the lot."

"What kind of pizza?" I asked, moderately interested. The community was generous and it wasn't uncommon to have donations of food or drinks, but if it was some trendy bullshit cauliflower base topped with quinoa, I was out.

"Gino's." He took another bite, talking around the crust. "Chief went bright red when he read the note, think it's some MILF who's sweet on him."

Note?

What kind of person would send pizza with a no—? Oh, yeah, my night just got a hell of a lot more interesting.

Unable to hide my smirk, I climbed down from the engine and wiped off my hands. I had a sneaking suspicion I knew exactly what would make the chief blush, and it wasn't some MILF. "Hadn't realized how hungry I was until right now. I'm famished."

Any doubts I had as to the identity of our pizza-godmother were put to bed when Chief swore under his breath. He shook his head, grabbing a slice and putting it onto a paper plate as I got closer.

"Eat your dinner, North. I've had enough trouble from you today."

"Me?" I laughed, raising my eyebrow. "Not sure what I had to do with it. I was just following you to make sure you didn't get in over your head." I peeked over at the four boxes of mostly consumed pizza. "Guess it didn't much matter though. So tell me, what did Quinn have to say?"

"No one said it was from Quinn." He shoved what I assumed was the note into his pocket. He'd done that a lot, shoving things in his pocket and expecting me to ignore them. But since acquiring further knowledge, I wasn't going to be as compliant.

"Who's Quinn?" Tibbs asked with a mouthful of food.

I folded my arms across my chest, unable to help myself. "Yeah, Chief, who's Quinn?"

It took a lot to make the Chief squirm, but women usually had an easier time at it. Not sure if it was his psycho ex wife, or that he hadn't dated in awhile but I was positive he'd rather attend three consecutive five-alarm fires than talk about the blond we'd spent our morning with.

"Nobody, just eat." He pointed to the box. "There's still work to get done, and anyone who isn't busy will find my boot in their ass."

A chuckle found its way up my throat, and if he thought I was letting it go then he was as crazy as his ex-wife. So it came as no surprise to either of us when I followed him into his office and shut the door. "C'mon, show me. We both know it was meant for me."

His ass sunk heavily into his worn-out chair, the thing creaking under his weight. Even though the guy was close to fifty, he was still built like a tank. "And how the hell do we *know* it's for you? She didn't address it to anyone."

"So it *is* from Quinn," I laughed. "And don't play dumb, Chief, you know why."

He swore under his breath, and then muttered a few audible fucks for good measure. But we both knew I wasn't backing down, something he'd seen first-hand when I'd shown up at that coffee shop. "Do not create a mess I'm going to have to clean up, North. You could be sitting in my chair one day, lord knows you've got the fucking talent. Pity your head is up your ass."

"I just love it when you sing my praises." I held out my hand, fighting the grin. "Makes me warm and fuzzy all over."

"You're killing me." The crumbled up note was slapped into my hand with a stern look, and a not-so-subtle, "Get the hell out of here." Having gotten what I wanted, I was only too happy to leave, barely getting into the hallway when I straightened out the rumpled piece of paper.

Well, well, well, never got hard over stationery, but I guess there was always a first.

The undeniably feminine letters curved on the page in some weird kind of taunt. Like she'd done earlier in the day, there was more than what she was saying. But rather than try to decipher her motives, or how she found out which station was ours, I decided to head out the door and do some investigating of my own.

"Heading out, be back in five, have my radio." The stream of words followed me out the stationhouse door before anyone could ask where I was going. I was probably going to catch some heat for it later but at the moment, I didn't care.

Chances of her being at Gino's were probably remote. She could have stopped in, placed the order and been on her way before the pizzas even left the building. But even if she had bailed, I had a burning need to go to the scene of the crime and see what I could find out. Was it dumb luck she'd picked the pizza place right around the corner, or did she secretly tail us so the chances weren't so random. Not even slightly unnerved that she might have followed us, the thought of her watching me getting me irrationally excited.

Great.

Get a handle on it, North.

Last thing I needed was to end up a news story because I'd developed some bizarre kink.

Gino's was busy any night of the week but on Saturday it became a different kind of animal. So it was unsurprising to see the place packed, the air filled as much with noise as it was with garlic and oregano.

"Hey, Riley." Vera smiled, giving me a look I knew was trouble. And not the good kind either. She was legal, barely, but her dad was a nice guy and I didn't shit were I ate—literally. So as much as she wanted to put her hand down my pants, it was going to remain a complete no-fly zone for her.

"Hey, Vera, you have a minute?" My eyes floated to the crowd around me waiting to be seated.

She sighed, leaning on her host stand as she batted her eyelashes. "Of course I have time, anything for you."

Ignoring the *anything* she was likely to volunteer, I instead pulled out the note. "Any chance the person who sent us the pizza is still here?"

Her pretty brown eyes rolled, huffing out a breath before pointing to the center of the room. "They've been here forever. Seriously, I could use that table already. Who takes two hours just to eat dinner?"

If the place hadn't been so crowded, or I'd taken a minute to look, I'd have seen her right away. She was laughing at something, her eyes closed as she threw her head back while her friend, Karli, didn't seem to share the joke. And it wasn't just me who'd noticed her, the pair of them getting eyes from all corners of the room. There was even one guy who seemed to be deliberating getting out of his chair and going over, the indecision likely the reason for the shuffle in his seat.

Back off, asshole; don't even think about it.

Not giving him the chance to find his balls, I strolled past him, shooting him a glare before stopping at Quinn's table. There was still a half-eaten panna cotta in front of her, with no indication she was in a hurry to leave, no doubt pissing off poor Vera.

"Ladies," I announced, catching them both by surprise as I pulled a chair from a nearby table and took a seat beside them. "While dinner was great, you seemed to have forgotten dessert. And I have to say, I'm a sucker for something sweet."

I didn't hesitate, reaching down to the abandoned spoon and loading it with some panna cotta, closing my eyes as I savored it. "Delicious." My lids slid open as I enjoyed the sweetness on my tongue.

Quinn's eyes flared as they strolled up and down my body, evaluating my uniform like she was giving me a station inspection. "Oh hey," she stumbled, only needing a second before recovering. "How did you know I was done with that?"

There was an edge to her voice. A taunting little tease that told me she wasn't mad per se but wanted to play nonetheless.

A grin formed on my lips, unable to help myself. "Whether you were done or not didn't matter, I still wanted a taste."

Yeah, it was cheesy as fuck and not my best work but seeing the heat in those beautiful blue irises was worth it. And if I hadn't been on duty—needing to get back to the station before Mack sent someone to drag my ass back—I'd have sampled her tasty treats a little longer. But time wasn't on my side. "Thanks." I licked the spoon one last time for good measure before returning it to her plate. I wasn't sure if she was going to continue where I left off, but the thought of putting what had been in my mouth back in hers got me five times as hard as I'd been before.

She didn't.

Either she was better at the game than I thought or she wasn't excited to swap bodily fluids, her eyes dipping down to the spoon before they came to rest on me. "You're welcome. It was my pleasure."

Her mouth lingered over the word pleasure and I liked the way it sounded. Wouldn't mind testing the theory, and finding out exactly what hers was, but Gino's wasn't the place to do it.

"So tell me," I leaned in closer, a different kind of hungry gnawing at my gut, "was it a lucky guess, or did you have some help?"

As far as I knew she hadn't used that number Mack had given her, but then again he wouldn't exactly volunteer that information. Nope, he'd keep that stuff to himself, especially since he'd been irritated with me since the morning. What can I say? I bring out the best in the chief, even if he couldn't see it. So instead of dealing with me and our little excursion, he'd done his best to avoid the whole conversation, burying his head in work and pretending like it hadn't happened. And if we'd been rotated off, and not had to go into work, I mightn't have been so willing to play along. Hard to be a pain in the ass for too long when there was work to be done. Still begged the question of how she found us, especially since as far as I knew he hadn't given her the station's address.

"I'm just naturally resourceful, it didn't take all that long," she answered innocently, her eyebrow arching.

Her resourcefulness was probably what I should have been thinking about, but it was hard concentrating on anything when my eyes slid to the front of her dress. I hadn't noticed when I'd walked to the table, but her outfit was doing a stellar job of showcasing her tits. It was nice, probably a little suggestive and I was pretty sure that was going to be burned into my mind for a while, and I couldn't say I'd be disappointed.

"Uh-hmm." Karli cleared her throat, hinting I'd been staring too long. And had I been like some of the other men she was probably used too I might've had the decency to be embarrassed.

But I wasn't.

Like them *or* embarrassed.

"Maybe you should have delivered it yourself. Then I could have given you a tour." Ironically, that wasn't a lie. While I didn't usually like women at the stationhouse—putting their hands all over my gear—something told me she wouldn't be like most. In fact, I'd stake my balls on it.

Her raised eyebrow suggested I meant a tour of a different kind and even though that hadn't been my intention, I was eagerly awaiting her response.

"Hey ladies, I'm sorry but Vera really needs this table." Gino—the younger version—appeared at the table, like the biggest cock block of all time.

I'd remember that next time I caught the kid making out in his dad's car in the parking lot.

"It's fine, Gino, we were just leaving." Quinn gave him a flirty smile, sliding out of her seat and giving me a better look at what she was wearing.

First things first, it seemed that Gino's terrible timing wasn't the only thing annoying me, the familiarity between the two of them making me irrationally irritated. There was no way he'd know what to do with a woman like Quinn, let alone earn that smile she gave him.

And secondly, my initial assessment of her dress being "nice" couldn't have been more wrong. There was nothing *nice* about her dress. It was tight and short, and curved her body like a sexy little bow begging to be pulled.

My mouth slammed shut before my tongue mopped the floor, my eyes roaming over her exposed skin like my hands were begging to do. Her body was insane, a combination of peaks and valleys in proportions that couldn't have been more perfect.

"Let me," I pulled out my wallet even though Gino hadn't even brought the check yet. "Since you paid for my dinner, I'd like to pay for yours." It didn't matter that I hadn't so much as tasted any of the pizza she'd sent over, my stomach still rumbling from the lack of attention. No, I liked the idea of buying her dinner, and hoped that the trend might continue.

Her hand reached out, touching my forearm as she held it still. "Already taken care of, seems you can't send that many pizzas just on good faith." She winked at Gino, making the kid turn three shades of red. "But thanks, tell Mack I said hi and not to forget about our date."

"Your *date*?" It flew out of my mouth before I'd had time to temper my reaction. If she was looking to get under my skin, her objective was achieved. I was also going to be having some serious words with the chief, because it was clear he'd been holding out on me.

She batted her eyelashes, her lips spreading into a grin. "Yes, but since you know him better than I do, maybe you can give me some suggestions. You know, to make it extra special since it's been a while."

I'd be the first to agree the whole Mack thing had been foreplay.

Not like that, you sick bastards.

Last thing I wanted to imagine was my boss in any scenario that involved sex, or Quinn for that matter. Nope, that was a visual I'd happily never entertain.

But since laying eyes on Quinn, I couldn't get my mind right. Not sure if was her crazy impulsive package, the effort she'd seem to go to for a friend or her seemingly free spirit, but she was a woman I wanted to know. There was also some crazy energy between us, and I wasn't sure it was only sexual.

The stupid ruse that neither Quinn nor I were interested in each other, was something we fell into, happily using the poor chief as a pawn while we figured each other out. It sure lit a fire under my ass, and I thought for sure it had done the same for her. Like some stupid ritual, circling each other and pretending like we didn't want to rip each other's clothes off.

Or so I thought.

She couldn't seriously be interested in the chief though, could she?

It wasn't like me to read the situation wrong, but I didn't really *know* her, and there could be a first time for everything.

My eyes went to Karli who was also wearing a smile, but if I thought she might throw me a bone, I was shit out of luck. Like it or not, her BFF was giving nothing up. So if Quinn was needling me, or she was genuinely interested, I wasn't getting confirmation one way or another from either of them.

"He likes quiet nights, not much for crowds." I sunk my hands in my pockets, hiding my clenched fists while I maintained my grin. "Dinner, but nothing fancy. He hates pretentious food and overpriced restaurants."

It was temping to sabotage their *whatever*, and feed her the opposite. One meal at an expensive French bistro followed by a trendy nightclub in SoHo would have guaranteed he never saw her again. But when it came to women, I didn't need to cheat my way to an advantage, and there was something rather unsatisfying about an unearned win.

So, regardless of why she was asking, she wasn't getting anything that wasn't the truth. But I was going to be paying very close attention to her next move.

I wasn't the only one paying close attention, her head tipping to the side like she was trying to work it out. I'd obviously surprised her with my answer, probably expecting some caveman bullshit where I told her not to waste her time with him. Again, I had no problem throwing a woman over my shoulder and getting primal. But only if that was what she wanted, and then all bets were off.

"Okay, thanks. That's a big help." She nodded, rolling her bottom lip with her teeth in a move that made me want to groan.

Funny how her mouth was saying one thing, but her eyes were saying something completely different. And that heated stare wasn't one of gratitude.

Yeah, I hadn't read shit wrong.

"I live to serve." I grinned, resting my hand on my heart. "Enjoy the rest of your night."

And without giving her a chance to respond, I strolled out of Gino's feeling cockier than when I walked in.

Game on, sweetheart.

Game.

On.

Chapter 5

Quinn

"**Y**OU ARE SO terrible!" Karli grabbed my arm, giggling as we left Gino's, the elaboration not needed as we strolled down the street.

"Please, he was playing me as much as I was playing him. You saw him sit down and help himself to my panna cotta. And newsflash, that wasn't the only thing he was trying to help himself to." I pushed her playfully, doing my best to stay upright when my pulse was racing.

It was true that I had sent off pizza like some crazy dough, cheese and saucy homing pigeon. I'd wanted to not only find him but tease out a response, hoping he'd come find me. It's the reason why we spent the amount of time we could have consumed a ten-course menu eating mediocre dinner and rather ordinary dessert.

But he'd been so goddamn confident, walking in with a smirk that meant trouble. And let's not gloss over how freaking hot he looked in his uniform. How could something so practical be so sexual? He wasn't even wearing his firefighting gear, the idea of him in a pair of turnouts a fantasy I didn't know I had.

And Lord, I'd never wanted to worship a pair of forearms before but I'd had to knot my hands in my lap and tell my tongue to behave. How could he have gotten even hotter? It was like being plunged into the depths of hell and poked by Satan's pitchfork.

And you didn't have to be a genius to know where the biggest fire was burning.

"Goddamn it," I swore both inwardly and outwardly. "I'm not going to become that girl. The one who turns into a quivering puddle because of some guy. And who cares what his uniform looks like?"

Karli laughed, "Uh, who mentioned his uniform? Although, did you see his forearms?" She fanned herself for effect.

"Yes, I saw them. They were nothing special," I snapped, trying to pretend like I wouldn't have erected an altar in their honor given half a chance. "Look, it's beside the point. I'm going out with Mack, so there's that."

"Yeah, about that. When did y'all make plans? Because I know that's something that you would have mentioned when we were sitting there for two hours *eating dinner*."

Her sly sideward glance told me she had me figured out, and my *amazing* bluff hadn't been so great.

I straightened my shoulders, ignoring pesky little details that served no purpose. "No plans have been made but they will. Trust me, I'll organize a date so outstanding Mack will be ruined for all future women. He'll be singing my praises, boasting about my prowess in what will go down as the greatest date of all time."

Karli shook her head, and while she was entitled to her opinion, she surely didn't doubt my ability for an award-winning date. I'd taken pictures of the "most perfect dates eva" at least thirty times in the last three months; it was a test I was more than studied for.

"Or you could just tell Mack that you really like Riley and be honest for a change."

"Or," I countered, "you could tell Brad you want to stick your tongue down his throat and inappropriately touch his *Dickens*."

"Very mature, Quinn," she laughed, pretending to not be impressed by my clever reference. "But fine, you have a point."

I sighed, happy because there weren't a lot of people who could out argue me. "Of course I do. So, since I hijacked the start of the night, I'll let you pick where we go next. Seedy bar, loud and trendy club, obnoxious lounge we need to bribe our way into." My smile widened as we walked without purpose or direction.

As long as we didn't go home, I didn't really care where we went. I was too buzzed to sit and watch trashy television like our original plans, and would probably obsess about every detail of mine and Riley's last two interactions if I ended up back home alone. Nope, I needed to be out, burning off energy and devising my next move. What that next move was, I had no idea but I hoped that at some point it would involve very dirty and hot sex with one of FDNY's finest.

"Oh, Quinn!" I was still lost in thought when Karli yanked my arm, stopping me from going forward. "Look, we have got to go in!"

"What? No! Come on, Karli, you can't be serious." I bristled, taking a step back tentatively, like any sudden moves might waken a sleeping cobra.

She pursed her lips, planting her hands on her hips and widening her baby browns like she always did when there were no plans to back down. "Did you not say it was my choice? You wouldn't be reneging on a deal would you? Because *this* is my choice, and we're going in."

Gah, she had me on a technicality, and I didn't renege.

"Fuck," I cursed, the luminosity of neon tube lighting emitting a weird pink glow on her skin while she grinned. "I hate these places. They're for suckers and idiots."

"And tonight, you're one of them." Karli pulled me to the door, the glass obscured by a beaded curtain and a cloud of patchouli.

Someone had obviously forgotten to pay the light bill, the room dim except for flickering white candles and trails of incense. The reflection of the neon pink hand permeated through the yellow—it might have started off as white—curtain, the inside packed with talismans, crystals, books, and enough salt to service the roads of the tri-state area next winter.

We seemed to be alone, no sales associate at the counter, with my heels echoing off the polished floorboards. "You don't need to be a fortune teller to know that we're probably going to get robbed." I laughed, slightly more nervous than I would have liked. Because as much as I believed it was bullshit, I wasn't dumb enough to mock the dark arts.

"They're called clairvoyants, psychics or mediums. Depends on their area of expertise," Karli hissed back. "Fortune teller is derogatory, you can't call them that."

"Are you kidding me? Fortune teller is derogatory?" I coughed, unable to hide my surprise. "I must've missed the important memo that circulated advising us of the proper terminology on how to address charlatans."

Karli shoved her hand across her mouth, trying to hide her giggle. "Shhh, someone is going to hear you."

My eyes squinted, looking around the store that was a con artist short of a scam, and tried to work out if we were being watched via security cameras. Sure, there wasn't a lot of value to take but it was New York, and someone would steal a park bench if it weren't bolted down.

"Non-believer," a voice boomed, the candle wicks flickering as a slight breeze flowed through the room. I had to hand it to the decorator, they had committed and were really putting on the hard sell.

"Yes," I stepped forward, despite Karli trying to hold me back.

This was how I was spending my Saturday night.

I could've been elbow-deep in dirty martinis, dancing on a hot and sweaty dance floor with some Norwegian tourist named Jonas who only knew one English word—yas. But no, instead I was talking to air in some dive shop in Midtown, which was probably a front for the Russian mob.

The black curtain pinned to the back wall separated, revealing that the wall was in fact a doorway.

Cue dramatic entrance.

Out walked a woman who was cloaked in mismatched crushed velour and silver chains. She was white—as in her skin was almost translucent—with wiry strawberry-blonde hair that was graying at the roots. Not sure if she'd been at it awhile or the gig was new, but as she walked toward me—her boney finger extended—she spoke again. "You're strong willed, resistant to the message. Yet you've come here, why?"

Ha, like I had a choice, lady!

"Listen, I didn't mean any disrespect." I met her eyes, not willing to be completely rude. "It's just I don't believe that you can peer into a magical glass orb and see what's on the horizon. Because surely if you could predict the future, you'd have put some money on a World Series win or two, or collected big in Powerball." Okay, so my attempt at being polite had fallen short, but surely someone who had the ability she was claiming to have could have gotten herself some fancier digs and a wardrobe that didn't scream Goodwill chic.

"Quinn," Karli hissed before standing beside me. "My friend is a skeptic, but don't hold it against her. I'm open to the message, and would love to hear what the universe has to say."

I had to hand it to her, Karli flashed that warm smile and let her accent thicken, and people were charmed beyond measure.

Not sure if it was because she was from the South and they taught that shit in school or her bubbly personality shone through. But whatever the reason, *Practical Magic* no longer looked like she was ready to curse me into a toad.

"Yes, yes, you have an open heart." She nodded as she moved closer, the bangles on her wrist jangling as she reached out for Karli. "Come, the universe has many messages for you. I'm Miss Lillian."

Trying to not roll my eyes and ruin what was obviously Karli's idea of a good time—we were going to have serious words when we finally left—I followed them as *Miss Lillian* took us behind the curtain.

Serious words.

Ah, and what a surprise, she'd kept the theme of the front room with more candles and crystals, the round table bare except for a faded black tablecloth and a candelabra that had seen better days. Still, there were chairs so at least we weren't going to have to endure the fiasco on our feet.

"Sit." Miss Lillian pointed to the chairs, taking one herself as her pushed up sleeves exposed a series of random symbols and shapes that looked like jailhouse tattoos. That was assuming they were real at all, there was a guy on the Highline who could give you some decent fake ones that lasted three weeks even with showering.

Miss Lillian closed her eyes, taking a cleansing breath before opening them and greeting us with a smile like it was the first time she'd seen us. "Now, all readings are fifty, no recording them on your phone and no refunds."

"Fifty dollars?" My eyes widened, even more confused if that was her going rate why she couldn't afford a lamp and maybe some decent drapes.

"That's fifty dollars, *each*," she clarified, because derogatory or not, fortune telling wasn't a charity. "And I have no control over the message, sometimes it's something you might not want to hear."

There was a surprise.

Money up front, no refunds and oh . . . the bullshit you might hear might not be to your liking. It seemed to make more sense to take out a fifty and light Ulysses S Grant on fire. I mean, at least then we were being upfront on who was getting burned.

"Of course. And I want a reading for Quinn too," Karli nodded, pulling out her purse, ready to part with her hard-earned cash for this shit show.

"Wait, I've got it," I groaned, digging into my small clutch and unfolding some bills. Even though I knew we were getting taken, Karli didn't earn anywhere near what I did. She never complained, or treated me like an ATM, but the book restoration business wasn't as lucrative as people's vanity. So if being lied to by a poor man's Stevie Nix was what she wanted, then I was going to be what she'd always been for me—a good supportive friend.

Besides, I'd spent more than that on the pizza, so maybe I'd chalk it up to my second act of community service for the day.

Miss Lillian counted out the money—because God forbid we short her—and when she was satisfied there was a hundred dollars in the pile, proceeded to reach across the table and grab Karli's hand.

I expected more theatrics. Maybe some weird groaning or chanting while she connected with the spirit world or something, but there was none of that. No flickering lights, or mysterious breeze either, just a long blink and then she opened her mouth.

"This guy you like, you need to either tell him what you want or move on. He's never going to make the first move."

Thank you, Jesus.

While I didn't believe for a second the Devine had bestowed its gifts on Miss Lillian, it had been an interesting message. And one I'd been trying to give my friend for months. If all it took was a strange woman and a hundred bucks to get Karli to find someone who was worthy of her time and effort, I'd say it was money well spent.

"What?" Karli turned to me, mouthing *oh my, God* before turning back to Miss Lillian. "You know about Brad?"

She shook her head. "I don't know his name, honey, just that he's gun-shy and scared he's going to screw things up with you. I'm not sure it will last, long term, but whatever happens will be on your terms. Whatever you decide though, you'll be happy with it. You know your heart, and you need to trust yourself when it comes to love."

"Wow, okay. Anything else?" Karli asked, watching with such rapture I almost felt bad for poking fun at it earlier. I mean, it wasn't really hurting anyone. And so what if it gave someone a false sense of happiness, wasn't that what alcohol did? At least with Miss Lillian there'd be no hangover.

"I also see . . ." she stopped, squinting like that enabled her to see it better. "You're going to get a promotion with a sizeable raise. You'll be heading the department."

Karli grinned, forgetting the shitty prologue she'd received and concentrating on the positive stuff. Classic Karli, and I couldn't say I blamed her. "Wow, thanks so much Miss Lillian."

"Okay, the non-believer's turn." She reached across to me and I used every ounce of willpower I had not to roll my eyes.

I was doing it for Karli, I reminded myself. It didn't matter what she said, I just had to nod, smile, hear the universe's message and then we could go find me a non-English speaking tourist to make out with. No point in the whole evening being a wash.

"You've recently met a man, who is your soul mate."

Okay, not exactly glaringly specific and something she could say to ninety-five percent of the straight, single and female population in Manhattan and be somewhat accurate.

"Want to help me narrow it down?" I laughed, not buying into it even though Karli's eyes were as wide as dinner plates.

Yes, if I believed a white woman from Long Island—she might have tried to cover the accent but wasn't fooling me—had the powers to see my past, present or future, then sure I'd have assumed she was talking about my *recent* interactions. But she was throwing darts at a board and hoping one of them stuck.

"This man, you didn't mean to meet him. Your paths crossed by fate," she continued, nodding to herself. "Sort of an accident, but not entirely."

"Oh my God." Karli grabbed my hand, squeezing it with enough excitement to stop the blood flow. "She's talking about Riley. The accident that isn't actually an accident."

"Let's not get too excited." I tried to quell my over-excitable friend and not give Miss Lillian any more information she could then use to back up her falsehoods. "It could be anyone. Like that guy I met at the airport who tried to steal my cab," I reasoned, refusing to believe we were talking about the man who I hadn't been able to get off my mind.

"No," Miss Lillian shook her head, seeming to be agitated. "This man . . . he . . . you gave him something. Something private. But . . . oh, I can't see what it is. But it wasn't intended for him, but the mistake was an accident, but it wasn't. He was supposed to get it."

What.

The.

Actual.

Fuck.

"Huh? Do you mean Mack?" It spilled out of my mouth on a gasp, incoherent words and jumbled thoughts tumbling through my brain while I tried to convince myself it had to be some trick. She'd had us followed, or someone was talking to her with an earpiece, or she was insane and the voices had gotten lucky. Any plausible—and a few implausible—possibilities were considered as her words echoed over and over again.

It was so freaking specific.

How the hell could she have known about any of it?

Unwilling to accept it as truth and unable to dismiss it either, I instead sat silent and waited for her to reveal more.

"He's your soul mate. The one you're supposed to be with. And if for some reason you deny your feelings, you will be destined for unhappiness. No one else has the right vibe."

What?

What!

Mack was not my fucking destiny.

I mean, he seemed like a nice guy, but I had to almost beg him to give me his phone number. He was not the guy I wanted to have hot, dirty sex with, who made my pulse race with just a smile. His eyes weren't rich chocolate brown, and I didn't want to discover every groove of his chest with my tongue.

He didn't even have the right forearms for God's sake.

"Listen, lady." I stood up, yanking my hands from her lying and fraudulent grasp. "Mack is not my destiny. You are wrong, and I don't know who the hell put you up to this, but it is not funny. I want sexy forearms, and he doesn't have them."

Miss Lillian looked at me calmly, ignoring the murderous vibe I assumed I was throwing. "Don't shoot the messenger, I'm just telling you what I see." She turned to Karli—who was clearly her favorite—and smiled. "You want me to see if I can get more from the spirits? Ask them what else is in store for you?"

"No, it's okay. Don't need the spirits, I've got Jesus." Karli looked at her watch-less wrist and grabbed my arm. "Oh, look at the time. Thanks so much Miss Lillian, you have a good evening."

Without giving me a chance to argue, Karli dragged me back through the black curtain, out of the smoky room, through the hanging beads, and pushed the glass door open until we were back on the street. My mind was still in free fall, wanting to challenge a woman double my age to some kind of medieval duel. Because that made sense.

So I'd become slightly unhinged, wild-eyed and ranting like a complete moron when what I needed to do was calm the hell down. Miss Lillian was full of shit, and I didn't care what she said, there was no one in charge of my destiny but me.

"Two possibilities," I huffed pointing to the door Karli was trying to distance us from. "Someone told her about Mack and Riley, and if it was you, Karli, you need to come clean," I warned. "Or she is one of those mentalist people. You know, they can read body language, pick up on cues we don't even know we have, then pretend they're being whispered to from the beyond."

Karli sighed, trying to keep up as I stormed down the street, ready to throw myself into traffic if that was what it took to get a cab. "Quinn, do you really think I had time to come here, feed her information, and then hope we'd *coincidentally* stop by? I didn't even know we were going out tonight, when would I have planned it?" Well, she did have a point. "And if any of this was my doing, we both know I would have made Riley your soul mate. Not to mention, I'd have made sure she told me I was going to marry Brad and have cute little babies sometime before I'm thirty-five, something that's apparently not going to happen if I leave it up to him."

Again, another excellent point.

So we could rule out Karli, but there were still other people who knew.

Riley.

"Oh, he's good," I laughed, annoyed I'd fallen for it like an amateur. "He probably saw us walk in and called her or something. That's probably why she was in the back when we arrived. He'd seen where we went and decided to have a little fun at our expense."

Granted, he'd left Gino's first and I hadn't seen which direction he'd gone—still none the wiser which of the three stationhouses he belonged to. But he could have easily laid in wait, hiding and watching us leave and then followed us.

"Sweetie." Karli scrunched her nose as she shook her head. "That seems like a lot of effort. You think he'd really go to all that trouble? And why? To push you into the arms of another guy?"

Uh.

Fine, she had a point.

"Yeah, so it doesn't make complete sense. Maybe it was Mack, maybe they were working as part of a team?"

Okay, I'd just heard myself and even to me—who usually didn't bat an eye at crazy—it sounded insane. Two grown men, who were supposedly at work, would not have had time or the inclination to mess with us. That was what it had come to.

Mentalist.

It was the only logical explanation, and Miss Lillian—or whatever her real name was—had read me and Karli like a book and told us what she thought we wanted to hear. It was the oldest scam there was and I couldn't believe I'd been dumb enough to actually believe it.

I grabbed my midsection, balancing on my heels and laughed uncontrollably in the street. "She almost had me," I gasped for air. "Please, like Mack is my *destiny*," I jazz handed for effect. "So ridiculous."

Karli's lips parted and started to laugh too. "Yeah, and as if she knows anything about Brad and whether or not he's going to ask me out."

"No, that part is true," I giggled, raising my hand to hail a cab. "But since our evening has taken such a dramatic turn why don't we head home."

"Trashy television?" Karli's eyes brightened with excitement.

I nodded as a cab stopped in front of us.

"Trashy television and a *lot* of wine."

Chapter 6

Riley

'D BARELY GOTTEN back to the stationhouse when we were off on another call out. And unlike the other ones we'd received, this one had been an actual fire.

A warehouse fire burning out of control in Hudson Yards put all thoughts of Quinn, the chief, and everything else unrelated out of my head while we battled the blaze. It was hot, intense and got me so excited my balls clenched.

I loved it.

Two engines and a ladder had responded, and every single one of those guys would put their ass on the line for each other and for me. That's the only way it worked. There wasn't any room for doubt when you were running into a burning building, you either believed they had your back or you went and got an office job and punched a clock.

The warehouse had been so old and unmaintained it might as well have been kindling. The windows had blown out, shattered glass littering the sidewalk while thick black smoke poured out of the holes like a demon was being exorcised. And I knew just the crew to send this bad boy back to hell.

Rev—or Bernard Mattis if you wanted to get technical—looked over at me and nodded. "You're lucky you got back when you did or you would have missed the good stuff."

He was in his mid-thirties and as comfortable on a hose as he was doing volunteer work at the local church. I wasn't much into religion, but had to respect a man who would roll up his sleeves on his day off and do whatever St. Martin's needed so the community had a place to pray. His wife was also ridiculously good in the kitchen, and if he ever divorced her, I was going to have to kneecap the guy just for the loss of her chocolate chip cookies.

"I had my radio on me in case you got lonely and needed to chat." I winked, watching as Leighton and Tibbs tackled the inferno from the side. It was almost out, and provided the wind didn't change, we'd have this sucker under control in record time. It was always a race, the risk to people or surrounding buildings rising the longer a fire burned.

Despite shooting the breeze like it was no big deal, there was nothing *casual* about our mood. Muscle memory and years of training were doing their job, and there wasn't one of us who didn't take the situation seriously. But business as usual just helped you not end up in a shrink's chair every week, and we were all about maintaining our mental health.

"Hot spot in southwest corner." The announcement came over the radio. "Maintain lines as we increase ladder access."

Rev nodded, indicating he'd heard it too. "Let's hope there's no more accelerant in that southwest corner, or this thing ain't going to be over as quickly as we thought."

He was right about that. The tinderbox had offered us nothing but bad news since we'd arrived on the scene and was backed up against a tire factory. If the fire spread beyond the lot, we'd not only have a second location to contend with but toxic fumes from the burning rubber.

Lucky for us—and the surrounding neighborhood—the additional line coming through the roof was the final nail in the warehouse's proverbial fiery coffin. It still took a while before the captain was satisfied we were safe to pack up and leave, but we'd managed to save the surrounding buildings.

Another job well done.

It wasn't until we were back in the engine on our way to the station that Rev turned his attention back to me. "So where did you disappear to? You're lucky you're in good with the chief, anyone else would have given you paperwork for sure."

In good with the chief wasn't really accurate, the man being the closest thing to family I had.

John—Mack—McPherson had taken me under his wing when I'd lost both my parents to a car accident.

Drunk driver—my dad being the drunk in question.

Luckily they hadn't taken anyone else with them. I'd seen the headline ticker of a crash while watching T.V. at home but never imagined that John and Jane Doe were Roger and Melissa North. Guess I shouldn't have been surprised though, both of them were a tragedy waiting to happen. And as much as I knew they were garbage, both of them drains on society with drug use and petty theft, they were still my fucking parents. I loved them even though it didn't make sense, hoping that once I got a steady job I'd get them the help they both needed. Sadly, I was about six months too late.

I was eighteen with nothing more than my high school diploma, and not a chance I could afford college. I didn't even have an inheritance, evicted from our *family home* when I couldn't make the rent and ended up couch surfing with the man who had attended the scene of my parents' accident. A lot of shit had changed in those ten years. He'd gotten married and divorced, made rank and become a pillar of the community. And I'd left the legacy of my white-trash upbringing behind, and followed into the footsteps of the only man in my life who'd been decent. So yeah, I'd say the shit between me and the chief was a little more than "in good."

"What can I say," I laughed, shrugging off the trip down memory lane, "he can't resist my winning personality."

Rev chuckled, shifting in his seat as we pulled into the station. "Yeah, that and the fact you're one of the most talented firefighters we've ever seen. And trust me, I hate admitting it, your head is already too big."

"Stop sweet talking me, Rev. I don't want your wife to get jealous." I shot him a grin that had him shaking his head.

After the truck had been restocked, I hit the showers and let the warm water wash over me. The suds felt nice, the comforting smell of Ivory soap filling the air as the steam rose. It was only after I washed my hair that memories of a certain blonde bombshell returned. Probably not the most convenient time when you're not alone and your dick was hanging out.

I managed to get the towel around my waist and keep evidence of my "thoughts" under wraps as I dried off and got back into my uniform. There was still a certain conversation I wanted to have with a certain chief, and barring another alarm, it was happening before we finished our shifts.

"Good work on the warehouse." Mack didn't look up, his hand signing some document as I took a seat opposite him while he sat at his desk. "Heard you didn't even aggravate Cap, that's progress."

"Geez, you, Rev, Cap—getting so much praise today, and it's not even my birthday." I smirked, waiting for him to meet my eyes. "I'd say it was making me uncomfortable but we both know I'd be lying."

He chuckled, tossing the pen across the desk and folding his hands behind his neck as he leaned back in his chair. "What is it you want, North? Other than to bust my balls which we both know you excel at."

"You. Quinn. What's going on there?"

I wasn't the kind of guy to draw out the bullshit with a man who was half father, half brother to me. And while I had a hunch where Quinn sat on the issue, I needed to hear it from the big guy himself.

"You mean the girl we met not even twenty-four hours ago? Who is probably the only other person on the planet more certifiable than you? *And* who you chased after like a bat out of hell when you should have been eating dinner with your team?" He shook his head, stifling a laugh. "Think it's pretty self-explanatory."

"She mentioned a date, asked what you liked. Did she call you?" It was hard not to sound like I was thirteen with pimples on my face and no hair on my balls, but that's where I'd ended up. Still, there was only one man I'd ever allowed to see me vulnerable and he was sitting right across from me.

Mack huffed out a breath, studying me before tossing me his phone. "She hasn't called. But I did get a text about ten minutes ago and it didn't seem to come from a sober person."

Mack,
When you free?
We have destiny even though you don't have forearms.
Miss Lillian can kiss my ass but just to be sure we'll date.
I don't need a hex right now.
Quinn.

"What the fuck?" I re read the text, trying to work out if it made more sense the second time around. It didn't, and unless I'd suffered smoke inhalation I wasn't aware of, it wasn't just me. "*We have destiny even though you don't have forearms*? Who the fuck is Miss Lillian?" I laughed, shaking my head as I read it a third time. "Do you think it's some kind of code?"

"Kid, you're asking me about women? Pretty sure my history with Melinda voids anything I'm going to say on the matter." He raised his eyebrow, warning me. "But the idea was to keep out of trouble, not go jumping headfirst into it."

He was right on both accounts. One, the message had most definitely not come from a sober person. And two, I was jumping headfirst into trouble. I'd also noticed he hadn't responded, the incoming message sitting ignored. And it wasn't polite to keep a woman waiting.

My fingers worked over the screen, typing out a message before Mack could snatch it back. "What the hell are you doing?" He launched across the desk but missed my hand and the phone.

Sucker.

Quinn,
Sober up and meet me tomorrow at
9 a.m.
I'll buy you breakfast.
You choose location.

It annoyed me a little that she would think it was coming from Mack and not from me, but that would all change in the morning. That was assuming she turned up. But considering her track record, I'd say my chances were better than average.

I didn't have to wait too long, the alert of the incoming message coming only a minute or two after I'd hit send.

I'm sobre now, Macck
I have a shoot in a.m.
Centree maX Mall.
Be there or be there.
Quinn

My shoulders shook as I laughed out loud; she was hilarious. I bet she looked adorable, glassy-eyed and relaxed. And hopefully somewhere safe like in her bed—naked and alone. While she still was not making sense, I assumed she had some kind of photo shoot at Center Max Mall in Brooklyn. But judging by her response, I wasn't sure she was going to be in any kind of condition to work.

"Want to swap phones with me Chief for a few hours?" I tossed mine casually onto the desk. "Pretty much anyone who's going to call you is already here. And if Melinda calls, I'll take a message."

His eyes dropped to my phone, shaking his head as he handed it back. "Nice try, but no. If you're going to text her, you do it on your own phone." He held out his hand, waiting for me to give his back, which I did, but not before taking Quinn's number.

Yeah, it wasn't like me to grab a person's digits under false pretenses but I'd take whatever bad karma came with it. And Mack was right, it needed to be on my phone. Of course it had occurred to me that she was probably drunk enough not to realize the response was going to be coming from another number, which would make things interesting. Either way, I would come clean tomorrow when I saw her, and let her yell at me if that was what she wanted.

"Wipe the grin off your face and go do some work. You're still on the clock." Mack pointed to the door.

I rose to my feet, giving him a two finger salute as I made my way out of the office and typed out my next message.

Are you home?
Safe?

She didn't miss a beat, responding to the new message thread with apparently no clue it wasn't the number she'd texted originally.

You had to go make it weird
If you ask what I'mm wearing I'm going to be very disaapointteded.

I chuckled, enjoying the exchange a little too much as I continued.

Not like I asked you if you were in bed and naked.
Which was exactly what I'd been thinking
I just wanted to make sure you got home safe or see if you were still out.

You're a nice really guy.
Home. Bed. Naked.
See tomorrow up 9.
Quinn

Fuck.

Her last message was like a sucker punch to the gut, first wrongly assuming I was a nice guy. Sure, she probably thought she was still talking to Mack who took being decent to a new level. But me, yeah, not so much.

And second, knowing she was in her bed naked made me harder than I knew it should. She was drunk and vulnerable, and I was excited by it? Refer to my previous statement about not being a nice guy. Still, I could argue logic until I turned up tomorrow at nine and it wouldn't make a difference. Because whether it made sense or not, there was an attraction between us. And I knew I wasn't the only one to feel it.

On a whim and maybe to clear my conscience a little, I sent one last text.

Mack is a nice guy, but you haven't been speaking to
him.
See you tomorrow.
Riley

Then I shoved it back in my pocket vowing to toss it out the window if I checked it again in the next few hours. I refused to be *that* asshole even if it did give me a warm feeling in my chest just seeing words on a screen that had come from her.

As I headed to the weight room I could hear the voices of Tibbs and Leighton going through some training with Evans, the rookie. He was only three months in but eager, and had I not had so much adrenaline pumping through my veins I might have joined them. But that would have to wait for another time, ignoring the chatter as I changed into a pair of warm up shorts and a tank and shut the door.

The place was empty, deserted except for a dirty towel someone had forgot on the bench press and a half-consumed bottle of Gatorade on the floor. And with some of the older guys already napping in the bunks, and the captain doing paperwork like the chief, I didn't expect that to change.

I liked the quiet. And the slow burn that spread across your muscles when you worked them to almost exertion.

It was a great reminder that unlike my parents, I was still alive.

I could've been in that car with them all those years ago, ended up in the same burned out wreck and rocking a tombstone. But for whatever reason, I wasn't and despite how it had started, I had a really great life.

And I was going to enjoy every last minute of it.

Chapter 7

Quinn

NO GOOD CAN come from a fortuneteller—sorry, *clairvoyant*. Firstly, because it assumed that your road was already mapped out. Your journey through life predetermined, driven by some invisible destiny while you were asleep at the wheel.

There wasn't a chance I believed that horseshit.

Refusing to accept that we—the people living the life—didn't one hundred percent control our own fate.

Secondly, the drinking that comes after is not helpful.

Fine, the drinking wasn't Miss Lillian's fault directly, even if her messages were questionable. Still, what were we supposed to do? Huddle together, accept the inevitable with an open heart and cheerful grin? Yeah, maybe Karli might have been able to manage it but I sure as hell could not. Which is why we did the only responsible thing and drank until we no longer cared. So reasonable or not, I was holding Miss Lillian accountable for my hangover the next morning.

I was also aware that I had drunk texted Mack at some point of the evening—sometime between bottle one and bottle two—and asked him out on a date.

Not sure which of those things made me want to puke, the excessive consumption of cheap white wine or the horror of being a fucking cliché.

I was positive the exchange wasn't my best work, but felt confident I'd stopped myself from saying anything completely mortifying. It could always be worse I reminded myself, with a history of previous drunk texts dissolving into drunk calls which inevitably led to drunk phone sex.

But when I woke up my phone was drained of battery lying facedown on the floor, my panties were still on, and my vibrator was still tucked away in the bottom drawer of my nightstand. So at some point I'd fallen asleep and whatever I'd said or done couldn't have been that bad.

Not something I probably would have been able to boast if I'd been texting Riley.

Ha, if he'd been my *destiny*, I'm sure I would have dissolved into inappropriate innuendo and a string of flirty suggestions. And all of them would have involved him getting his fine sexy ass to my apartment and making sweet, sweet love to me.

See, that was why I knew I couldn't be trusted. Because who the hell talked like that? Surely not anyone with any decent seductive technique.

So rather than relive what I'm sure was a bunch of bumbling messages where he was probably being more polite than he should, I plugged my phone into the charger and got out of bed.

As much as I wanted to enjoy a lazy Sunday morning laying around in bed and fantasizing about sexy firemen, duty called. I had a shoot for a social media campaign and they needed me there at the ridiculous o'clock otherwise known as nine a.m. on a weekend. Still, no rest for the wicked and it was nice to have something local for a change. Maybe it could start a trend where I could sleep consecutive nights in my apartment, pack away my suitcase, and adopt a dog.

Okay, maybe I was getting a little ahead of myself, grimacing at my reflection in the mirror before I stepped into the shower.

Ugh.

So wasn't a smart move.

I wasn't sure exactly what I was chastising myself for, whether it was the drinking or accepting the *Marty and Jenn's* shoot I apparently needed to be at in the next thirty minutes. Thank God, it wasn't far from my apartment, Center Max Mall only a fifteen-minute leisurely stroll or seven minutes if it wasn't so leisurely.

Ordinarily when I turned up to shoot for a client, my appearance was on point. Hair, make up, fancy clothes—it was all about the image even if I wasn't the one in the photograph. You wouldn't want to buy a Mercedes from a man driving a beat up Honda, so my work followed the same logic.

But the day's gig was a freebie, a favor I was throwing Marty and Jenn's way because they'd been such great friends of my dad. He'd known them both since college, but had unfortunately died before seeing their dreams of an ice cream and dessert emporium become a reality. In a small way, it made me feel like he was still with me, his old Pentax camera stuffed into my messenger bag even though I probably wouldn't use it. It was also the reason why I forewent the makeup, the flashy clothes, pulling on a pair of sweats, a hoodie that was two sizes too big and sweeping my hair into a ponytail.

Hey, I was decent, and Marty and Jenn had seen me look ten times worse.

Thankfully none of the stores opened until ten so when I entered the mall via a side door, the only *shoppers* were gray-haired, athletic-wearing retirees doing laps.

"Quinn!" Jenn grabbed me, engulfing me in a hug that was probably more suited to greeting a ten-year-old. "Look how beautiful she is, Marty, isn't she just stunning?"

Marty nodded behind her, beaming like he always did. "Of course she is, and smart and talented. We saw Carrie and her family last week, three perfect little girls. Your mom is so proud."

Mention of my mom and sister had me swearing under my breath. In the rush to get ready and out the door, I'd forgotten my recharging phone. And while I didn't see my family much these days especially during the week, Mom hadn't missed a Sunday morning call in forever.

"Ah, yeah. They're great," I lied, hoping to God my mother hadn't called the cops yet. "Hey, do you mind if I borrow your phone really quickly. I need to call her so she doesn't freak out. I forgot mine at home."

Fussing over me not to rush, Jenn handed me her fancy new smartphone, insisting it would give her time to make waffles. My grumbling stomach didn't help convince her I wasn't hungry, choosing to pick my battles as I agreed and dialed about the only number I knew by heart. At least if I was ever arrested, I'd have one less thing to worry about, the call connecting almost immediately.

"Hello," the frantic edge in my mother's voice evident as she answered. "Hello?"

"Mom, it's me. Sorry if you were worried. Karli and I had a late night and I forgot to charge my phone. Please tell me you haven't called 9-1-1." I breathed into the phone, feeling terrible for making her worry as I stepped to the side.

She was so understanding, totally supportive of my fly-by-the-seat-of-my-pants lifestyle as long as every Sunday morning—regardless of where I was—I let her know I was okay.

"Quinn Iris Rhodes." She three-named me, reinforcing I was in big trouble. "I was thirty minutes away from getting in the car and driving to New York, and you know I hate that stupid traffic."

I tried to laugh, taking a seat on a nearby bench for some privacy while I reassured her. "Mom, there's traffic in New Jersey and I'm fine. I'm here at Marty and Jenn's emporium, ready to do a shoot."

If I thought mention of work would get me off the hook, I was sadly mistaken. But it was my fault so I let her yell at me a little longer, and then told her about my week. Of course I left out mention of the two men I'd met yesterday and the debacle with Miss Lillian, but I was used to giving her the curated version, not hanging up until she was satisfied I was safe and happy.

"I'm sorry." I turned to hand Jenn her phone, my *quick* phone call taking at least twenty minutes. "Now, let's get this show on the road before the mall opens for real."

Oh.

My.

God.

Sure, Jenn was there—brandishing waffles like she promised—but standing right beside her was the hot sexy firefighter I'd been having improper thoughts about. And Jesus Christ did he look good.

Dressed in a pair of jeans, faded t-shirt and a smile, he was every bit as delicious both inside a uniform and out. Freshly showered, smelling like soap and deodorant, I breathed him in like it was the first time I'd had oxygen.

"Riley?" I asked, wondering if they hadn't piped some weird hallucinogenic gas through the mall vents in an effort to increase spending. Lord knows if men like him were around, I wouldn't be in a hurry to leave either.

He waved, the cheerful expression on his face confirming I was not seeing things, his eyes moving up and down my body as he took me in.

FUCK.

Too bad my expedited morning ritual meant I looked like a college student ready for a drive-by. And to think I was high-fiving myself earlier, reassuring myself that no one who gave a damn would be seeing me on a Sunday morning at the Mall. It had to be retribution for cursing Miss Lillian and her bogus destiny bullshit, making my mother worry, or scandalous thoughts about sex with Riley up against a fire truck. Or maybe it was all freaking three, thank you very much universe!

He smiled, his lips curling into a grin as he moved closer. "Eventful evening?"

Ha! If that weren't the understatement of the freaking century. "What are you doing here?" I managed to string a sentence together while being unable to hide my shock. Not that being composed was riding high on my list of priorities. Checking to see I was actually wearing a bra, and the consequences of Jenn's beaming smile much more important.

"Oh, Quinn, you brought your boyfriend to meet us. I could cry. Marty, look how handsome he is. And tall. She always did like the tall ones. They're going to make the most adorable babies."

I was going to die.

"Wow, look at those waffles. I'm starving. Famished." I grabbed the plate out of Jenn's hands, ready to bathe in maple syrup if it would help the situation. Good news, I had remembered my bra but I was fairly certain my hoodie had a pizza stain on it so I was holding off on celebrating the victory.

Riley raised an eyebrow, watching as I shoveled a forkful of waffle into my mouth like a savage, while Marty patted him on the shoulder like he'd won a third-grade spelling bee.

It was the beginning of the end.

That stupid hex Miss Lillian had warned me about was coming home to roost, and somehow I was going to end up a sexual pariah.

Without warning, Riley curled his beautiful big hands around my plate, saving me from asphyxiation by baked goods as he took it away. "Let's take a quick walk." He handed the waffles to Jenn who was already promising to whip up another batch.

"You forget or not remember?" Tingles moving through my body as his hands gently clasped my arms. I liked their weight, firm but not aggressive.

I shook my head trying to remember if I'd said something back at Gino's. I'd mentioned a date with Mack, flirted, let him check out my boobs in my nice dress—no, nothing that would help explain what he was doing there.

"What was I supposed to remember?" I leaned forward, trying to find some bravado. "And you still haven't answered me as to what you're doing here."

He rolled his eyes, puffing out a breath like I was the one being unreasonable. Not sure why he was annoyed, I wasn't following him around like a stalker, turning up on his doorstep when he looked less than ideal. Not that I thought it was possible.

"You sent Mack a message. I responded. We made plans." His dazzling chocolate eyes not showing any hint of a lie, his grip tightening as a rather enthusiastic retiree lapped around us. He'd given us a dirty look, grumbling under his breath for us to move aside.

"No, I sent Mack a message, *he* responded. I'm fairly sure I flirted badly and then I went to sleep. We didn't talk." I left out the part about there being no phone sex because I was concerned that my assessment might have been incorrect. After all, I'd apparently made plans, giving him details on where I was going to be. Heavy breathing and touching myself didn't seem like such a big leap anymore.

"Quinn, it was me the entire time. I took his phone initially and when I texted you from mine, you didn't notice it was a different number. It was probably a dick move not to clarify, but you sounded so adorable. Anyway, when I said goodnight, I *told* you it was me. I assumed you knew."

I opened my mouth and then shut it again, no words coming out as I tried to work out if I was angry or glad it had been Riley the entire time. It wasn't cool that I'd assumed I'd been talking to someone only to find out it was someone else. Even if there'd been some veiled attempt to tell me, it was still kind of shady. Although I hadn't exactly behaved in the most honorable way either, so I wasn't about to throw stones when there were so many glass windows around.

"Quinn?" Riley asked, his cocky smile not so sure. "You don't seem like the kind of person who is usually speechless."

He was right about that.

My mouth was legendary, getting me into trouble and out of it with equal regularity and I was rarely short of something to say. It helped when I worked, able to make conversation even in the most difficult circumstances. But as he stood there—a real-life action hero—I couldn't find words.

"So . . ." he prompted, waving his hand, waiting for me to continue.

God, I liked him.

Not sure why, but there was something about him that fascinated the hell out of me. And maybe it was because I was used to men who didn't challenge me or maybe it was the hunch he'd call me on my bullshit. He was exactly the kind of guy who could be more than just a one-night stand. The kind I'd like to stick around and get to know. But he was no longer a stranger, and at that point in my life I wasn't exactly stellar relationship material. Hello, commitment issues!

"I can't date you," I blurted out, regretting it the minute it came out of my mouth. It hadn't been what I'd wanted to say, and yet clearly it was exactly what I'd meant. Because as much as I would have loved to push him up against a wall and have dirty hot sex, relationships always complicated things.

His brow creased, his gaze slightly confused before his lips twitched at the edges. He chuckled, keeping his hands on my arms as he smirked. "Did I ask you to date?"

Um.

Well.

"I guess you didn't." I shrugged, not really sure why I was disappointed when I'd been clear I wouldn't—or more realistically couldn't—date him. Still, no one liked a rejection, even when you were pretending not to want it in the first place.

"Okay, so it's settled. We're not dating," he said matter-of-factly like he was commenting on the weather. "You want to go eat some breakfast? Those waffles looked amazing, and if the way you were shoving them into your mouth is any indication of how they tasted, I want in." He tipped his chin to Jenn, whose lifted plate looked like the Pride Rock presentation of *Simba* in the *Lion King*.

Um.

What?

"What do you mean breakfast? Didn't we just decide we're not dating?" I tried to find some reason, some semblance of cognition where *breakfast* made sense.

"Yeah, but I'm here and I'm hungry. So let's go eat." His hands which up to that point were maintaining contact with my arms, slipped down to my waist and spun me around. "Hint, it's that way."

My ungraceful twirl—because clearly I was winning at life—made me unsteady on my feet, just narrowly avoiding a collision with a spritely, Lycra-wearing lady old enough to be my grandma.

"Hey, careful there," she huffed as she passed by.

"Wait a second." I turned back to face Riley, resting my hands on his chest.

I mean, I hadn't started the touching thing but since he started it, I wanted my turn. *Mmmm. Nice chest. So firm and toned and*—shit, I was getting sidetracked, and if his smug raised eyebrow was anything to go by, he knew it too. But I wasn't moving my hands. I had to get something out of it, especially since I crawled out of bed looking like an extra from a French play set in the revolution. You know, ones that had dirty, haggard street whores who looked liked they were dying of tuberculosis.

"Wait a second," I repeated. Hey, anything to keep my fingers on him a little longer. Man, he must work out. A. Lot. "So we're just going to eat?"

"Yeah, we can talk if you want to. Especially since now you seem to have regained the ability." He chuckled, glancing down at his chest, which would probably be sporting indentations of my fingers very soon. "But we might want to move, we're currently being heckled by mall walkers."

He wasn't wrong, shaking heads and unimpressed glances shot our way for apparently being in their path. "Oh, well that will not do." I lifted my chin, throwing off their judgmental stares with a defiant one of my own. "The nerve of us."

My sarcasm must have amused him, a bright and warm laugh escaping from his mouth, making his chest shake. I liked the sound of it, and the things it did to his face. Not sure he needed any more help in that department—he was already basically a God—but Riley laughing was perfection.

"Right? So let's go eat some of Jenn's waffles before we start any more trouble." His beautiful chocolate-colored eyes threatened exactly the trouble his mouth said he was trying to avoid, his wicked grin confirming it.

"Sure, waffles," I agreed, excitement coursing through my veins as my skin heated. "Or trouble, I'm game." My shoulder lifted, taunting him in an unintentional dare.

Or maybe it had been intentional.

I was pretty freaking good at trouble.

"Yeah, I am too."

Oh-uh, apparently I wasn't the only one.

Chapter 8

Riley

USUALLY WHEN I came off a twenty-four-hour rotation I went home, slept and ate. Twenty-four on, forty-eight off meant my free time was whenever the hell it landed. And weekends, holidays and special occasions were just another day. Either on or off, it didn't much matter.

But I hadn't even had time to go home, showering and changing at the station and leaving as soon as the new crew clocked on. Mack had given his usual spiel, telling me to make good choices. But I think even he knew there wasn't a lot that could stop me from making my morning meet up with Quinn.

She hadn't responded to my last message—but she hadn't tried to cancel either—so I wasn't entirely sure what I was walking into. Unpredictability and Quinn were sort of a package deal, and it was a little unnerving how much I liked it.

With no idea where I was supposed to meet her at the mall, I'd strolled casually knowing she was the kind of woman that I wouldn't be able to miss. It helped the mall was still largely empty, finding her made easier without the crowd.

Turns out, I didn't have to look too hard, discovering Quinn talking animatedly on the phone not far from an ice cream shop. And fuck me, if I didn't want to walk right up and fucking kiss her.

Last night she'd looked like a bombshell. Her hair, her makeup, the outstanding dress that looked like it had been painted on—every single part of her was mouthwateringly delicious. And I was hungry and thirsty for every last drop.

But this morning, she was different. Gone was the makeup, the sexy dress, the styled hair, and in its place was a woman that was more gorgeous than anything I'd ever seen. She was stunning—no tricks, no distractions—her bare face and pulled back hair making her look even more beautiful. And as for her wardrobe, I could've had her out of those sweats and hoodie in twenty seconds flat. Nothing sexier than a woman who was comfortable in her own skin and owned it, and my dick was so hard it was losing circulation.

Down, boy.

Not so surprisingly her recollection of our text exchange wasn't great, but she was sadly mistaken if she thought I was going to wave her goodbye and leave. Yeah, not a chance in hell.

Usually when a woman looked at you like a deer in headlights at the thought of dating you, it wasn't a good sign. It was a hint to tip your hat, bid her goodbye, and move your attention to someone who wanted it. I'd never forced a woman to do *anything*, let alone spend time with me, and I sure wasn't going to start now. But her little declaration didn't even leave a mark, amusing the hell out of me. We'd do it her way, and if dating wasn't on offer than I'd be anxious to see what else was.

Not bothering to ask whether Quinn wanted me to keep touching her, I led her back to *Marty and Jenn's*, my hands firmly around her waist. Wasn't sure who was wearing the bigger grin—them or me—as we resaid our hellos, Quinn and I directed to a small table.

"A fireman!" Jenn—which best I could work out was some kind of surrogate aunt—clapped her hands excitedly. We'd met briefly while Quinn was on the phone, but she was only just getting to proper introductions. "Wow, you're so brave. Marty, he's so brave, isn't he? And handsome? So handsome."

I chuckled, watching Quinn's cheeks pink. The girl could send a random guy a pair of lacy panties and not bat an eye, but an overly enthusiastic aunt calling me *handsome* did her in. It was clear the opinion of Jenn and Marty was important to her, and I liked that she had people around her that obviously cared.

I came up a little short in that department. Who knew if I had any aunts or uncles—blood related or otherwise. I'd never met any, and none bothered to come forward after the funeral, so I assumed my parents evolved out of thin air. Or they were such deadbeats they'd burned every bridge, which was probably more likely. Still, families, can't pick them.

"Good for you, son." Marty indulged his wife, smiling at her while he served us milkshakes. "A very honorable career choice, exactly the kind of man who's deserving of our Quinn."

Their Quinn rolled her eyes, mouthing an apology and trying to smile. As much as I could tell she hated it, she would rather let them embarrass her than hurt their feelings. It said a lot about her, and reinforced what I already knew—there was something about her that was undeniably special.

"So how are you guys related?" I asked, not sure if it was too personal a question. Still, I was eating breakfast with a woman who forty-eight hours ago I didn't know and now I couldn't leave alone, being hosted by members of her family. Normal conventions really didn't fit.

"Her dad and I were best friends. No finer man than Tom." Marty rested his hand on Quinn's shoulder in what I assumed was an act of comfort. And judging by the tense he used—the past—Tom aka Quinn's dad was no longer with us. Weird to think we had that in common, though I could assure you no one would ever talk in glowing terms about my old man. That was where the similarities stopped.

"We never had any children of our own. So we count Quinn and Carrie as ours," Jenn added, beaming like she couldn't be prouder. "And to think she took time out of her busy weekend to help us with photos for the shop. For FREE!" She waved her hand, looking like she might cry. "She's an angel. A perfect, talented angel."

"Okay Jenn." Quinn's cheeks heated. "You're going to inflate my ego's ego. And I told you, it was nothing. I'm happy to help."

"Carrie's my sister." Quinn felt the need to explain. "She lives in Jersey where she obviously isn't being nominated for the Nobel Peace prize like I am, but hey, we all can't be so selfless."

Jenn and Marty laughed, well versed in Quinn's sarcasm, but I found her latest installment interesting. Was she sassy or deflecting? Something I was definitely going to try to work out.

"You're from Jersey?" I playfully bumped my shoulder into her as I leaned closer. "You don't sound like a transplant."

"Whatchatalkin' about?" She pursed her lips, pretending to give me attitude. "Yew sayin' I don't got an ax-cent. Wud-ever."

This time I laughed too, because as beautiful and talented as she was, she was fucking hilarious.

Man, this girl.

Where the hell did she come from?

"Okay, as much as I'd *love* to sit around and continue talking about myself." Her hand dramatically fluttered at her chest. "We should probably finish breakfast and get shooting."

We polished off what was left of the waffles and milkshakes, insisting I help Marty clear the plates while Jenn and Quinn set up the shots.

She got creative with a couple of ice cream cones, rigging a set up with fishing wire and Perspex to make them look like they were floating midair. Then dumped one upside down onto the counter, positioning M&Ms so the melted ice cream looked like it had transformed into candy.

Not saying a word, she twisted back and forth with her camera, her lips moving silently like she was talking to herself. She was in her own world, the melting ice cream and her camera the only thing getting her attention. It was hot, the crease at the bridge of her nose crinkling whenever she took a break and looked at the camera display.

It was fascinating to watch her, the attention to every detail amazing, as she moved things up to seven times before she was satisfied. Freebie or not, Marty and Jenn were getting the full-service treatment. And if I hadn't loved ice cream before, she'd have converted me without a doubt.

She'd spent almost an hour, a crowd gathering behind us as people got curious about what she was doing. It was weird, Quinn looked almost startled when she turned around, like she'd been in her own world and just realized where she was. She recovered quickly, slipping on the confident smile I'd seen at the coffee shop, and encouraging the spectators to try the mint-chip, which was apparently her favorite. *Good to know.*

By the time she packed up her equipment and said goodbye to Marty and Jenn, I was struggling not to yawn. I never got any decent sleep when I was on duty, napping sporadically but nothing of any real substance.

"You know," She slung the messenger bag over her shoulder as she came out to meet me. "If you yawn one more time, I'm going to have to go back inside and let Jenn top up my ego. Geez, way to make a girl feel special." Her smile fucking beaming.

"I'm just trying to keep it real for you. Balance it out. Participation ribbons and gold stars for everyone are destabilizing humanity. Maybe," I leaned closer, her hair smelling of cotton candy and vanilla ice cream, "you aren't that great."

"Ha!" She scoffed, pushing roughly against my chest as she laughed. "I'm fucking awesome. A delight! You should be so lucky to know me."

"Don't know, Quinn." I bit back the grin. "I mean, I save *lives*. Did you not hear how honorable and brave I am? What about handsome? Sounds to me like *you're* the lucky one."

Her body shook as she giggled, her eyes and face lighting up with what could only be described as pure magic. Everything about her was animated, beautiful and raw. There was a vulnerability to her, a realness—something I just couldn't quantify.

And then she stopped, noticing her hands wrapped around my chest and mine were around her waist. Not even sure how we'd got there, like some magnetic force had pulled us there and neither of us had been conscious of it.

"Well, I should let you go sleep." She untangled her arms from me and I fought the urge not to pull her back. "I really don't remember the messages, but I guess I didn't mind your stalking too much. I'll go relive our conversation when I get back to my apartment, I'm sure I was hilarious." Her smile slipped a little as she took a step back.

"I could drive you home? I mean, you already know where to find me, seems only fair that I get an address too."

It was the most pathetic attempt to prolong a goodbye I'd ever seen. It wasn't smooth, or even the slightest bit inviting, the offer sounding so fucking creepy I'd have turned down my own ride. But I didn't want it to end. Dead tired and no idea what the hell an extra few minutes would achieve, I just did not want to leave her. And despite common sense arguing I should play it smart, and stop acting like a moron, my gut told me different.

She hesitated, the mental pros and cons being weighed in front of my eyes as she shifted on her feet. "Okay," she agreed, the answer seeming to surprise us both.

"Okay." I grabbed her hand, lacing her fingers through mine and making an exaggerated motion toward the exit. "Let's get out of here."

If I'd known she lived only a few minutes away, I'd have offered to walk. Not because I didn't love having her in my truck, but because it would have given me more fucking time. Hell, I'd have crawled, that would have given me a good forty-five minutes easy.

But when she said she lived in Brooklyn, she was talking about the flashy part, just over the bridge. You could still see Manhattan, and fuck me if it wasn't like five minutes from the fucking mall.

And as I pulled up to her brown brick stylish apartment building in DUMBO—which literally meant Down Under Manhattan Bridge Overpass— I was all out of excuses. She was going to open the door of my beat-up Ford Explorer and I was either going to embarrass myself or she was going to walk away.

"I *don't* know," she said suddenly, her hand hesitating on the door handle, answering some question I didn't remember asking.

I reached across, unable to stop myself from touching her as my fingers grazed her cheek. "Don't know what, beautiful?"

She swallowed, blinking before meeting my gaze and pushing whatever reservations she had about what she was going to say to the side. "I don't know where to find you. I sent pizzas to three stationhouses, and even now, I have no idea which one was yours."

I hadn't meant to laugh, wanting nothing more than to close the gap between us and just fucking kiss her. It had been an urge that was getting difficult to ignore, and something I wasn't going to be able to resist if I sat with her much longer. But her revelation was beyond amusing.

Man, she was perfect.

So fucking perfect.

And I no longer cared if I embarrassed myself or not.

"Now whose ego needs help," I leaned in closer, chuckling. "Which other companies got my Gino's? I didn't even get to have any. By the time I got back, it was all gone. Now I find out, I wasn't even that special? Thanks a lot, Quinn."

The heat between us wasn't just one sided. Her pupils dilated, licking her lips as she watched my mouth while I hovered just a couple of inches out of reach.

"How did you know it was for you? I could have been sending it to M—" I cut her off, resting my finger on that pretty pink mouth. I didn't want to play anymore, and I sure as hell didn't want to hear her lie.

"I'm going to kiss you, Quinn. It can be a one-time deal, or I can do it again. I'll let you decide. But if I don't have that mouth of yours right the hell now, I know it's going to be the biggest regret of my life."

It felt like there was a boot on my chest, my skin too tight and I was losing my mind. The second between watching her nod her head and my lips on hers feeling like it took a fucking eternity.

And then, there was no stopping me.

My fingers wrapped around her ponytail, bringing her closer as my mouth attacked hers. She moaned, the parting of her lips all my tongue needing to get the advantage. But it wasn't just me. Her hands cupped my face as her body strained to get closer, the center console stopping her from getting too far.

"Riley," she breathed my name between kisses, her hands moving down my neck to my chest. "God, you're hot."

"Too late now, Quinn." I sucked on her neck, my need to have her against me driving me insane. "You already did a hatchet job on my ego, saying nice things won't fix it."

Truth was, I didn't fucking care what she said. She could send pizza to every company on the eastern seaboard, and tell me she didn't want to date. But as long as her mouth was on mine, and I was touching her, she could spill whatever lies she wanted.

"I need to be closer," she begged, keeping her lips fused to mine as she contorted herself into my lap. It was tight, the steering wheel digging into her back till I released the seat and rolled us all the way back.

It wasn't ideal, my windows tinted just enough to shield us from an audience but not enough to avoid a charge if a cruiser happened to pass by. Not sure getting a ticket wouldn't be worth it, my hands moving from her back to her ass as she ground into my crotch.

Jesus.

Fucking.

Christ.

I couldn't stop, moving from her lips to her chin, her neck. My mouth kept busy kissing, sucking and biting her skin, while my hands did their own exploring. Like an animal who was out of control, my hips rocked into her so she could feel exactly how hard she made me.

There was no way I was going to fuck her like this, not a chance I was going to waste what I knew would be monumentally awesome. She deserved better, and I wasn't going to disrespect her by treating her like a cheap hookup. But I needed more of her, and at that moment, fucking her mouth with my tongue was all I could get, and I was gonna take it.

Her sweet breath panted against my mouth, her hoodie hindering me getting the full effect of her tits pressed to my chest as she circled her hips. I knew it was making her wet, the idea she was using my cock to get her off making me want to bust through my jeans.

"We should stop." My voice escaped past my clenched jaw, my hands locked around her hips and holding her still. "Quinn, we *need* to stop."

She nodded, agreeing with me while teasing me with kisses like she couldn't help herself. It was not a good way to be, one of us needed to pony up and be responsible and it was clear it wasn't going to be her.

"Quinn, you're fucking killing me," I groaned, closing my eyes as my dick throbbed. "Is that what you want? Because I'm really fucking close."

There hadn't been any reported cases of a man dying from blue balls but I was sure it was possible. And not wanting to test the theory out, I yanked her ponytail slightly, pulling her away just enough to give us both a moment.

The windows were fogged up, and we'd drawn some rather interesting stares from a few people who'd happened to stroll by on the sidewalk. It was still morning, and a classy neighborhood, and dry humping in a truck was frowned upon I was sure.

"I don't want to kill you." She traced my lips with her finger, breathing heavy.

It was a dangerous question, but one I couldn't stop myself from asking. "Then what do you want?"

Because whatever it was, she'd pretty much get it.

Her eyebrow arched as her mouth hesitated. "Can you come upstairs with me and not expect sex?"

"Quinn, I don't expect anything." My hands cupped her face. "And right now, I'd probably go to hell if you fucking asked."

That earned me a smile, and a big one at that, her lips brushing against mine one last time before reaching across to the passenger side and fishing out her bag. "So come with me."

I couldn't help the smirk.

"Not like *that* you jerk." She pushed against my chest. "I can already tell this is probably a bad idea."

She was probably right, my fingers interlacing with hers as I brought her hand to my lips. "And I can already tell you are full of bad ideas, and I'm going to love every last one of them."

Chapter 9

Quinn

PROBABLY NOT THE smartest decision to ask Riley to come up to my apartment, but I was a flawed woman and there wasn't a lot I could do. I accepted that when it came to smart choices, I didn't always make them, and was totally okay with it.

I embraced it.

It was who I was.

It also meant there was less chance of us being cited for public indecency for using him as a sex toy, so really, I was more responsible than it seemed.

Yay, me!

But as much as I wanted nothing more than to close the door behind us and attack him like a wild hyena, I hoped the ground rules I'd put on record would help me stay on the straight and narrow.

Unfortunately for him, being incredibly sweet with Jenn and Marty had ruled him completely out of being a fling. Flings only worked if there were zero emotional feelings, and exposure to personal details and private life were kept to a minimal. That's why my last guy had worked out so well, English as a second language was a handy little buffer.

So whatever slim chance he had before—which realistically had been more wishful thinking on my part—I'd waved them goodbye when he crashed my morning.

Firstly, he'd seen me looking like hell. No fling is allowed to see that. Nope, you have to be perfect—and so do they—to maintain the sexual chemistry because that's all you have going for you. We don't know each other really, so no, we're not together for moral support and sharing our hopes and dreams. It's physical. That's it. Sure, you're allowed to dress down a little, keep it casual with some jeans and a top, but the minute you look like Old Navy chewed you up hard and spat you out, it's over.

And assuming I granted leniency, letting the less than perfect appearance slide, there had been too much personal conversation. He knew my sister's name, he'd met people from my inner circle, he knew details. It was like an exposure to an infection and we were too far gone. Once the bubonic plague takes hold, there's no going back.

So there we were, unable to use him for casual sex, with feelings I didn't understand, and a relationship track record that didn't do me any favors. But I liked him, and I was selfish, and wanted him in my life even though it probably didn't make sense.

The door closed behind us, my body pressing against it as he kissed me. "You smell like ice cream and mischief, and I want to lick them both."

Whoa.

So not helping.

"I should take another shower," I groaned against his lips. "Make myself look less like a homeless person."

His kiss deepened, his mouth taking desperate pulls while his fingers pressed against my hips. "You look fucking perfect, except for this." He lifted a hand, pulling the band from my ponytail. "I love your hair down."

My resolution was dissolving quickly, and a full Riley attack with his mouth and his body could only be resisted so much.

I was just about to say we need to slow down—his tongue currently doing wicked things to mine made it hard to say *anything*—when he seemed to back off.

He was pressed against me, holding me hostage between the wall and his amazing body while his hard-on teased me with promise. His head was bent, dropping languid kisses against my mouth and my jaw, a groan making its way up his throat when I accidentally—or maybe it was on purpose—arched into him.

"No sex." He closed his eyes, either reminding himself or me as he gently pulled away, his breath coming out hard and fast. "Why don't you show me some of the photos you took today? I promise I won't yawn too much."

"Ah shit!" I exclaimed, feeling like an asshole. "You must be exhausted."

While my fatigue and seediness had been self imposed—or delivered at the hands of Miss Lillian if we were still blaming her—Riley had spent the whole night working. I'd been so preoccupied kissing Riley and feeling his amazing chest through his T-shirt, I hadn't even asked how his shift had been or whether he needed a nap.

"It's not so bad." He kissed my forehead. "I'm not a great sleeper so I've gotten used to getting by on a few hours."

The way he said it tugged at my heartstrings, the idea that something I took for granted wasn't easy for him. "Is it because of your erratic hours or . . ." I asked, curious as to why.

"Is this where I tell you my deep dark secrets?" He smiled. "I'll make you a deal, you tell me *some* of yours and I'll tell you *all* of mine."

On paper it was a pretty sweet deal.

All I had to do was volunteer a few random bits of information—which in all honesty could have been lies, he'd never know—and he'd give me the keys to the kingdom. Granted, his deep secrets could be lies too, so maybe I wouldn't be getting much at all.

"Fine, but let's get you into bed." I tugged at his arm, his brow knitting in confusion as his feet stayed planted on the floor.

"If you're going to try and use your body to distract me, Quinn, it won't work. I still require tit-for-tat," He warned, refusing to move no matter how hard I yanked.

So many other men would have followed me into the bedroom with no questions asked. They'd have taken my "no sex" proclamation and used it as a challenge. Or at the very least, happily yielded if it seemed like that was what I wanted.

But Riley was like a tree.

A massive oak with snarling defiant roots capable of tearing up a house's foundation.

He was rock solid, and he wasn't budging.

"I am not using my body to distract you." I gave up trying to move him. "We're not even getting naked. But what we are going to do is lay down. You can close your eyes and rest while I talk. That way if you do fall asleep we can blame my amazing bed, and not that you were bored."

He eyed me suspiciously but seemed satisfied it wasn't some obscure seduction technique that would plunge our virtues into peril. "I won't be bored." He followed me into my room, watching with interest as I led him to my bed.

"Of course you won't. You'll be lulled into the best night sleep of your life by my ridiculous thread count and outstanding memory foam like I already told you. Jeez, Riley, try and keep up." I game show waved at the mattress before pushing him down on it. "Also—fair warning and everything—you falling asleep will give me time to go through your pockets and snoop."

He laughed, settling his hands on my hips and pulling me into the space between his legs. "You have no game face, none. And completely lost the element of surprise by telling me your evil plan. But I'll make it easy for you." His hands dropped from my hips and dug into his pocket, pulling out his phone, his wallet and his keys. "Not much snooping material, sorry. Next time I'll come prepared with a stash of bank statements and a list of my passwords just to make it more interesting for you."

"Fine." I raised my hands dramatically before letting them drop. "But include your health records too. I need to know important details like if you've had Chicken Pox or if your body is a genetically engineered prototype they built in some lab."

His body shook, his hands scrubbing the front of his face as he laughed. "You're crazy, but I really like it. So lay with me, talk to me, and tell me one of your secrets."

He leaned back, kicking off his shoes and shuffling his large mass up to the pillows. His arm stretched out, creating a space while offering a silent invitation. My RSVP was swift, kicking off my sneakers and crawling into the nook his muscles had created. It was a nice nook, one I could imagine spending a lot of time in, his arms coming around me and covering me like a built-in blanket.

It was strange to feel so safe, to feel so comfortable with someone I barely knew. I'd invited him into my home, into my bed with no idea of whether or not I'd wake up in an ice bath missing a kidney. But whether or not it was logical, it just felt right.

"I miss my dad." My first admission something I barely told anyone. "Marty was right, he was a good man. It was like he'd been frozen in time, he had a lot of old school values. Not bad ones—he wasn't a chauvinistic pig who believed women belonged in the kitchen or anything like that. But man was he big on work ethic—you worked hard and you earned your success. He didn't believe in shortcuts."

It almost felt too personal to look at Riley while I spoke, keeping my face pressed against the warm firm lines of his chest while I spilled things I didn't think I'd told any man. "He was an architect—so crazy talented—but turned down working with major contracts if they had a reputation for short changing the laborers. He just *really* cared about everything he did, and had more personal integrity than anyone I've ever known." I swallowed hard, a lump forming in my throat. Riley's hand moved, gently stroking my arm as he listened patiently, not prompting me either way.

I probably could have left it there. Insisted I'd given him one of my secrets and collected on my bounty. But funny enough, I wasn't thinking about the prize any more, a weird emotion coming over me while we laid together. I didn't want to stop. I wanted to tell him more, because in some stupid way it felt right to share it with him.

"He wore these tragic turtlenecks," I laughed, remembering how many times I begged to take him to the mall and restyle him. "And these hideous rimless glasses. And oh my God, his car—it was this ugly old SAAB that he refused to upgrade. He died just before my twentieth birthday. Heart attack—it was sudden." I sighed, his face in my mind so clear it was hard to believe he was gone. "He was like an old leather satchel and freshly sharpened pencils—authentic in every way that mattered. And I loved him so much."

A tear rolled down my cheek as I blinked furiously, the last thing I wanted to do was cry. What a buzz kill. Still, it would pretty much guarantee we wouldn't have sex. A crying emotional basket case killed libido every time. So if nothing else, I guess I solved one problem, so there was that.

The quiet stretched between us and I wondered if I'd made a mistake. If at that moment he was calculating in his head an exit strategy so he could leave without looking like an asshole. *Thanks for sharing your feelings but I really only came up here to touch your boobs, maybe some other time.* Lord, he hadn't even done that; poor guy was probably feeling really short changed.

And I was just about to let him off the hook—or check to see if I'd bored him to sleep—when I felt the softest pressure of his lips against the top of my head. It was barely there—a whisper of a kiss—and I'd have almost missed it if his hands didn't tighten around me at the same time.

"I'm sorry, Quinn. He sounds like an amazing man." Another kiss. "Thanks so much for sharing that with me."

His fingers reached down and tilted my chin, and whether I wanted to look at him or not, I no longer had the choice. "I know I'm the last person on earth that has any authority to say this to you, but I'm sure he loved the hell out of you."

Our mouths met and I wasn't sure if I'd moved first or he did, and it didn't matter. The kiss was everything he needed to say without the words—that he cared, that he was sorry, that he didn't think I was a basket case, that maybe he still wanted to touch my boobs.

It was sexy, it was sweet, it was gentle, yet demanding—all the things I wanted without the pity I hated. He was kissing me because he wanted to, and I liked the way it felt so much.

"God, you're beautiful." His lips moved to my chin. "And there is nowhere I'd rather be right now."

"Really?" I chuckled, wondering how he could find the disaster of my stained hoodie, old sweatpants, and now messy hair attractive. "Wow, you must not get out a lot."

He laughed against my neck, the vibrations tickling my skin. "I get out *plenty*. And you were supposed to say something nice, like, you enjoy being here with me too."

My lips curved, the sadness I'd felt only a few minutes ago dissipating. "Riley, it's so nice being here with you."

"Prompted doesn't count, Quinn." He shook his head, grinning. "And I got fucking *nice*? Wow. Brutal."

It was crazy.

Like he had some wonderful superpower to turn things around, to make me laugh when I'd wanted to cry, to make me feel empowered when I'd felt vulnerable. I didn't understand it, or ever seen someone with such an incredible gift. But I liked the warm feeling I got over my skin and the way it squeezed my heart.

"Okay, so pay up." I continued with the playful tone, waving my hand like he was trying to short change me. "I need your secrets. ALL of them. And I really hope you weren't a boy scout because I'm counting on you to give me some juicy stuff."

He dropped a soft kiss on my mouth, pulling my bottom lip with his teeth to tease me. "Was never a boy scout but don't think for a second I don't know my way around a knot."

"Ohhhhh, yeah?" I mock moaned. "Anytime you want some help earning badges, let me know."

His hand dipped down and squeezed my ass. "I'll give you all my secrets, Quinn. But I don't need your help earning badges, I like to get things on my own."

And I didn't doubt him for a second.

"Now who's using their body as a distraction?" My eyebrows rose in suggestion. His superpower was also his ability to turn me on. Zero to a hundred in five point two easy.

"If I wanted to distract you, I'd take my shirt off," he taunted.

Make that zero to a million.

"Nope," I lied. Those warm and fuzzy feelings I had in my chest traveling a little further south. "I want information, now gimme!"

Chapter 10

Riley

ABSOLUTELY HATED talking about my parents.

Hated it.

And not because I was ashamed of them—even though they weren't great—but because I refused to believe that they or anything else in my past defined me.

But.

And here was the kicker.

I wasn't going to lie to Quinn.

If she wanted to hear about my life—our losses the same but so vastly different—then that's what I was going to give her. Even if I wasn't sure how she was going to react. Not that it worried me much, strange because it should have been the biggest concern.

It was crazy how ridiculously fast I was having feelings for this girl. We'd met yesterday? It didn't even seem possible, feeling like I'd known her for years. But Mack always accused me of jumping first and thinking later, and I guess it was one of those times I was happy his criticism had been right.

So.

Where to start?

"My dad was *not* a good man." I took a breath, letting my hand trail up and down her spine as she settled against me. "Neither was my mom."

I felt her body stiffen, anticipating probably the worst-case scenario. "No, not like that." I looked down at her, giving her a weak smile. "They weren't evil, and they never intentionally hurt me. They just weren't *good*. They were drug addicts, alcoholics, gamblers, con artists—they were always working a scam. But for all their faults they did their best when it came to me, even though by most people's standard it wasn't much."

I shook off memories of a childhood of being hungry and dirty and continued. "Anyway, I loved them—or at least I thought I did—because it was all I really had. No other family to speak of and it was hard to make friends when your parents are taking turns being out on bail. I wasn't a popular kid if you get my drift."

It was exactly what I was trying to avoid, the flicker of pity passing through her eyes before I had a chance to stop it. "Don't feel sorry for me, Quinn. Just like my dad, I'm not a *good* man."

She screwed up her face in horror, ready to fucking argue or save my soul or whatever bullshit she felt I needed to hear. But I put my fingers on her lips and went on. "I was eighteen when they both died. And at that point, it was the best day of my life. They were both high, drunk and driving and thankfully, they'd only killed themselves. I wasn't with them because they'd pissed me off, I was angry that I had to be the grown up. And then, they were gone and they were no longer my responsibility. I could just look after myself for a change."

Her eyes soften, sadness replacing the pity but I kept my finger on her lips, looking at her while I talked.

"Anyway, Mack was one of the first responders on the scene and the one to tell me. Not sure if he felt sorry for me or he was trying to earn brownie points with the big guy, but he took me in. Gave me a place to stay, a safe place to land and a kick up the ass when I needed it. He'd been the first person who'd cared to even bother." The humorless laugh making its way up my throat. "That's *why* I'm not a good man, Quinn. Because I'm glad they're gone and I refuse to feel guilty for it."

I was sure by some definition that made me a monster. That I could be happy about being suddenly orphaned, and so flippant over two lives lost. And people were free to form their own opinions 'cause I sure as shit wasn't an authority on it. But when it came to that day, I refuse to feel anything other than fucking relief and gratitude. The second chance it gave me, the most precious gift I'd been lucky enough to receive.

"You shouldn't feel guilty." She shook her head, her next words surprising me even more. "And I'm glad they're gone too. They didn't deserve you."

Maybe she was right. But people got shit they didn't deserve all the time, both good and bad. Who was to judge one way or the other?

"It doesn't matter." My fingers grazed against her jaw. "It's in the past and I've moved on. But I didn't want you to think we shared the same feelings. I am genuinely sorry you lost your dad, Quinn. But there's only one of us who's mourned a parent and it wasn't me."

She swallowed, squeezing my hand and silently thanking me for being honest. I liked the way it felt, and that she was no longer looking at me with pity.

"Well . . ." she left her sentence trailing and I had no idea what she was going to say next. A grin that could only mean trouble edged across her lips. "Guess that would make it a little awkward if I married Mack. Whoa! Would that make me like your stepmom?"

I laughed, wondering how the hell I'd gotten so lucky. "Wow, that is wrong on so many levels. He didn't adopt me, you deviant."

"Hey," she waved her finger at me accusingly. "How am I the deviant? I was just picturing us having pecan pie all together at Thanksgiving, not sure where *your* mind was at. But I bet," she drew in a breath, pretending to be shocked. "I can guess."

"You make pie?" I groaned, the idea of her naked in an apron covered in flour making me inappropriately excited.

Never going to look at pie the same way again.

"Pfft, no, of course not," she scoffed. "I *buy* it like every other normal person."

"I'd be a little careful throwing that "normal" word around. Not sure it applies here."

She mock punched me, screwing up that perfect mouth and knuckling me right in the side. "Easy there, Riley. Or I'll wait until you're asleep and then shave off your eyebrows."

I raised one of the brows she was threatening, unable to help myself. "And *that's* supposed to convince me you're normal? You suck at this game."

She erupted into laughter, her face morphing with pure joy as I caged her in with my arms. I felt exhausted—tired on every level—and yet didn't want to miss a second of it. Her laugh, her smile—was pure oxygen, and I was inhaling every last drop like I'd forgotten how to breathe.

Her giggles tapered off and she settled back against me. I liked the way she fit, and more importantly how she felt and was wondering at what point I was overstaying my welcome. Not that I wanted to leave, willing to lay in her bed with her until she threw me out.

"You can sleep," she mumbled against my chest. "I'll do my best to be normal."

Funny how it was the last thing I wanted from her.

"Don't be normal, Quinn. You're too amazing to lower yourself to that standard."

I was expecting a comeback, maybe a little quip about me saying something sweet in an effort to get into her pants or something else. But it didn't come. Instead she snuggled against me and whispered, "You too."

I didn't remember falling asleep, but at some point I must have closed my eyes and lost the fight I'd been having with fatigue. I wasn't sure how long I'd been out, but judging by the sunlight coming through the bedroom window, it was obviously late afternoon.

As I tried to move, I stiffened, registering why I was so hot. Quinn's body was curled around me like a snuggie, her arms locked around my neck while her foot was hooked around my leg. I wasn't going anywhere unless I wanted to wake her, and judging by the gentle whoosh passing by her lips, that wasn't happening any time soon.

So I guess I was sticking around for a while, either that or figure out a way to extract myself from her without trying to manhandle her.

Yeah, not an option.

I could think of a million things I'd rather do—like stub a toe, break a rib or suffer second degree burns, all of which I've had—rather than peel her off me. So I was just settling in for the long haul when there was a pounding at Quinn's front door.

"Shit!" She jumped, almost kneeing me in the balls as she woke in a start, looking around slightly confused by what had woken her.

"Jesus, Quinn. I know you said we weren't having sex but I'd like to be able do it again eventually." I laughed, watching her face morph from bewilderment to concern as she realized where her knee had landed. "Someone is trying to beat down your door. Want me to go see who it is?"

"Crap. Sorry. No. I've got it." She unhooked her limbs, rubbing her eyes as she leapt from the bed.

She might have said she didn't want me to see who was at the door but I wasn't going to hide out in her bedroom either. She lived in a decent part of town, in a place that had excellent building security, but that didn't mean someone hooked on drugs or intending to rob a place couldn't get in if they wanted. Thanks a lot, Mom and Dad.

So without asking, I followed her as she dashed through her open plan living area and threw open her front door without even bothering to ask who it was.

"Quinn!" Karli shrieked, her face pale like she'd seen a ghost. "Oh my God, I just got off the phone with work and—" She stopped short, her eyes widening when she saw me. "Oh my God!"

Not sure if the *oh my God* was directed at me, the fact Quinn and I were together in her apartment, or it had something to do with her call from work. What I did know was a conversation needed to be had and at some point I was going to be the topic of it.

"Hey, Karli, everything all right?" I asked, deciding the conversation would happen sooner than later. It wasn't like we'd done anything wrong, and if I had my way, she was going to be seeing a lot of me with Quinn."

"Um, oh hey, Riley." She smiled on a dime, pretending like she hadn't been freaking out not twenty seconds before. "Fancy seeing you here. How was work last night? How's your day been so far?" She didn't even blink, friendly salutations tossed my way like she was on stage for a pageant. "Nope, nothing is wrong at all. Everything is just peachy."

Yeah, and I believed that.

I settled in behind Quinn, making it clear I wasn't leaving and probably being an asshole for not giving them privacy. "Well that's great."

"So what happened with work?" Quinn asked, ignoring what I thought were some pretty obvious cues that her friend didn't want to discuss it in front of me.

"Um. Oh. Well, nothing too exciting." Karli continued to lie, trying to maintain the cheery disposition and happy face. She certainly had a talent. "Lorraine had a fall this morning and broke her hip. Poor Lorraine. I should get to the florist and pick up an arrangement. Flowers always make things better, don't you think? You want to come with me and help me pick?" The words came out in a rush, Karli needing to take a huge breath as her eyes widened.

"Lorraine? As in your boss Lorraine?" Quinn rubbed the back of her neck, squinting her eyes like she was trying to solve a riddle.

"Yep, that's the one. Going to be out for a while too. It was a nasty break." Karli's eyebrows rose, willing Quinn to pick up whatever telepathic message she was sending.

And then like a light had been turned on, Quinn's face changed. She blinked, her eyes widening and her mouth dropping open as she glanced over at me. Whatever frequency they were on, clearly I wasn't.

Quinn's voice dropped. "So . . ."

"Yep."

"Wow."

"Oh my God, I know."

Who knew a whole conversation could take place with just a few words? Glances ping-ponged between them in silence while I stood there like the only idiot in the dark.

"You want me just to leave?" I joked, wondering at what point it would get awkward. It was clear they had something to say but didn't want an audience. And asshole or not, I was man enough to leave when someone needed space. "Don't want to mess with your vibe."

"What, what did you say?" Quinn turned suddenly, her eyes wide.

She looked scared, or worried, or . . . Jesus, what the hell? "Quinn, are you okay?"

"What did you say?" she repeated, grabbing my arm and squeezing like every word I said needed to be echoed back verbatim.

Even Karli had stopped, dropping the fake smile and merriment, my flippant remark tripping a switch in both of them. "I asked you if you wanted me to leave." I looked between them, hoping my words weren't going to make them stroke out or something. "That I didn't want to mess with your vibe. Look, clearly there's something going on between you and it's fine if you don't want me to know. It's cool, you're friends, I get it. I can just go."

"No, no, you don't have to leave," Quinn scoffed, trying to laugh but coming up short. "We don't have anything going on between us, do we Karli? Karli's boss had an accident. Accidents happen all the time. No reason for them. They just happen. It's unfortunate. It just means Karli's the boss for a while. It's fine. It's nothing. No one said it was permanent."

If I thought either of them elaborating would clue me in more, I was mistaken. I had no idea what Quinn was talking about, and what Karli's boss breaking her hip had to do with it and why me saying I didn't want to *mess with the vibe* was freaking everyone out. Not to mention it meant her friend getting a promotion seemed like the worst news ever.

"So you're going to be the boss?" I asked Karli, hoping she might make more sense.

"Yes. That's right. Brad and I started at the same time but I have more experience so I'll replace Lorraine."

"But it's temporary," Quinn interjected.

"We don't know how long." Karli shrugged. "Depends on Lorraine's recovery."

"Okay, so is this new boss thing," I tried to spitball, working out why everyone was acting so weird, "a bad thing because you're trying to date Panties Brad?"

I hadn't forgotten that Brad was the intended recipient for Quinn's lacy red panties. I wasn't going to even get into the whys of it, but I personally thought a man who couldn't sack up and ask a woman out was a dipshit. But it wasn't my place to tell some girl who clearly liked the guy, who to date.

"Oh my God, I'm going to be Brad's boss!" Karli screamed, her voice booming off the walls like it hadn't occurred to her until I'd mentioned it.

"Okay, ladies." I shook my head, willing to concede defeat. There were some of life's mysteries I just wasn't going to know. And clearly this was one of them. "Karli, congrats on the new job. I'm sure you'll be amazing. Quinn," I turned around to face her. "When you get around to checking your phone, you'll see you have my number. I have another day before I'm back on duty, let me know when you're free. Breakfast, lunch, dinner—whatever."

It wasn't usually my style to leave it so open ended, but things were different with Quinn. There were no rules, and nothing we were doing was conventional. There wasn't a chance she was going to blow me off, not after everything she'd told me about her dad and after listening to me about mine.

"And we're the stationhouse on W 38th in case you decide to send more pizza," I grinned. And without bothering to ask if she was okay with it, I lowered my head and kissed her. Nothing too flashy, but enough to leave her wanting more, the whimper against my mouth proof I'd done my job correctly. "Call me."

With my shoes and keys all in Quinn's bedroom, I had no choice but to turn and head back there. I pulled on my boots, shoved my phone and wallet into my pockets and fisted my keys. It wasn't until I turned around that I saw Quinn standing in the doorway looking at me.

"Enjoying the view?" I laughed, watching as she slowly walked toward me and pressed her face against my chest.

"You didn't touch my boobs." She lifted her head and looked me in the eyes.

Jesus.

"Quinn." I breathed out her name trying to be respectful with her friend in the other room. My free hand tangled in her hair, bringing her closer to my mouth, and I kissed her again. "I want nothing more than to touch your boobs. Trust me, I want to *touch* all of you. But it's fine. Go be with your friend and call me later. I want to see you tomorrow. Can you do that for me?"

She nodded, lingering on my mouth. "Okay."

Before I did something stupid like pull her back on the bed and show her exactly how much I wanted to touch her, I headed back into the living room. And with one final goodbye, I left and went back to my apartment.

To sit by the phone obviously.

Chapter 11

Quinn

KARLI'S TEMPORARY PROMOTION meant nothing.

Miss Lillian was full of shit.

I was not destined to be with Mack.

And there was no way I believed different.

Riley left my apartment Sunday afternoon probably believing I'd lost whatever grip I had on reality. Not that any of that was going to matter since I hadn't called him yet.

Oh, I'd meant to.

Wanted to ask him to come back the minute he'd left and tell him to spend the night with me. My Monday was light, with only a couple of shoots in the afternoon, and I figured there was actually a lot of leeway in no sex.

And I was willing to explore all of them.

But after having a crisis meeting with Karli, and reevaluating everything that Miss Lillian had said, I decided to just let things *breathe* for a while. Which was code for basically avoiding it all and burying my head in the sand.

It wasn't bad enough that I was already dealing with really *liking* a guy for the first time in ages, we had to go add a possible dooms day clause to it. Because that made sense. Shit like that didn't happen when I was kissing some nobody in a club. But I finally find a man who was smart and funny and so good looking my eyes hurt and damn, someone better cue the apocalypse.

Riley had messaged me only once, and that was to wish me good morning. Literally that was all it said. *Good morning, Quinn.* But however short, it was sweet, and I loved that he was thinking of me. I stupidly hugged my phone, closing my eyes and remembering how he said my name.

Quinn.

I involuntarily shivered.

So wanting to get back to hearing him saying it real time, and throwing ridiculous notions out the window, I decided to put Miss Lillian's prophecy to rest once and for all.

If one part of it proved to be untrue, then it stood to reason it was *all* untrue. And it was.

All of it.

Moving my clients around to earlier in the day meant I had most of my afternoon free. I didn't make a habit of rescheduling but when needed, I used my reputation and the fact I was in high demand to my advantage. Sometimes you just have to break out your inner diva. So the minute my schedule was cleared, I sashayed my ass to Willow and Lynn.

Set on the Upper East Side, guaranteeing no scoundrels would wander in looking for a comic, the red brick building was quiet like a library. The sales associates were dressed in cardigans and tweed jackets with patches on the sleeves, while an aroma of faded pages wafted in the air.

It was a literary delight, a bibliophile's fantasy and the workplace of my best and dearest friend.

But I wasn't there to see her.

Careful not to arouse suspicion, I strolled past the exposed shelves—regular books—around the glass cabinets—expensive books—and down the stairs to the basement—rare books. You couldn't go down there without an escort or a pass, but I'd stealthily blended in with a houndstooth dress and chignon. And despite being five-eleven, I was invisible.

"What are you doing here?" Brad looked up from his desk, hearing the door open. "Quinn? Is that you?"

Strolling over as fast as I could—Karli had a buyer's meeting but who knew how long those things lasted—I arrived at Brad's workstation, surveying the area to make sure we were alone. "Yes, it's me."

His shoulders relaxed, easing back into his seat as he smiled. "Oh, you just looked different. Karli's not here, she had a buyer's meeting."

No shit, Brad.

"Yeah, actually, I'm here to see you." I casually leaned against the partition wall and prayed he didn't think I was trying to flirt. Still, he hadn't clued up with Karli and she'd been trying. "I just had some questions I needed to ask."

"About books?" He scratched his chin, probably thinking it was the most logical. But considering I was contemplating some spirit-talker's take on my romantic destiny, I'd say logic was in short supply.

"No, not books." I shook my head. "Look, these questions might sound weird but they're important. Just a yes or no answer is fine." *Well here goes nothing.* "Are you married? Engaged? In a serious relationship?"

His brow creased. "Umm . . .no."

So far, so good.

"Gay, have an aversion to women, or any issues with their anatomy?"

"No," he answered looking utterly bewildered.

"Have any trauma, PTSD, dating issues, social issues, or anything that would rule out enjoying an evening with a woman?"

"Quinn . . . what—"

I held up my hand. "Just a yes or no, Brad. Trust me, this is harder for me than it is for you."

"Fine," he huffed out a breath. "No."

"Do you find Karli attractive?" I lifted my chin, waiting for his answer.

Look, I knew what I was doing was terrible. Meddling in people's private business, getting involved in issues that didn't concern me, blah, blah, blah. But I was under no delusions I was a selfless human being who would float up to heaven like a baby angel with fluffy white wings.

I had no time for that.

So instead of fighting nature, I was taking shit into my own hands and working this stuff out.

"Brad, do you find Karli Kelly attractive?" I repeated, in case there was any confusion as to which Karli I was referring to.

"Yes."

"I'm sorry," I leaned in closer, making sure I hadn't misheard. "Did you say yes?"

"Yes. Jesus, Quinn." He threw his hands in the air, exasperated. "Of course I find Karli attractive. She's beautiful."

My eyes blinked, my legs taking a step back as I tried to stop reeling from the shock. "Then why the hell haven't you asked her out?"

There I was, thinking Brad was either going to admit to having five kids, a wife and a minivan in Vermont or that his last date had been named Karl. And on top of no wife, no kids, no minivan and a preference for vaginas, he didn't have any standing mental, social or emotional blocks against dating. So many wins I couldn't keep count.

So why my friend and the guy who *dog-eared her pages* weren't at least getting to second base behind the shelves of the poetry section was beyond me.

Brad shook his head, apparently not as clear as I was on why it could've already been a done deal. "Because we work together. This is a specialized industry, it's not like there's a million book restoration and antique book curating jobs in the city. If I ask Karli out and for some reason we end up breaking up, what is going to happen? Either one of us leaves or we have to soldier through being awkward. And I like her too much to have her uncomfortable or hate me."

I was stunned.

Here I thought Brad had either been clueless or had no spine, but in truth, he was just a really nice guy.

Goddamn it!

"But . . ." I tried to reason, "You guys might be great together and end up some nerdy old-book-saving duo. How are you going to know unless you take that leap? And seriously, what the hell are you going to do to make her uncomfortable or have her hate you?" The idea so ridiculous I was struggling to find even a viable scenario. "Burn a first edition Fitzgerald or ask for an orgy with the Brontë sisters?"

"Well, that would be difficult considering they're all dead, Quinn." He laughed.

"Brad, I *know* they're all dead." I rolled my eyes. "Look, I get it. You guys see one tragic love story after another. Love, loss—some stuffy-shirted asshole ignoring some pale billowy-dressed virgin. Or maybe they get together and one of them dies of dysentery or fucking syphilis leaving the other broken hearted. But it doesn't have to be that way, you can have a relationship and it can work out. And if it doesn't, you can be two regular modern-day people who aren't hurling yourselves off a cliff or drinking poison in a tomb."

Huh.

What do you know? I was actually making sense and judging by Brad's softening expression, he was thinking it too.

He shifted on his feet, straightening his tie as he lowered his voice. "So I should ask her out?"

Seriously, Brad?

"YES! Yes, you should ask her out." I waved my hands dramatically. "Go to a movie, dinner, visit a museum—something."

Brad snapped his fingers, bravado or inspiration taking hold as his face animated with excitement. "Oh, there's an adoption day at the shelter on West Broadway. And I know she'd love a cat. I could help her pick one."

"Whoa, Brad." *Jesus, and I thought I worked fast.* "Don't you think it's a little fast to be picking out pets together? Maybe work up to it slow. Start with coffee, roll a meatball to her from a shared bowl of spaghetti."

He scoffed like I was the one being ridiculous. "She's a vegan, Quinn. She doesn't eat meatballs."

"Brad, you seriously need to work on your ability to read sarcasm if we're going to continue to be friends." I shook my head, the mystery on why a good-looking and friendly guy, with a great paying job was still single was solved. "But fine, take her to the adoption day. I'm sure she will love it even if she doesn't walk away from it with a cat."

What was the harm? He couldn't do any worse, and maybe it would work out and the two of them would fall in love over an abandoned tabby. That shit worked in Christmas movies all the time, all we needed was a house renovation and some frosted cupcakes and we were set. Maybe I should tell Brad to bring cupcakes, just to be sure. I had no problem stacking the odds.

"Thanks so much, Quinn." He caught me by surprise, throwing his arms around me in a hug. "You're the greatest."

My eyes widened as I awkwardly tapped Brad on the shoulder. Most we'd ever shared was a handshake so the hug was very unexpected. "Heeeeeeey, that's okay, buddy. Here to help. I just want to see my best friend with a good guy."

And wasn't that the truth.

But I also wanted to prove once and for all that Miss Lillian's predictions were as reliable as the weather forecast. Not that I was sharing that little nugget.

And yes, I realized how absurd it was I believed in any of it at all, but no more ridiculous than believing I was falling for a guy I'd met two days ago. I mean, it was too quick, and lasting relationships needed weeks if not months to build. So if it was possible to be infatuated with Riley, it was equally plausible that Miss Lillian had the *spirits* on speed dial.

Hey, I needed to cover all my bases.

His face beamed as he pulled away. No doubt he'd have an extra spring in his step for the rest of the day, his hazel eyes bursting with excitement. "Okay, it's this Saturday, opens at eleven. I can pick you both up."

"Huh?" I leaned forward, assuming I hadn't heard right.

"Well, I know neither you or Karli have a car so I'll come get you both, and we can drive together," he said, confirming that I hadn't been day drinking and in fact, I'd somehow been added to the equation.

"Why would I be there? It's a date. You're a smart guy, you must know how it works."

"Yes, I know *how* it works," he chuckled. "But things are different for us. We already know each other and like I said, the last thing I want to do is screw it up. So I thought, what better way to ease into it than invite you along with us. You can leave after a little while if you want, or stay. I don't mind."

If there ever was a prize for someone who could convolute their lives, I'd be standing proud on the podium wearing a crown of laurel leaves.

"Brad, don't you think me being there as the third wheel is going to make it worse? Or I don't know, defeat the fucking point." I swear, at this rate I was going to have to give poor Brad a slide rule and diagram and even then there'd be no guarantee.

He shrugged. "So invite a guy, we'll double date."

Yeah, right.

I was just about to open my mouth to tell Brad I wasn't going to ask some poor random guy to suffer through his sweet but bumbling effort to woo my friend when it dawned on me.

I didn't need to find a random guy.

There was a guy who would—at least I hoped he would—go with me and wouldn't be phased by crashing Karli and Brad's weird first date. Nothing rattled Riley, he even seemed to have fun watching me snap photos at the ice cream shop even though it was boring as hell. Not to mention I could kill two birds with one stone. Prove Miss Lillian wrong and get the guy.

And we were definitely kissing again.

A lot.

"Quinn?" Karli's voice came from behind me, her surprised look toggling between Brad and I as she got closer and gave me a hug. "What are you doing here? Did we have plans I didn't remember?"

"No, no plans. I was just in the neighborhood, thought I'd stop by. I forgot you had that meeting so I was just chatting with Brad to pass the time." I waved my hand, acting as nonchalant as I was able while trying to contain my excitement.

"Just in the neighborhood, huh?" She eyed my outfit with suspicion. "Nice dress, is it new?"

Busted.

"Please, this old thing. I've had it for years." Which technically wasn't totally a lie. *Someone* had had it for years, and then donated it to Recycled Rags which was where I found it earlier in the morning. Not that I was fooling Karli, her knowing smile letting me know she was aware I was lying but wasn't going to make a scene. Gotta love those southern manners.

"Okay, well, I better dash. Great seeing you, Karli." I gave her another hug. "Brad, great chat." I hoped my thumbs up were enough confirmation I was on board. If not, well there was no hope for any of us.

"Okay, see you at home," Karli chuckled, no doubt compiling the list of questions for my inquisition. "You have any other plans?" Her southern manners only went so far, wanting to know if I was seeing Riley.

"Yeah, I have *a lot* of plans. And I should go get working on them." I shot her a smile as I pulled out my phone.

I was going to call Riley.

And it was going to be amazing.

Chapter 12

Riley

NOTHING.

So much for not being worried about Quinn blowing me off.

Had to admit, part of me was expecting her to text or call later that night. Not like I hadn't made it abundantly clear I wanted to hear from her. But sure, I wasn't unreasonable and figured her secret women's business with Karli had taken longer than expected.

Fine.

And while most guys would have said that texting the next day made you looked desperate and needy, I didn't buy into that shit. If I wanted to text a girl, I would and no one would tell me different.

But I wouldn't beg.

Which was why when she responded to my "good morning" with nothing more than a smiley face emoji, I shoved my phone in my pocket and didn't text again.

Then I pretended I wasn't pissed off, hitting up the grocery store and doing my laundry and washing my Explorer like it was just another day off.

Except it wasn't.

Because ordinarily I wouldn't have jerked off twice in the shower and still been hard. Or feel the burning need to cross the bridge into Brooklyn. Or be so moody I had to wonder whether I was going to start menstruating.

Jesus.

This. Fucking. Woman.

I laughed at myself because honestly if it were happening to another sucker it would have been hilarious. At the station it was like our favorite pastime, taking enjoyment over one of the guy's tragic and clueless behavior and giving them all kinds of shit. Yet there I was, sitting with my phone in my hand and willing it to ring.

And it did a few times.

But not one of those times was Quinn.

"Hey." Mack's call the latest in a series of ones I didn't want to take. "You coming over for the card game tonight? Rev's wife is making us meatloaf."

I scrubbed the front of my face, trying to laugh even though my skin itched and my balls ached. "Dude, do I look like a retiree to you? You know the last thing I want to do is throw spades with you ugly ass jerks. Isn't it bad enough I have to see you at work?"

Mack liked to yank my chain, inviting me to their standing card game even though I had zero interest. I insulted him, he insulted me and then I'd usually blow him off. I'd occasionally turn up when one of the guys was having a tough time and needed the company or when it was Mack's birthday and he'd refuse to do anything interesting. Not that I was in the mood for it at the moment.

"You hear from Quinn?" he asked, going off script and forgetting our usual banter.

I breathed out, wondering which of the assholes I'd ran into at the Laundromat had said something. I hadn't mentioned anything, pretending shit was fine as my clothes went through the rinse and spin. But we all knew each other too well not to pick up on when someone was being cagey, and Leighton and Tibbs were worse than a pair of old women. "Tibbs?"

"Leighton," he chuckled. "Couldn't tell me fast enough how you looked like you slammed your balls in a car door. I assumed your surly mood has to do with the tall beautiful blonde that's recently come into your life."

"Yeah, well. I thought we were going to see each other today." I pinched the bridge of my nose thanking small mercies Mack wasn't in my apartment with a front row seat to witness the misery. "Guess I got my wires crossed."

"It happens."

"Yep."

There wasn't a doubt in my mind the bastard was grinning, I could hear it in his voice.

"Anything else you want to add, Chief? Or can we save it for when I come over later to change your colostomy bag?"

Mack laughed. "You keep saying stuff like that, kid, and I'm going to hold you to it. Think I'd like to spend my twilight years, shacked up with you as my nurse. Your bedside manner needs work though."

"Yeah? Let me just add it to my vision board."

Honestly, as irritated as I pretended to sound, talking with Mack was never a hardship. The amount of shit I put him through when I first moved in, should have had me tossed out on my ass in a week. But no matter what I did or said, Mack was there. And for the longest time, the only thing I could count on.

"You want to talk about it?" he asked, filling the silence.

I shook my head, not really sure what I wanted to say. "Not really."

"Then come eat meatloaf and I'll let you win a hand or two."

Classic Mack, he never pushed.

"*Let me win*? Did the drug store mix up your script and give you LSD instead of Viagra?" I snorted, the idea making me laugh.

Mack was many things, and being horrendously bad at cards was one of them.

"Rev's wife is also making cookies."

"So what time is this thing?"

Rev's wife's cookies weren't something I was going to turn down especially since my evening plans hadn't gone beyond . . .yeah, nothing.

"First hand is at five at Cap's house. Pick up some beer on your way so you don't look like an ingrate. Domestic."

I rolled my eyes, shaking my head. "You know this is how it starts. You invite me over to *hang* with you and before I know it I'm drinking Pabst Blue Ribbon and shitting the bed."

"I'll save you the seat closest to the bathroom then."

"You're all heart."

We ended the call without bothering with the goodbye and I went into my room to change. I'd lived alone for the last five years, and liked the one-bedroom studio I rented. But Cap was married with two twin daughters in high school so he was over the bridge in—you guessed it—Brooklyn.

Refusing to be like some creeper and do a drive by, I got into my Explorer, picked up some beer and made my way over to Brooklyn Heights.

Cap's wife had book club on Monday nights so as long as we didn't mess up her house and the girls were able to do their homework, she didn't mind having a house full of men. I think the girls kind of liked it too.

So it was no surprise when I knocked on their door a little past five that it was one of the twins opening the door.

"Hi Riley," she smiled a little too enthusiastically as she leaned against the doorframe. "Dad didn't tell us you were coming over. Bring any beer?"

"I did, but last time I checked you were a long way from your twenty-first birthday, Holly. Pretty sure there's nothing wrong with my math."

Holly was cute, smart and liked getting into trouble. She was also incredibly underage and I wasn't dumb enough to engage. A. Because I wasn't a deviant who was interested in children and B. because she was Cap's daughter.

Even if she had been legal, that right there put her out of contention. Not to say I didn't applaud her ingenuity—hell of a lot smarter than I was at her age—but if anyone gave her an inch, she'd take ten miles and some change.

She rolled her eyes, tossing her long red hair over her shoulder. "I'm sixteen, you honestly think I haven't had any?"

"I'm sure you have but you won't be getting any from me."

"You know, I used to think you were the fun one, but you're just old and boring like the rest of them," she groaned, standing to the side so I could pass. "They're in the dining room."

I laughed, wondering how many heart attacks she was going to give her father before she turned eighteen. Luckily her sister, Hannah, was an angel so at least they balanced each other out.

"To what do we owe the pleasure, North?" Cap grinned, taking the two six-packs and shaking my hand. "You heard about the cookies, huh?"

"Well it wasn't the company that's for sure." I tipped my chin hello to Mack and Rev. "You guys better have left me some, I'll be pissed if I made the trip out here for nothing."

Dinner was just about to start with Cole—an EMT—dishing up plates of meatloaf. "Hey Riley, hope you're hungry."

I was just about to tell him I'd had a late lunch when my phone started to buzz. And without even looking at it, I just knew who it was.

Quinn.

Of course it was.

Mack coughed into his hand to hide his grin, watching me shake my head as I pulled it from my pocket and checked the caller ID.

"Hello?" I answered casually, wondering whether she'd felt a disturbance in the force when I drove into Brooklyn or she'd been bored. Didn't like the idea of being an afterthought but clearly wanted to hear what she had to say.

"Riley, so I know I was supposed to call you earlier but today has been a DAY. But I was hoping that if you didn't have plans already, we can do something? Touching my boobs is still on the table."

I didn't want to laugh, annoyed that she sounded so fucking sweet and it was making me forget how annoyed I'd been earlier. *It wasn't like she dodged you for a week, asshole. When did you turn into such a pussy?* And fuck me if I wasn't talking myself into getting back in my truck and going wherever the hell she wanted.

I stepped to the kitchen to give myself some privacy. "Sorry, but I'm already out."

Because that was smart, letting my pride do the talking and ending up punishing myself in the process.

When the human race eventually became extinct, I'd know the exact reason why. Because we were stupid, present company included.

"Oh, okay then." She didn't sound too disappointed, the smile still in her voice. "What's the address?"

I chuckled in disbelief. "Excuse me?"

"Where. Are. You?" She paused between each word for emphasis. "I'll come there."

This.

Fucking.

Woman.

"Rather presumptuous of you. What if I'm in the middle of something?" I couldn't wipe the grin off my face if I tried.

"Why would you answer your phone if you were in the middle of something? That's kind of dumb. I thought firemen were supposed to be smart."

"Haven't had a chance to get an IQ test. Saving lives and being a pillar of the community has taken up most of my time."

She laughed, the sound hitting me like a concussion grenade right to the chest. "Well since you're so selfless and charitable, I have a proposal for you."

"Yes, Quinn, I'll go out with you." I bit the inside of my cheek to stop myself from laughing. "But saying it's charity is a little sad. I thought you had better self esteem."

"Ha! You're so funny. But this is a serious proposition and I need a reliable wingman."

As entertaining as it was to let the conversation go on—I don't think I could ever get bored talking to Quinn—I was done pretending I didn't want to see her.

"I'm texting you an address. I'm here with a few of the guys at the captain's house. But I'll understand if you want to give it a pass."

Pretty sure watching a group of men play cards was the last thing on her mind. But I'd just arrived, and leaving wasn't the right thing to do. So if her offer was still good, I was going to take it. If not, I'd toss a few hands, bail early and then go directly to her place. Didn't even care how needy it looked.

"Oh that sounds fun! I get to meet your friends." She sounded genuinely excited. "Great, send me the details and I'll be there soon."

"Yeah, not sure I like how enthusiastic you are to meet my friends. You really are going to start giving me a complex." I shook my head, the excitement going both ways.

She laughed, the sound filling my ear. "I promise they'll only get half of my attention. Almost so little they'll think I'm being rude. Except for Mack, because . . . well, we have history."

"You're enjoying this way too much." I bit back the grin.

"Yep, I'd apologize but we both know it wouldn't be sincere."

I hesitated, unable to say goodbye just yet.

"Quinn."

"Yeah?"

"I'm glad you called."

"I am too."

Chapter 13

Riley

WASN'T SURE which would be worse.

Warning the guys to be on their best behavior, or letting the chips fall where they may. Ultimately I decided Quinn was more than capable of handling herself so I informed the congregation we were expecting company and prepared for the onslaught.

Rev set up a kitty, each of those bastards putting in fifty bucks to see how long she'd last before she got bored. There was a reason no one brought their wives, and girlfriends usually didn't get invited.

"I'll get it," screamed Holly, racing to the door before I had a chance to intercept. I should've just waited outside and escorted her in, but sitting on Cap's stoop until she arrived was just too pathetic even for me.

"Oh heeeeeeeey," I heard Holly's voice as I rounded the corner. "Wow, I love your top. Are your highlights real?"

"Oh thanks." Quinn smiled, seeming completely at ease. "I use lemon juice once a week. I mean, I need them for the tequila, not like I don't always have them around." She laughed. "Um, wait. How old are you?"

"Twenty," lied Holly, "I'll be twenty-one in June."

"She's sixteen." I strolled to the front door, my dick inappropriately hardening the minute I saw Quinn. "And an opportunist."

"Not a very nice thing to say, Riley." Holly glared at me. "Are you Riley's girlfriend? You seem too classy for him."

"Hahahaha," I mocked laughed, wrapping my arms around Quinn and giving her a smile. "Aren't kids just a hoot?"

"I'm not a kid!" Holly stomped her foot, poorly arguing her point. "Why do people keep calling me that!" She stormed back up the stairs and slammed her bedroom door.

"The president of your fan club?" Quinn grinned as I lowered my mouth, not getting to ask anything else before I kissed her.

It wasn't until my lips were on hers that I realized how desperate I'd been. I hadn't even bothered to say hello, taking what I wanted and tasting how sweet she was on my tongue. I didn't even care how impolite it looked, willing to take a chewing from Cap for making out in his entranceway if that's what it took.

"Hi," she breathed against my mouth. "I brought snacks." She raised the shopping bag in her hand.

"First pizza, now snacks." I shook my head, chuckling. "I'd say better be prepared for a marriage proposal or two."

Her face lit up as she laughed. "Now, now Riley. Don't be jealous that they're going to like me more than you. I can't help it that I'm so popular."

I kissed her again, reaching down and squeezing her ass as I pulled her closer toward me. She smelled amazing, like citrus and summertime, and I'd never wanted to rip someone's jeans off more in my life.

"Um, should we go say hello?" she asked, pulling her lips from mine and letting her hand trail down my chest. I liked her hands on me, giving her a nod in approval as she kept it there.

"Yeah, come and I'll introduce you." I slid my hand to her waist and tugged her to my side.

She looked amazing, dressed in a pair of dark blue jeans and a purple top that did amazing things for her eyes. Her hair was down the way I liked it, her lips covered in a pink shimmery gloss that tasted like cherries. I was probably wearing more of it than she was, not that I gave a shit.

Quinn followed me into the dining room not hesitating as we walked in. The noise of the room died, eyes swinging around toward us as I introduced her.

"Quinn, you already know Mack. But this is Cap, Rev, and Cole." I pointed each of them out, the guys taking turns at either nodding or giving her a wave. "And this is Quinn."

"Hi, so glad to meet you." She grinned. "No regular names, huh? Good for you."

"I'm Elliot but the wife is pretty much the only one who calls me that." Cap stood up and put out his hand. "Sometimes it takes me a while before I realize she's talking to me."

"Cap it is." She accepted his shake. "I brought snacks."

Rev and Cole took turns in giving Quinn their "real" names, but she proved what a team player she was by using the same ones we did. Even Mack, who she was surprised to find out was actually named John.

Quinn settled down in a seat beside me watching as we played a round of Spades. I was partnered up with Mack, the two of us winning the hand before Rev switched to Texas Hold'em dealing everyone in with a pair.

"You're not some prodigy who is going to sweep the pot, are you?" Rev laughed nervously as Quinn peeked at her cards. He was smart enough to know there was more to her than a pretty face.

"Why don't you put your money where your mouth is and we'll find out." She winked, smiling like she had a pair of aces.

Not like I had them, the two of Hearts and the seven of Clubs in my hand not doing me any favors.

Cap tossed her a small bag of Skittles, the currency we were using for the night, and filling her in that if we were using real money Cole would've retired already.

Rev dealt more cards, turning over the flop and the turn before I finally tapped out. Cap had folded just before me, leaving the table just long enough to put out some of Quinn's snacks and refresh everyone's drinks. Mack and Cole were still going strong, while Quinn either had the worst poker face of all time or was working the biggest con of the century.

No one had a clue, Mack and Cole looking at her and then at me like I had any better idea. My shrug and raised hands were pretty clear that I wasn't on the inside and I was riding blind like the rest of them. And we were just about to find out if she'd been bluffing when Holly ran into the room, bright faced and squealing.

"OHMGEE." She jumped around, her phone in her hand. "You're Quinn Rhodes."

It was the kind of declaration made when someone was famous but with Holly, you just couldn't tell. If Quinn was a movie star or a singer, then she'd done an amazing job keeping that on the down low, everyone turning to her as she confirmed it. "That's me."

"You did a shoot with Martja in Paris! Oh! My! God! Did you get to go in her private jet? I heard it has a Jacuzzi in it and everyone has to get naked. Did you get naked? And please tell me she's not that pretty in real life, I'll just die if she is."

"Holly, what's gotten into you?" Cap shook his head, like the rest of us not really following the conversation. "And not sure that's an appropriate conversation to have with a guest."

"Quinn's like a big deal, Dad." She rolled her eyes, throwing the teenage attitude around like all of us were morons. "And I knew she looked familiar."

My eyes darted to Quinn, her usual bright smile dropping slightly. "Trust me as much as my ego would love to let you believe that, I am really *not* that big a deal. I take photos, people post them, that's about it."

"Famous people, rich people," Holly added, in case anyone needed clarification. "*Hot* people."

If the attention was making Quinn uncomfortable, she wasn't showing it. Taking it in her stride as she elaborated. "Not all the time. I have regular clients as well. Photos are photos, and each subject is just as special."

Holly was about to argue, or scream or do whatever else teenage girls did when they got excited, when Quinn stood. I thought for sure she was going to toss in the card game, make her apologies and leave. And who could blame her? But instead of making some bullshit excuse, saying goodbye and hitting the road, she instead got closer to Holly and the phone she was waving around. "Want me to show you how to take foolproof selfies?"

"Are you kidding me?" Holly screamed, grabbing Quinn's arm like a life preserver. "Um, YES! Like that's even a question. Hannah, bring your phone, Quinn Rhodes is going to give us a one on one." She turned, running back up the stairs to get her twin.

Moving from my place at the table, my feet went directly to where she was standing, lightly touching her arm. "Quinn, you don't have to do this."

In fact, of all the things I imagined that would be a good time for her, showing Holly how to pose like a supermodel would be dead last.

"She gets distracted easily," Cap offered, chuckling to himself. "We could ask her to go to the mall or something?"

Quinn smiled. "It's fine, it will take like ten minutes. Trust me, I'll be back in a second."

Giving me a squeeze on the forearm, she turned, disappearing in the direction Holly had taken off in search of her sister. Most people would have waited, but not Quinn, she wasn't the kind of girl who wasted time looking for permission. And I fucking loved that.

"She's too good for you," Cap laughed. "I know you like the pretty ones, but this one seems different."

"She *is* different," I answered without hesitation. "And since when have you taken an interest in the women I'm with?" I raised a brow, curious since he'd never commented on anyone before.

He chuckled, grinning at Mack like they were sharing some secret joke. "Since you brought one to my house, you moron."

Well, he had a point.

There wouldn't have been a chance I'd have invited some other girl to Cap's house, especially not one I'd just met. That shit was reserved for people who'd earned their place on the inside, the kind who were sticking around. And Quinn and I hadn't even started dating yet. And what was weirder was that it hadn't even occurred to me. That I asked her to come without thinking.

Interesting.

"So we going to finish this game or what?" Cole asked, drumming his fingers on the table. "I'll call if it makes a difference."

"Tell you what. Why don't you guys do whatever the hell you want. I've got some different plans." I smirked, patting my pocket and making sure I had my keys.

I'd done my part, and been as polite as I was able to. But I no longer wanted to sit around playing cards, and share the most amazing woman I'd ever met. Nope. I wanted to be selfish, have her all to myself and see if I could get any deeper in that head of hers. Besides, that kiss at the door wasn't even close to what I wanted to give her.

Rev chuckled, pulling out the cash he'd taken from each of them and handing it over to Mack. "And we have a winner."

I rolled my eyes, ignoring how pleased Mack was as he stuffed the cash into his pocket looking smug. "It doesn't count, assholes. She hasn't asked to leave so the bet is moot."

Mack tipped his chin to the door and grinned. "I didn't bet on her, North. My money was on you."

I laughed, shaking my head as I waved goodbye to them.

Didn't even care what they thought.

Quinn and I were getting out of there.

I wanted her alone.

She'd been surprised when she found me at the bottom of the stairs waiting for her. But she didn't ask any questions when I pulled her against me and kissed her. Her hands gripped the bottom of my shirt, a little moan escaping from her lips as I took her mouth.

Yeah, we needed to go.

So she said a quick goodbye to the guys and then we got into my truck, heading back to her place because it was closer than mine in Midtown.

And while I managed to get to her apartment without breaking any traffic laws, we'd barely made it inside before things started to get indecent.

"This was such a good idea," she moaned between kisses. "I'm so glad I thought of this."

I pulled her mouth from mine, holding her chin in my hand, stopping her from getting more of what we both wanted. "Whose idea? I think you'll find that it was mine."

"Ummmm, did I *not* go to your friend's house and seduce you? Yeah, pretty sure I did."

"Oh, so *that's* what you were trying to do? Sweetheart, your seduction game needs work."

In truth I didn't give a shit whose idea it was. Considering how the night started off, I'd have said the chances of seeing her would've been remote. She still hadn't told me why the hell she hadn't called or why the sudden change of heart, but we'd get to that later. Too hard to be concerned about conversation when I had her right where I wanted her.

In my arms and kissing her like I'd been the first one to discover her mouth.

Fuck, she tasted sweet.

Everything about her so fucking delicious I didn't know what I wanted first. And for the first time since I'd met her, I was giving myself permission to *really* touch her.

My hands glided down her neck as our tongues tangled, my descent to her tits making me hard. They were full—not huge but felt fucking amazing in my hands—palming them over her top as I sucked in a breath.

I'd wanted to before—to feel if they'd be as perfect as I'd imagined them in my head—but I'd stopped myself from going there. I knew it would've been too hard to stop once I'd touched her, and I was right. She might not want to have sex and I was fine with that, but there wasn't a chance in hell I wasn't going to touch her everywhere and make her come at least once. My hand, my mouth, my cock—whatever she wanted, but it was happening and it was going to start with my mouth on those sensational tits.

Acknowledging we had a tit-for-tat agreement, I pulled my hands away from her briefly to yank off my T-shirt. Her eyes widened as I tossed it on the floor, her hot gaze roaming over my chest as I fingered the hem of her top. "Your turn."

She didn't hesitate, nodding as I peeled it off her to reveal a plain cotton bra with pretty pink hearts on it.

Fuck, it was hot, groaning as I lowered my mouth and kissed the soft skin teasing out the top. "I thought you were more a red lace kind of girl," my fingers curling round the cup and pulling it down.

"I told you I was seducing you, dummy," she chuckled. "And you told me you had a thing for cotton."

I wasn't sure if it was the taunt, the contradiction of the innocence of the bra against her sex bomb body, or her fucking sensational tits. But appreciating her lingerie wasn't going to happen.

My fingers got busy with the back clasp, unhooking and sliding it off her. I was fairly sure I tossed it to the floor but I didn't bother to check. My mouth and hands curled around each of her breasts, my tongue swirling around one of her nipples. It hardened in my mouth, a whimper coming from her lips as I moved to the other and repeated.

"That feels so good." She arched into me, her hands gripping my shoulders as she closed her eyes. "So. Good."

I didn't stop, licking, sucking and pinching—teasing her until she was almost begging. I bet I could've made her come just like that, her body humming with need as she tried to rub up against me.

"Take off your pants," she moaned, my body kept just out of reach. "And take mine off too."

"Do I look like I'm finished?" I chuckled against her skin, my balls so heavy they were starting to ache. "I'll get to your pants when I'm good and ready."

Little did she know I was more than fucking ready. My cock strained against the fly of my jeans, desperate to get in on the action. But I wasn't rushing any of it, even if it meant also punishing myself.

She growled, her eyes snapping open as she pushed roughly against my chest. "I said, take them off and get naked."

Not giving me a chance to comply, she took matters into her own hands and tore at my button and zipper. Her eyes got hungrier as she yanked down my jeans, taking my boxer briefs with them and letting my dick spring free. Her nails grazed my skin, the contact making me hiss as she stared at my cock.

"This what you wanted?" I asked, liking the way she looked at me as I gave my hard length a stroke. "Now what?"

She licked her lips, her eyes not moving from my hand as she unbuttoned her own jeans. "I'm going to blow you."

Gripping my cock and squeezing was the only thing that stopped me from coming. The heat jacked up my spine as I watched her tear off her shoes and pants, and finally a pair of white pink hearted cotton panties that joined its matching bra on the floor.

She was completely bare, walking toward me while I stood there—literally—with my dick in my hand. And I'd never been more turned on in my life.

Chapter 14

HE.

Was.

So.

Fucking.

Hot.

Not sure what I was expecting when clothed he looked like a god, but he wasn't even fully naked and I was going to lose my mind. Lord, he must work out a lot because no amount of a good metabolism got you a body like that. He was lean, but tight, with every single muscle cut and toned like a poster they hung in gyms for protein drinks.

And that wasn't the only thing that was *hung*.

Thank you, Jesus.

Before I could reach for him, he wrenched off the rest of his clothes and shoes and gave me what I'd asked for. And lord, I thought I was going to pass out.

Just like he'd done, I'd started at his chest, my fingers tracing the grooves and my tongue adding its own show of appreciation. His fingers tangled in my hair as I moved lower, feeling his abs flex under my lips and his core so completely engaged, I could have parked his truck on it. He was a tightly wound spring and I was itching to unravel him.

My hands gripped his hips, sliding down his strong muscular thighs as I sunk to my knees. I wanted him, and I didn't care whatever reasons I'd told myself before that it wasn't a good idea.

It was suuuuuuuuch a good idea.

"Quinn." He pulled gently on my hair. "You're not sucking my dick without me tasting you. We made a deal, you give me something first and then you can have whatever you want."

He didn't let me argue, scooping me up in his arms and carrying me to my bedroom. Man, he was strong. Those muscles weren't decorative, not breaking a sweat as he tossed me onto the bed, my mattress absorbing the weight.

We'd spent time on it before, but we'd both been fully clothed and slept. Pretty sure that wasn't his plan, his hands wrapping around my ankles and dragging my ass to the edge.

"But—" The sentence lost as he sunk to his knees on the floor.

He raised an eyebrow, daring me to stop him before his long agile fingers touched my clit and I almost screamed. I was so wet, hot and needy—his earlier attention to my breasts working me up into a state.

His thumb circled, barely touching my most sensitive spot with large and small circles with no apparent pattern. My legs opened wider, unabashedly exposing more of myself to him as he brought his mouth closer and licked while simultaneously sticking a finger inside.

"Oh. My. God," I moaned, clutching the comforter as my body bowed, the sensation making me feel like I'd been electrocuted.

He didn't stop—circling, licking, sucking, penetrating—alternating between his lips, tongue and his fingers until I felt like I was going insane. I was stuck in a tortuous loop of wanting to come and not wanting it to end that I honestly didn't even know what I wanted anymore.

Except.

I hadn't had my turn.

Summoning all my strength, I reached down and pulled on his hair, forcing him to lift his face while I squeezed my knees shut. "You want to continue that, you need to give me your cock. So what's it going to be?"

The brown parts of his eyes were almost black, a smile creeping across his lips as he edged off his knees and pressed his erection against me. "Is that so?" He ground against me, using the ridge to rub and tease me.

"Yes," I hissed out, reaching down between my legs and gripping it. "Now get on the bed."

And for what was probably the first time in his life, he did what he was told. He shuffled me further up the mattress, smothering my body with his as he kissed me on the mouth. I tasted myself on his tongue, and it kind of made it hotter, my hand going back to his cock as I gave him a pull.

"Fuck," he gritted out, hardening in my grip as I tried to jerk him off. His hands punched the mattress as he moved to reposition. "You need to come first."

That wasn't going to be a problem, his hands and mouth going back to my core as he curved us sideways in what had to be the hottest yin and yang ever.

And finally he gave me what I wanted.

The blunt of his cock smacked against my lips, my tongue circling it before I sucked the tip gently. He was long, and thick, needing both my hands to grip him as I pulled him into my mouth.

We both groaned, the vibrations on my clit tingling through my body as I pushed him further down my throat. There I teetered, hanging off the edge while I sucked and licked him, my hands locked around him as they traveled up and down his length.

I needed to come, unable to concentrate as my movements became sloppy and uncoordinated, his assault on my core continuing relentlessly until I exploded on his mouth.

"Oh my God," I gasped, a surge of energy pulsed through my body as everything contracted and then released, like he'd willed it to do so.

And I couldn't feel my legs.

He pressed his mouth to my clit, kissing me gently as the waves rolled through me, over and over like a never-ending tide.

"I thought you'd be more vocal, didn't scream my name once," he chuckled against my thigh. "Clearly, I need to do better."

Moving from his position between my legs, he twisted around and wrapped his arms around me. His lips hit my collarbone, nibbling my skin as he palmed my tits, his voice gravel. "What's your current stance on sex, Quinn? Because I can go down on you all night if that's all you want."

Holy.

Freaking.

Shit.

My eyes widened, gripping his shoulder as his hard-on pressed into my hip. While the idea of him doing that all night sounded amazing, there wasn't a chance I didn't want more.

"We're having sex." My words like my limbs were unsteady. "I want—"

"Why don't you let me take care of what you want, Quinn." His smile edged wider. "I think I'll be pretty good at working it out."

He kissed me.

Or I kissed him.

Our mouths smashing together as he hauled me on top of him like I weighed nothing.

Ha! His mistake.

From my current vantage point, I was in control, rocking my body against him until he steadied me with his hands.

"Quinn," he warned, hissing my name out like a curse. "Please tell me you have a condom."

It was tempting to say I didn't, see if he had one handy or if he'd run into the street naked and get one from the corner store. But I wasn't that cruel or that stupid.

"I've got a whole box." I leaned down, licking the shell of his ear and reaching across to the decorative jewelry box that sat on my nightstand. It was metal with painted roses on the top, but more importantly light tight and cool. Meant it kept the integrity of the latex, and if anyone tried to rob me all they were getting was a fist full of Trojans.

I handed one to him, watching him tear open the top before reaching down between us. He kept his eyes on me, one hand holding the condom while his other hand slid in between my legs. My body involuntarily lifted, his head nodding in appreciation as my knees sunk into the mattress and I circled my hips.

"Just give me one second." His eyes dipped down to his twitching cock, stretching the latex over it and giving it a firm tug. "Now let's see about giving you what you need."

Holding his cock at the base, he used it to circle my opening while his other hand held my hip. It felt amazing, my hips rocking as he slid in one agonizing inch at a time. I'd tried to sink down, take him all in one hit, but he shook his head, both hands holding me still as he eased me down.

He was big, so it was tight, my internal muscles needing a minute to adjust, as he filled me all the way to the root.

"God you're beautiful." He tilted his pelvis, pushing in just a little deeper. "I want to make sure I see you come this time."

Starting to move, he bucked up from under me, encouraging me to roll my hips while his hands held my thighs. He didn't break my gaze, watching me as the feeling inside of me started to build again and he quickened the pace.

"Yeah, that's it," he encouraged, each thrust a little faster and deeper. "Touch those amazing tits for me, Quinn. Squeeze them like you know I will later."

My hands slithered up my body, pressing against my breasts and holding them while I tried to ride him.

"Touch yourself, Quinn. Pinch them, I want to see how hard those ends get with my cock buried inside you."

My body bowed, my fingers twisting and pinching my firm peaks as he seemed to get deeper and deeper. I was on fire, my skin burning as he moved one of his hands to where we were joined and started to rub.

"Riley." My voice was a hoarse whisper, my eyes widening as he touched my clit. It was still sensitive, the barely there pressure of his knuckle sending me into overdrive as I tried to increase the tempo.

"I'm right here, Quinn." His stare locked with mine. "Right here."

It was too intense.

Everything too much as my body felt overwhelmed by sensations. My breasts felt heavy, my nipples hard as diamonds, and my pussy full while he continued to stroke me.

I was either going to come or die.

And neither was going to be a disappointment.

Unable to take it any longer, I let go of my tits and grabbed onto my headboard. My hands found purchase, using it to steady myself as he fucked me into oblivion. With a blinding white light—so of course I wasn't sure I hadn't died—the orgasm tackled me from behind and I unraveled like cheap knitwear.

Over and over I chanted his name, my body shaking as he tensed, following me over the edge with his own release.

"Quinn," he groaned, his fingertips digging into my thighs as he jerked into me. "You feel so fucking good. Fuck. Quinn, I can't stop."

True to his word, his body didn't stop, teasing the last tremor out of me until the only thing holding me up were my hands on the headboard and a decent spine. Even then I couldn't be sure I wouldn't collapse, my body feeling completely boneless as I panted his name.

"Come here, beautiful." He pulled me down, my body crumbling like a rag doll.

Thank God he was basically a giant. If he'd been a normal man I'd have probably crushed him and totally ruined my chances of a repeat.

His mouth found mine, kissing and curling my body against his; limbs intertwining liked they'd been magnetized.

"That was amazing." I pressed my lips to his chest, hoping the feeling in my legs would return soon. "You are amazing."

"You know, if you are trying to make me feel good about myself, you shouldn't sound so surprised. It kinda negates the compliment." He laughed as he kissed the top of my head. "And you're not so bad yourself."

"Oh, *not so bad?*" I lifted my head, trying to shoot him an evil glare but failing miserably. "Now who's shitty at giving compliments?"

We had such a strange dynamic, and being around him was effortless. He didn't have that veneer most people had when you first meet them, where the alternate "better" version was presented until you got to know them. He was just Riley, and I could just be my usual, unedited self.

It was refreshing and exciting, and unbelievably unnerving all at the same time.

He excused himself and went to the bathroom, leaving me to lay in post orgasmic bliss until he returned. I used the opportunity to get under the sheets, propping myself up on pillows and trying to look like I hadn't been screwed within an inch of my life. He didn't flinch when he saw me checking him out, smirking proudly as he casually strolled back and slid into the bed beside me.

"So, you want to tell me why you changed your mind?" He strummed my shoulder, letting his fingers run through my hair. "Because I have a feeling, us ending up here wasn't your original plan."

I swallowed hard, the inevitable conversation happening sooner than I thought. He was a smart guy, but I could've probably lied about why I hadn't called earlier. Told him there had been some client emergency, or bullshit about the day just getting away from me. But I didn't want to, and he deserved better. And being the usual, unedited me meant telling him the truth, even if it did sound ridiculous.

"I was avoiding you," I admitted, forcing myself to look in his eyes even though it would have been easier to bury my face in his chest. Firstly, because it was nice there, and I still couldn't get over how hot he was. And secondly, because maybe I wasn't so positive he would understand.

There was zero anger or resentment in those beautiful brown eyes, his hand stroking my cheek as he smiled. "Quinn, I know you were avoiding me. I asked you to call me and not only did you not, but you sent me a fucking emoji when I texted you. I'm not going to pressure you for anything, but I thought we had fun yesterday. But if you're not into this, then you need to tell me. I'm a big boy, I can handle it."

God, he was sweet.

Really, really sweet and I was going to be pissed if it fell apart because I was an idiot.

"This is so dumb, but Karli and I went to some fortune teller after we left Gino's and she told me I needed to be with Mack.

That he was my soul mate and I'd be miserable and doomed if I ended up with someone else. And I know it sounds ridiculous and people can't see the future, but she was so eerily accurate on the details."

I waited for him to laugh, to get out of the bed and run because he'd just slept with a moron who believed in carnival magic. Because seriously I was hearing myself and I wasn't doing myself any favors.

"She said Mack was your soul mate?" he asked, raising a brow and surprisingly not leaving. "What else did she say?"

"That's just it. We walked in randomly, like right off the street, there's no way she could have known about me, or you, or Mack or Karli." I shook my head, still wondering how the hell it had been possible. "But she knew about Brad, and how he was never going to ask her out. And then she said some bullshit about Karli getting a promotion. So when Lorraine broke her hip, and Karli got a promotion, it seemed like it *had* to be true."

His hand pushed the hair out of my face, still not making a move to leave. "So we're doomed, Quinn? If we're not supposed to be with each other, sleeping together can't be helping the situation." He leaned in and whispered, "But I won't tell the universe if you don't."

"I know," I groaned, pulling my face into my hands. "That's why I had to prove Miss Lillian wrong. If Brad asked Karli out, then she had to be wrong about everything else. So I convinced him to take a chance and ask her, and now he thinks going on a double date with me and a cat is a good idea."

I still wasn't sure it had made anything better. Karli hadn't called me with news of an impending date, and I didn't want their failed relationship ending up in a custody battle over a domestic shorthaired named Mr. Darcy.

"Wait a minute." Riley pulled my hands from my eyes. "He wants to take you and a cat on a date with Karli? Because I have to tell you, Quinn, that's crazy even for you."

I laughed, amused he thought it was even a possibility. "No, he wants to take her to an animal shelter to adopt a cat. He wants me and a *friend*," I gestured to him, "to go with them."

"Is that your version of asking me out?" His smile widened, enjoying the whole thing more than should be allowed.

"Well assuming he asks Karli out, the dooms day prophecy of my love life should be a bust too. I say we risk it."

His hand lowered, pinching my ass as he laughed. "That is literally the worst. You can't ask someone to go out by saying *you'll risk it*. Jesus, woman, you're killing me. Not to mention, the love triangle with one of my best friends and my boss. Are you sure he's not the one who's supposed to go pussy hunting with you?" His brow rose suggestively.

"He would probably be more mature about it." I rolled my eyes. "And I don't make the rules. Miss Lillian is the one who said the guy who got the package that wasn't for him—"

He started laughing.

Uncontrollably laughing.

His whole body shaking so much I was worried I'd broken him. It would be just my luck too, ruining him before I had a chance to properly enjoy him. Either that or it was Miss Lillian.

"Quinn," he rumbled, bringing me in closer. "The package was delivered to me. It was *my* apartment."

What the what?

"But Mack—"

"But Mack was convinced it was sent by some kind of psychopath. His wife was one so he should know, so he warned me not to go. Not only did I flat out tell him I was going but we argued. I thought if someone went to the trouble to send panties and a note, I should at least show up, he didn't agree. So to appease him, we made a deal that *he* would meet whoever it was first. I thought the idea was bogus but since he'd not been on a date in forever, I figured it couldn't hurt. And neither of us could have ever anticipated you."

I assumed this was what shock felt like.

It felt like my heart stopped, the room getting blurry because being bug-eyed wasn't compatible with proper vision. I wanted to move, to talk, to question—but all of those things came up short as my opened jaw and rigid frame flopped around with no command of my nervous system. My lungs also let me down, burning with possible paralysis while I tried to form sentences and words didn't make sense.

"You? You?" I pointed wildly not really sure what I was asking.

Was he sure it was his house?

Was he the one who got my panties?

Was he my soul mate?

He chuckled, kissing my still gaping mouth. "Just call me Hot Stuff. Because there isn't a chance in hell I'm giving back those panties."

Chapter 15

Riley

HOUSE FIRE.

The second-story apartment perched above a shop front was billowing smoke from the roof while the bright red glow of the interior screamed bad news. And worse, there were no residents on the lawn out front.

Two engines, a ladder and a medic had responded, Cap shouting orders the moment boots were on the ground as we tried to work out if anyone was home. No one had seen the elderly couple or their fox terrier since the neighbors called 9-1-1.

"North and Tibbs, get your masks on. Both of you are on search and rescue." Cap pointed to the building. "Do not take any chances."

"Gotcha, Cap."

"All good, Cap."

We shouted out our matched responses while lines tried to make a dent in the flames. It was hard to see where it was coming from so we entered through the metal fire escape on the side. Last thing we needed was the roof collapsing, and until we had confirmation exactly where the fire was, going in blind wasn't only stupid but dangerous as well.

I hauled myself up the stairs, taking the rungs two at a time as I climbed to the second floor. Tibbs was right on my ass, both of us hoping it was going to be a rescue and not a recovery.

"Looks like it's coming from the north." My hand pointed to the side. "I'm going in."

Glass exploded as I swung my axe, clearing the shards from the edges before I poked my head inside. The room was filled with smoke, but it wasn't on fire just yet, my hand signaling to Tibbs we were going in.

It was hard enough for someone my size to get through a window, but add the turnouts and a breathing apparatus and it was one hell of a squeeze. Not that I let that stop me, barreling through the hole I'd created and stepping in.

"Hello?" I called out, even though I knew it wouldn't do much good. Between the water, the fire and my voice being muted by the mask, no one was hearing anything.

Tibbs was beside me, our time starting to run out as we moved deeper into the thick black cloud. We had one shot to find these people and it was already getting toasty.

The living room was clear, no people or pets—living or otherwise—so we moved down the hall.

Fuck.

A closed door was alight, and I had to hope whoever we were looking for wasn't in there. It looked like it could be a bedroom, but we couldn't be sure. The flames licked under the frame spreading across the hall and making it difficult to get to the rear of the house. But there was another closed door, a dim light peering underneath the jamb through the smoke further down. That had to be where they were, trapped by flames with no direct way out.

As I plowed through the door, I heard a distinctive cough. Someone was in there, momentarily relieved to see a shivering figure huddled in a corner under wet towels.

"We got one," I shouted at Tibbs, his nod confirming he understood.

There was no more time for thinking, my hands lifting the towels just to let them know they were safe and we were going to get them out.

"Help me."

Jesus.

The girl had to be no older than seventeen or eighteen and in her lap was a frantic fox terrier who was trying to get loose.

"Please, please get me out."

I yanked off my mask, giving her a few good breaths. "Is there anyone else in here?" I shouted over the roaring fire and looked around. "Anyone in other rooms?"

She shook her head no, her eyes getting wide with the crack of timber exploding.

"Are you sure there's no one else?" I handed the dog to Tibbs who had already grabbed another wet towel. "No one will get in trouble, but we need to know right now if there's anyone else in here."

She pulled my mask from her face, her chest heaving as she started to cough again. "Grandparents." Cough. "Vacation." Cough. "Watching Jack."

Tibbs signaled to the hallway which was already on fire.

Fuck.

We were out of time and needed to get out of there like five minutes ago.

He led, holding the dog close to his body, shielding him from the flames. I followed behind, leaving my mask on the girl as I carried her out.

Adrenaline pumped through my veins as we entered the living room. A wall of heat hit us, ashes and plaster falling from the ceiling making it almost impossible to breathe and even harder to see. My lungs burned, the smoke so thick each breath felt like I was sucking on the back of a bus. It hurt too, like a million tiny needles were jabbing into the soft tissue between my ribs, and I knew there was only a minute or two before shit turned critical. Not that there was a chance I was taking back my mask, the girl in my arms needing it a hellva lot more.

Tibbs was out the window first. My first gasp of outside air sucked down my throat as I followed, watching as he stepped out to the landing and then descending down the fire escape. The dog had stopped barking which wasn't a good sign, but we didn't have time to stop and assess.

I was right behind him, sticking to his back as I maneuvered the girl in my arms so I could navigate the stairs.

It was only once we were on the ground I realized how hard I was breathing.

"Medic," I yelled, my voice hoarse and raw as my throat burned. "Need," I spluttered. "A medic."

And then someone was taking her, my hands reaching down to my knees as they handed me back my mask. "Put it back on," yelled Darcy, a young EMT. "We need to get you back to the truck and check you out."

I shook my head, watching as they tended to the girl and the dog. "I'm fine," I squeezed out. "Just look after--" My voice dried up, a coughing fit taking hold as I shut my mouth and put the mask back on.

It didn't take long for smoke to get to you, and in most cases you were dead from lack of oxygen long before you ever felt the flames. We'd been lucky the girl had the presence of mind to get low and cover herself with the wet towels, but another minute or two and it wouldn't have mattered anyway.

My ass dropped to the grass as I concentrated on each breath. It hurt like hell and was going to feel like shit for the next few days but, I'd live. Two other boots joined Darcy's as she helped me back up to my feet. "Girl and the dog are going to be okay. Both are heading to the E.R. to get checked, and you, my friend are going to be joining them."

"Cap." I pulled the mask from my face and coughed. "It's not that bad, I don't need a hospital." The subsequent coughing didn't help my cause as I put the mask back on.

Cap shook his head. "Oh, I must have missed it when you got your medical degree. This isn't up for debate— you're either going voluntarily or we'll strap you down to the stretcher. Rev has already offered to be the one to do it. And Mack will meet you at the hospital."

There was no point arguing.

For one, my throat felt like I'd French kissed a blowtorch and my lungs ached. And if I wasn't at that hospital by the time Mack got there, he'd tear me a new asshole. *Sucked when the boss was also your emergency contact.* Not that he wouldn't have been on immediate speed dial even if it had been one of the other guys. But me, yeah I knew it was different.

The cap took my SCBA while Darcy peeled off my turnouts, got me onto a stretcher, and gave me a shot at their oxygen. She was young, but skilled and didn't do drama. And her current look told me I needed to shut up, do as she said and not give them a hard time. First responders always made the worst patients, and I was living up to that stereotype as they wheeled me into the back of the ambulance.

When we arrived at Mount Sinai West my head was feeling a little dizzy as my eyes focused on the overhead lights. It had been an amazing week and it sucked it had ended with me flat on my back, needing oxygen and not from going ten rounds in bed with Quinn. If nothing else I hoped they could give me some decent drugs and I could get some sleep.

"How you feeling?" Mack pulled back the curtain. I'd already had my blood drawn and a chest X-ray and was really not feeling the hospital gown. "You look like shit."

"Thanks, I'll let my stylist know. And I'm fine." It still hurt to talk so I kept my words to a minimum, the oxygen tube up my nose making it easier to breathe. "Any chance you got my phone?"

When I was in that fire, the only thing I could think about was getting that girl and that dog out safe. There'd been no room for anything else. But on the ride to the hospital, my mind couldn't help but wander.

I needed to hear her voice.

"Nope, but I've called Quinn."

Fuck.

I scrubbed the front of my face, not sure whether to thank the guy or yell at him.

It hadn't even been a week since we'd met, and to be honest, I hadn't even taken her out on a proper date yet. But we were together, and I was going to do everything I could so that didn't change. Hell, our big debut with her friend Karli and Panties Brad was supposed to be tomorrow. And I'd really been looking forward to it, especially since she no longer thought Mack was her soul mate and dating me was going to put her love life in the toilet. Had to admit, it had all been pretty funny. One, that she believed in psychics and two, that she was willing to roll the dice, sleeping with me before I'd confirmed that I had been the one to receive the panties.

"How did she sound?" I coughed out, fairly sure it was too soon in our relationship to be having a crisis.

"She umm . . ." Mack rubbed the back of his neck. "She was worried sick, kid. Was on her way before I got off the phone."

"Will you let her back here when she arrives? Don't let the nurses give her a hard time because she's not family."

I wanted to see her.

I wanted to look into her beautiful blue eyes and feel her lips on mine, and then everything would be okay. They could pull out the line, take away the oxygen and I'd be good to go. But I needed her, and until she was in front of me it just didn't feel right.

Mack shook his head, pulling up a chair and taking a seat. "I've known you a long time, Riley. Have seen you chase a lot of women, seen a lot of women chase you. Ain't never seen you fall so fast or as hard as you have for this one."

"Who says I've fallen? Maybe they should check you for smoke inhalations." I tried to look bored, not willing to admit he'd read me like a fucking book. It was crazy to even think about it, but he wasn't wrong.

It made no sense. And lord knows it wasn't something I'd been looking for, but I felt more for Quinn than I'd ever felt for any woman.

Didn't care how insane it sounded, or how smarter it would be to pump the brakes and slow the fuck down. I wanted nothing to do with the alternative.

We belonged together and I sure as shit wasn't going to stop it.

"And yet, you didn't deny it," Mack laughed. "And of course I'll get her when she arrives. I'd be more worried about the nurses though, something tells me being in the way of something that girl wants wouldn't be a pretty sight."

Man, he had that right.

It hurt to laugh, my lungs giving me the finger as my body shook. She was a handful that was for sure, and I loved every single crazy, impulsive and spirited tendency. There wasn't a thing about her I'd want to change either.

Mack put out his hand and squeezed my arm. "Just do me a favor, kid, and take it slow. Our life isn't for everyone, and today's call is probably not the last she's ever going to get if she sticks around. Not everyone is up for that, and last thing I want is for you to get hurt."

It was tough to hear but I knew he was right. It wasn't a mystery why the divorce rate was high especially for people like us, it was a lot for a significant other to take. The hours, the worry, the job itself—looked more attractive on T.V. than it did in real life. It was probably why I hadn't had a steady girlfriend in over a year, preferring to have casual relationships rather than deal with the arguments.

But I didn't want that with Quinn, and it took me lying in a hospital bed wanting to see her, to know it. I didn't want casual, not with her. And it was the first time in a long time I wanted— no *needed*—to take that risk.

I say we risk it.

They'd been her exact words and even though the context had been completely different, I couldn't have agreed with her more.

"Thanks, Mack. But no need to worry, I'm not going to end up hurt."

Mack's phone buzzed, his grin telling me exactly who the message was from. Ordinarily I'd be pissed he'd gotten my girl's number before I did, but given the circumstances, I was glad.

"I'm going to get her before she gets tazed by security," he chuckled. "Then I'm going to go find the doc and see how long you need to stay in. Give you guys your privacy."

"Thanks, Mack," the lump in my throat for reasons other than the smoke. "Really appreciate it."

Mack nodded, not one to make a big deal. "I've got you, kid. Just rest up."

It didn't take long for Quinn to burst through the curtains, her face wild as she took me in. "If you wanted to cancel our date tomorrow, you could've just said."

I grinned, no longer feeling the pain as she walked closer. "You're delusional if you think tomorrow counts as a date. Pretty sure you'd need to actually agree to one before I could cancel."

"Is this some elaborate way of asking me out, Riley? Because saying no when you saved a girl's life and are in hospital would make me the biggest bitch alive." Her hand slipped over mine, interlocking our fingers and squeezing.

"Beautiful, I don't make the rules. But if you want to be heartless and turn me down, have at it."

She leaned closer, her lips just out of reach. "Am I allowed to kiss you?"

"You don't ever have to ask." I closed the rest of the gap.

It wasn't even close to how I wanted to kiss, annoyed I couldn't pull her onto the bed with me and do it properly. But the contact was enough, making me feel better than any of the pain meds they'd given me.

She was the first to pull away, settling into the chair Mack had vacated, and went back to holding my hand. "How long are you going to be in here? I have no shoots for the next two days, so am totally ready to be your nurse."

My dick stirred at the idea of Quinn in a sexy nurse's outfit, making sure I knew his stance on the topic. "Hopefully soon, but it depends on what the doctor says. I'm trying to be good so they can let me break out of here early, I'd rather be home in my own bed."

"Well then, I'll just have to stay here and keep you company." She picked up my hand and kissed my knuckles. "And by the way, yes."

"Yes?" I asked, wondering if my thoughts of her being in that bed with me had been spoken out loud. Sure would make staying in it a hell of a lot more interesting.

A small smile edged at her lips. "Yes, I'll date you."

My chest heaved as I tried not to laugh. "Like you had a choice."

Despite telling everyone I was fine, they kept me for twenty-four hours, only releasing me when I assured them I wouldn't be alone. At the time, I had been lying through my teeth. Mack was still on rotation and it wouldn't be the first time I'd gone home to get through an injury alone. I just kept my phone beside the bed and entertained a revolving door of visitors, each of the guys stopping in for a few hours when they weren't on duty.

But as it turned out, Quinn's offer to be my nurse wasn't just talk. Her overnight bag was packed and already in the trunk when she and Mack picked me up from the hospital.

"Thanks so much." She threw her arms around Mack, surprising the poor guy as he hugged her back. "For calling me and . . . well, everything else."

I had a hunch there'd been a conversation or two I hadn't been a part of, Mack's cheeks flushing all but confirming it. "It's fine, Quinn. Just let me know if you guys need anything. He can be a pain in the ass when it comes to doing what he's told. So if you need reinforcements, either me or one of the guys can come and muscle him around for you."

"Ha! Like you'd have a chance, old man!" I chuckled, easing into my La-Z-boy. "And quit trying to hit on Quinn, you had your chance and she's not into senior citizens."

He rolled his eyes, shaking his head before pointing at me. "Watch your mouth, kid, or I'll have to embarrass you in front of your girlfriend."

"Don't you have a rookie to yell at or paperwork to file?" I flipped him off. "You can leave any time."

"I'm going." He waved, saying one last goodbye before leaving me alone with Quinn.

"He called me your girlfriend." Quinn's brow rose, shimmering as she sat on the edge of my recliner.

I smirked, tugging her back until she landed in my lap. "So he did, how about you get naked, *girlfriend*."

"The doctor said you need to take it easy for the next few days." She wiggled her ass gently against my crotch. "We both know you won't be able to do that if I'm naked. Not that I blame you, I am almost impossible to resist."

My hands grabbed her hips and gave them a squeeze. "Why don't you let me worry about what I'm able to do. And stop pretending like you're not trying to get me hard with your ass."

Her arms circled my neck and she leaned down, the smell of her citrus shampoo wafting up my nose. "Was it working?" Her lips brushing against mine.

"You know it is." I lifted my hips, showing her the evidence. "We can have sex, beautiful, we just need to take it slow."

She bit her lip, looking guilty. "I hate that I want it right now, that I can even think about it. I just . . . I don't know, need to feel you. Be with you. And figured if I wasn't directly responsible for it then I won't feel bad."

"Quinn, you're *always* responsible for my hard-ons, but there's no reason to feel bad. I want you too. So get naked and let me show you how slow I can go."

Chapter 16

Quinn

I KNEW WHAT he did was dangerous.

And that every single call out was a risk.

But hearing Mack's voice tell me Riley had been taken to the hospital was a fear I hadn't felt in a really long time.

Bile had risen up my throat, banging on Karli's door and begging her to get me an uber while I got dressed and out the door. I'd been so scared, not reassured by Mack telling me he was okay, and only relaxing when I saw him awake and alert.

He'd looked comical, his huge body taking up all the real estate on that tiny hospital bed. But I could tell he was hurting, his breathing labored and his voice raw. It brought back memories of losing my dad, but unlike that trip to the emergency room, I wasn't going to have to say goodbye.

And even though we were no longer there, relocated to his Midtown apartment, the memory of it still sent shivers down my spine.

"Kiss me, Quinn." His hand brought my head closer, my legs straddling him in the chair. "Let's make us both feel good."

God, I wanted him. Wanted to just feel him safe and whole with me, to really know he was going to be okay. My heart squeezed at his cheeky smile, his other hand sliding suggestively down my back.

"Slow, and you'll tell me if I hurt you, right?" I peppered kisses against his jaw, my own hands on a journey of discovery.

He was so hot, my fingers fisting his T-shirt and lifting so I could feel the hard planes of his chest. Nothing had changed, his body was exactly as I'd left it. There were no visible marks or injuries with everything just as it should be.

"You won't hurt me, Quinn. Now take off your clothes, don't make me beg," he warned, tugging at my bottom lip with his teeth.

I loved it when he did that, the slight sting of pain giving way to pleasure as my lower gut tightened. My body got hot, tingles spreading across my arms and legs as I shifted from his lap and let my feet drop to the floor.

He toed off his shoes and pulled off his T-shirt, watching me as my hands slithered down the front of my dress. He'd said he wanted slow and that's what I was going to give to him, taking my time to move to the back where I could undo the zipper.

His eyes darkened, biting his lip as I dropped my dress to the floor. I'd worn cotton panties with a matching bra—pale blue—and the way he was looking at me you'd think I'd been wearing crotch-less panties and nipple tassels.

"Take them off," he gritted out, lifting his hips and shoving down his jeans and boxer briefs. His cock was already hard, bouncing off his tight abs as he tossed his clothes to the floor and removed his socks.

My gaze dropped to his cock, his hand gripping it hard as a bead of pre cum spilled at the top. I loved how much he wanted me, that he was just as desperate as I was.

"Like this?" I flicked off my bra, sliding it down my arms before bringing my hands to my breasts. They moved slowly, squeezing, my fingertips pinching my nipples as I rolled my hips.

"Jesus, Quinn." His hand moved up his shaft, giving himself a few good pulls while I played with my breasts. My hands moved lower, teasing my stomach and hooking on the edge of my underwear.

"Yes, Riley?" I grinned, slowly turning around before bending and pushing my ass in the air. I heard him groan, taking my time as I slid down my panties and giving him more of a show.

"Fuck," he cursed, watching as I turned and moved my hand between my legs, my fingers circling my opening as I got even wetter.

His hand was busy too, keeping a steady rhythm as he fisted his cock. Tight abs flexed as his thighs kicked open in invitation. "I want you."

"I want you too," I moaned, letting my head drop as I continued to play. But it wasn't enough, my hands not satisfying me the way I knew he could.

I strolled over to the doorway where my overnight bag was sitting, his head craning as he watched me pull out a condom, waving it at him before heading back.

He'd gotten impatient, pulling me into his lap and kissing me hard as he rocked against my core. His hard-on hit right where it needed to, making me whimper as he grabbed the condom out of my hand. "You think I'm going to be able to go slow after that? What the hell were you thinking?" The edge in his voice made me more excited, my body clenching as I got even wetter. He hurried to sheath himself, rolling the latex to the base before pushing inside of me in one long thrust.

"Ride me, Quinn." His mouth sucked on my neck as his hands found my tits. "I want to feel you come."

My hips moved, circling and thrusting as he pushed into me. It felt so good, my skin tingling as he bit my shoulder and pinched my nipples.

Deeper.

Harder.

Faster.

Each one of our rocks got me closer until I couldn't take it anymore. My body tensed, his mouth crushing mine as he swallowed my scream.

"Riley, I'm—"

"I'm right there with you, beautiful." He thrust into me, grinding his hips until I felt him explode inside of me.

Both of us unraveled, his cock jerking into me as my core pulsed around him. His kisses unrelenting as he whispered my name against my lips.

"Are you okay?" he asked, moving his hands to my chin as his mouth continued along my jaw.

I laughed, loving the soft kisses. "I think I'm the one who's supposed to be asking you that. That was so *not* slow."

"Well, if anyone is to blame, it's you." He grinned against my skin. "Teasing me wasn't a nice thing to do. Besides, Mack said to call if we need anything and they have oxygen at the station. It was totally worth it."

Panic rose up my throat, grabbing his face and searching it for any sign of discomfort and wheezing. "Please tell me I didn't hurt you. Can you breathe okay? I can move."

"Don't you dare move. And I'm fine. I was kidding about the oxygen." His arms locked around me, keeping me still.

While he wouldn't admit it, I knew he was still hurting. His breathing was heavy—and not just because of sex—and his voice was rough around the edges. But he was a grown man and not very good at being told what to do. Okay, so maybe I had that problem too. But as irresponsible as it was, we both needed it.

God, I liked him.

I liked him a lot more than I even wanted to admit.

"What are you thinking about?" He raised his eyebrow, catching me mid contemplative stare.

I shook my head, not wanting to ruin the moment by talking about feelings. "Nothing."

It took some convincing, but I managed to get Riley into bed. I'd propped him up on enough pillows so he looked like a ruling emperor, turning on the television for him to watch whatever macho sport was playing. There was less chance of doing damage if he was distracted, and I used the opportunity to order some food from a local Italian place and had it delivered.

Unfortunately—for Brad—being Riley's nurse meant I had to gracefully bow out of our planned double date. Brad had eventually worked up the nerve to ask Karli, mumbling something about going to check out cats on adoption day. Of course, the man, while sweet, was terrible at asking women out, not making it clear to my bestie it was in fact A DATE. Sworn to secrecy and because it was mildly entertaining, I decided to wait until *after* to fill Karli in. So he picked her up, took her to the animal shelter and I hoped it didn't end up a total disaster.

"Hello?" I answered my phone quickly, Riley having dozed off a little while ago.

"Hey girl," Karli's warm voice filled my ear. "So I know you're busy but was hoping you had some time to talk."

I tiptoed out of Riley's bedroom, closing the door before settling on the couch. "Of course, Riley is sleeping so I'm all yours. How was your . . ." not sure what word we were using, "*thing* with Brad?"

She waited, blowing out a frustrated breath. "It was fine, I guess. But we spent all that time and then he didn't get a cat. It was so weird."

I shook my head, trying not to laugh. "Wait, you thought you were there to get *him* a cat?" Lord, it had been such a huge train wreck I was almost disappointed I missed it. Did he talk to her at all? Like even give her the tiniest bit of a clue?

"Of course we were there to get him a cat, he asked me to go with him to an animal shelter on adoption day. Why else would we be there?"

Poor Brad.

I was positive he was sitting somewhere in his house, replaying the afternoon like bad game day footage. And I'm sure even with the retrospective, he still had no better idea.

"Don't get mad," I warned, biting my lip. "And remember how much you love me."

Karli groaned, "What did you do?"

"I *may* have suggested that Brad should ask you out. I figured since my last effort had been so successful, why not interfere again."

"Quinn, do I need to remind you that your last effort was *not* successful."

"Speak for yourself, sweet cheeks. I think it worked out pretty freaking awesome." I grinned to myself, the outcome more than I could've ever imagined.

"Just give me the details so I can decide how mortified I need to be on Monday."

Taking a breath, I divulged my covert plan to get Brad to ask her out so I could prove Miss Lillian was a hack who knew nothing. Of course, had I known Riley had been the recipient of the package and therefore my soul mate, proving her wrong wouldn't have mattered. But hindsight was 20/20 and I had issues. So, there we were, me convincing Brad to man up and take a swing and his counter offer of dipping a toe in.

"The location was completely his idea. I'd tried to talk him out of it, but he knew you loved kittens so I guess he hoped it might work in his favor. Probably would have helped if he'd actually told you though. So yeah, you weren't there looking to adopt a cat for him. He was trying to put the moves on."

"Quinn!" Karli laughed, "Oh my god, you're terrible. Oh, and to think I missed out on a kitten."

"Honey, you both missed out on pussy." I laughed, unable to help myself.

Karli shrieked, "Oh God, now when I see him, that's all I'm going to be able to think about."

"Well, it's a start, and maybe now he's done it once, he'll do it again. It can't get any worse."

Karli sighed, still giggling over the situation when she asked. "How's Riley? I'm assuming you're staying with him."

My eyes darted around the room, making doubly sure I was alone but dropping my voice just in case. "I think he's okay but the more I read about it on the internet the more I freak out. I can't even think about what might have happened." Nothing good ever came from Googling medical conditions. One minute you're looking at home treatments for mild smoke inhalations and the next you're tumbling down a hole of esophageal burns and cancer from chemical exposure. "It feels ridiculous to even say it out loud, but I'm petrified about him going back to work. I mean, he's a firefighter for God's sake, what did I think he did?"

"Ah, Quinn. It's normal to be scared but his job is part of who he is. I doubt he'd take any unnecessary chances."

With every fiber of my being, I wished I could agree. But I didn't, believing deep down in my heart if it came down to Riley's own life and saving someone else, he'd be the goddamn heroic bastard I'd fallen in love with.

Well. Then.

Love.

Was I in *love* with him?

Oh Fuck.

"You're right, Karli. He wouldn't take any unnecessary risks," I lied, my throat feeling tight. "Hey, is it okay if I call you later? There's something I need to do."

"Sure Quinn, let me know if you need anything and give Riley my love."

Yeah, that's what I was going to do.

Give him Karli's love when I couldn't even give him my own.

And to think I used to think I was such a badass.

Yep, not so much.

Chapter 17

Riley

"GOOD MORNING." WAKING up to Quinn's smile was one of the best parts of my day. "You want some breakfast? I can go hunt and gather, see what I can make us."

She turned like she was about to leave, my arms stopping her from going anywhere. "You didn't wait for my answer." I pulled her warm body against mine. "And I wanted to tell you what I was hungry for."

Here's a clue, nothing that was in my kitchen.

"Are you trying to ply me with your body?" She mock gasped, feeling my hands wrap around her tits. "Riley, I was talking about *food*."

"As long as we eat, what's the difference?" I laughed, letting my hand slide a little lower. My hard-on pressed against her ass, his agenda pretty clear.

Being on medical leave sucked balls, but there was no greater silver lining than extra time with Quinn. Having her in my bed—something I was already getting used to.

"Well," she spun around in my arms. "You need to check in with Mack and I need to call my mother. If she doesn't hear from me on Sundays, it can get ugly. Don't think us making those calls while you're giving me an orgasm is appropriate. I know, I know—so old fashioned."

Well, she had a point.

"Fine, food it is," I groaned, releasing her from my arms. I'd relent for the time being, but only because we had a whole day to play.

She slid from the bed, shooting me a grin that had me reevaluating my stance as she grabbed some clothes off the floor. And I didn't take my eyes off her until she'd disappeared down the hall.

My arms stretched above my head as a satisfied grin settled on my face. Things were going pretty fucking awesome and by some miracle I'd scored possibly the best girlfriend ever. Not that I'd taken her anywhere yet, but I was going to be changing that ASAP.

I grabbed my phone off the nightstand and decided to call Mack. Quinn was right about me needing to check in. Last thing I wanted was for him or one of the guys from the station dropping by unannounced.

"Kid, how you feeling?" Mack answered before the call had barely registered. He was old school liked that, preferring to talk rather than text.

"Pretty good, Chief. And I'm good to go. Which is lucky for you too because I know how much you're missing me." I watched the door, waiting for Quinn to return.

"You know the drill, North. Not allowed back in rotation until you've got medical clearance. Your appointment is Tuesday, everything checks out, you can come back. If it doesn't, you're on the bench."

Mack had always been a rule follower so his spiel wasn't all that surprising. But I was young, healthy and knew that I was fine. And it seemed like a waste of resources to have me sitting at home when I could be with my guys. Besides, Quinn would probably go back to work on Monday and I was going to be bored out of my mind.

"Come on, Mack. You know I'm solid, and you guys need me."

"What I *need* is for you to be one hundred percent. You go out on a call less than that, and you become a liability. To me, to the crew, and to yourself. It's not happening, North. So don't argue."

"Fine, but we both know I could be half dead and would still give you more than most. I'd never allow for you or any of the guys to be in danger, and this whole thing is bullshit." I huffed into the phone, annoyed it was probably going to be Wednesday or Thursday before I'd get to go back. I was going to need a fucking hobby.

"Relax, North," He laughed. "It's not a personal flaw to need a few days. And while we're on the topic, when was the last time you had a vacation? Took some personal time? Might be worth thinking about, do something with Quinn."

I knew what the Chief was doing and while I appreciated it, I didn't like being handled. He knew it too, which was why he hadn't brought up my lack of *personal* time until now. The other guys had families—either ones they'd created or belonged to—so it made more sense for them to get first dibs. Plus, I was the lucky son of a bitch who got to see my family every day; there was no need to be greedy.

"I'll think about it." My noncommittal response the best he was going to get. "Tell everyone I said hey, and make sure Tibbs keeps out of my fucking locker. That asshole keeps taking my deodorant and forgetting to put it back."

Mack chuckled, probably shaking his head that on top of all the serious shit he had to do, he had to run interference with us too. "I'll pass on your regards. Stay out of trouble."

We said our goodbyes and hung up and Quinn still hadn't returned. I assumed she'd gone to the bathroom, heard me on the phone and decided to give me some privacy. Either that or she'd gone to the kitchen because she was serious about food.

Tossing my legs over the side of the mattress, I reached down and pulled on some sweatpants. Quinn in my kitchen wasn't something I wanted to miss, strolling out of my bedroom and down the hall with a huge grin on my face.

I still had that fantasy of her naked making pie and I didn't care how impractical it sounded.

But when I got to the kitchen, it was missing one hot blond. And a quick scan of the bathroom turned out to be fruitless too. Had she left? She wasn't wearing any shoes. And where the hell did she have to go?

I was just about to go grab my phone and call her when I heard the front door open. Quinn—just as disheveled as when she'd left my bedroom—stopping a beat before she came back in. "Hey, did you call Mack?" she said casually, like she hadn't been trying to sneak back into my apartment.

"You have an early morning crack deal?" My chin tipped to the door. "Or did you forget to rob me and were coming back for my wallet."

She laughed, rolling her eyes as she closed the door behind her. "I checked your wallet while you were asleep and it wasn't even worth my time. Your medicine cabinets are boring too."

Her quip should have reassured me everything was cool—sarcasm was her baseline—but there was something that made me feel uneasy. I didn't like to think of myself as paranoid, but I wasn't an idiot either. "You going to tell me where you went, or we going to pretend that you didn't just come back?"

An emotion I couldn't quite place flashed through those beautiful blue eyes, not making me feel any better.

"I didn't go anywhere, I was just outside. I knew you needed to call Mack and I was trying to give you your space."

"Space?" I tilted my head, confused. "To make the call? Quinn, anything I need to say to Chief, you can hear, you know that. So did you step outside because of me, or because you wanted to talk to your mom and didn't want me to hear?"

It was natural she might want to have her conversation in private; I got that. And I wasn't so insecure to think it had anything to do with me. But leaving the room was one thing, leaving the whole goddamn apartment was something else. Like she not only wanted me not to hear, she didn't want me a part of it. "Something else you want to say?"

Quinn didn't do uncertainty, but her face was full of it when she lifted her chin. Whatever had transpired on that conversation, it wasn't making her feel good, which of course I instantly disliked.

"I haven't called my mom yet," she confessed. "I had to rearrange my work schedule."

"Work? I thought you had today off?" I scratched my chin, wondering if I'd gotten my wires crossed when she'd told me her day was free.

"Not today, I have a shoot on Tuesday in Connecticut."

Well that wasn't worth worrying about, we could take the drive together if she wanted the company. And it's not like I didn't know she had to work.

"So, that's not so far. Why would you cancel?"

"Because I want to go with you to the doctor's, okay? And if you knew I had to work you'd go without me."

She was right; I would go alone. Why should her day be thrown into disarray because I had a stupid appointment I was more than capable of attending solo. But it was strange hearing the concern, and not only because it was her giving it. Just wasn't something I was used to or expected, and to be honest, really even understood.

"Quinn is something going on that I don't know about? Because I don't expect you to babysit me 24/7 and I'd probably drive you crazy if you did. There were no burns on the X-ray; I'm fine. The appointment is just routine."

Her eyes lifted, looking so unsure it was adorable. "I really like you, Riley."

"Well, that works out since I really like you." I laughed, unable to shake the feeling I was still missing something. "Why don't you tell me what else is on your mind."

She took a breath, her chest lifting while the tension lingered in her shoulders as she locked her gaze on mine. "I'm going to sound so pathetic right now, but you wanted to hear it so you only have yourself to blame when all the mystique is gone."

I closed the distance between us, wrapping my arms around her. "I think I'll survive, go on."

"I haven't liked a lot of guys like the way I like you."

"I get it." I winked. "I'm *liked.*"

She rolled her eyes, jabbing me roughly in the chest. "Stop making fun of me or I'll Photoshop your face onto porn. You know I have the skills to do it."

"Okay, Okay." I lifted my hands in surrender. "As interesting as it would be to see myself with a twelve-inch penis, might cause some issues with HR. Proceed."

"So these feelings I have for you are not only new but intense, which is silly because we just met. I mean, we've been together like five minutes. It's crazy. But there they are, whether they're practical or not. And then I got that call, and now I'm paranoid." She sucked in a breath, continuing, "You would know better than I do how short life can be. Gone. In an instant." She snapped her fingers. "My dad hadn't even celebrated his fiftieth birthday. Fit, healthy—gone. And I just got you."

"Quinn." I pulled her close to my body, unable to process how I'd gotten so lucky. "Listen to me. You are *not* going to lose me. I'm sorry if I scared you, but I'm okay. And if you want to come with me to the doctor and hear it for yourself, then of course I want you there. But look at me." I lifted her chin. "Don't think for a second that what we have isn't real because it was fast. When you know, you know, right? Life is short, so let's not waste time trying to work out the whys. And the only way you're going to lose me is if you walk out the door yourself."

I kissed her, taking her mouth because it was mine, and still not feeling like I was close enough. She moaned, leaning into me as she clutched at my skin. Mack had been right, the life wasn't for everyone and it was easy to get scared. But I'd do whatever I had to and make sure we'd be okay. Even if it meant following orders for a change.

"Hey." I pulled her mouth from mine. "How heavy is your workload for the next few days? Apart from the obvious shoot in Connecticut you already canceled."

She scrunched her nose, doing the mental calculation. "Monday and Wednesday are both shit shows but the rest of the week I can shuffle. Why? What did you have in mind?"

"Well," I kissed the tip of her nose gently, "while you were hanging outside my door like a stalker, Chief reminded me I have a butt load of vacation time. Figured maybe we'd take off somewhere together, give the guys a chance to really miss me."

"Go somewhere, like just for fun?" Her eyes got wide.

"Yeah, I hear people do it all the time. Sometimes a couple of times a year. Sounds like something we should definitely try."

"That sounds perfect." She pressed her face against my chest, squeezing me for all it was worth. "Oh my god, I'm so excited."

"Quinn," I whispered against her hair. "Just promise me if shit is on your mind, you'll talk to me. I can handle anything you need to say."

She chuckled, her lips tickling my bare skin. "You sure you're ready for that level of commitment? I say some pretty out there shit."

"Bring it," I taunted, not the least bit scared.

"Fuck!" Her head snapped up, looking at me with concern. "I still need to call my mother. I swear one of these days I'm going to end up on the missing person's page."

God she was adorable.

Crazy, but goddamn adorable.

"Why don't you do one better, call your mom and tell her we'll stop by. Give you a chance to show off your amazing new *boyfriend*."

"You really do think highly of yourself, don't you?" She laughed, twisting her mouth into a grin. "Okay showoff, let's go meet my mother."

Chapter 18

Quinn

AFTER CALLING MY mom and informing her of our impending visit, she was even less convinced that I was fine. It wasn't like I didn't stop by, making it a point to at least visit once a month. But what I didn't do, was bring a date.

Last guy she'd met was my eighteen-year-old boyfriend, and that had been accidental. I'd snuck him into my room when I assumed everyone was asleep, but had miscalculated the variable that was my mother.

Oh, she didn't bust in and embarrass me while I was getting hot and heavy, instead letting us finish, which was ten times worse. It was only after we were both dressed, and attempting to sneak him back out, that we found my mother at the bottom of the stairs drinking tea. Calmly smiling as she confronted us. And then—after daintily taking another sip of her Darjeeling—she informed him that she'd raised two strong, independent women who had their whole lives ahead of them. And if he fucked—yes, she actually used the word—that up by getting me pregnant, there was going to be hell to pay so he'd better have used a condom. Then she invited him to join the family for our next Sunday dinner, but funnily enough we broke up shortly after.

So, the fact I was voluntarily bringing a man—who I was dating—to the house after such a long hiatus, had her rightfully questioning my state of mind.

Had to say, I didn't fully disagree.

While my parents had originally lived in Woodbridge, they moved to Montclair right before I was born. My dad was literally in love with the architecture, spending evenings dragging us out to look at houses in the neighborhood. I'd hated it when I was younger, wishing I could be inside watching T.V. like regular kids instead of trawling the streets like weirdos. But I'd learned more about art and composition on those walks than I ever learned in college.

Mom still lived in the same house, making sure it was as pristine as it had been when my dad had still been alive.

Riley smiled, glancing over to me as he drove up the driveway. "I'm sensing a theme between you and fancy neighborhoods."

"Yeah, don't believe the hype. Unlike some of my neighbors, I never got a trust fund. My dad picked up the vacant lot on a bank sale and designed the house. We were far from living on the poverty line but we didn't vacation in the Hamptons either."

"Shit, Quinn." He bit back his grin, pretending to be disappointed. "I'd kind of counted on you being loaded. A lot of time and effort to put in for no payday, probably something you should have told me up front."

I shook my head trying not to laugh. "Easy there, gigolo, I'm self-made and have done pretty well for myself. Just play your cards right and you'll be a kept man in no time."

I couldn't even keep a straight face, the idea that Riley would mooch off anyone let alone a woman, hilarious. He'd sooner starve, and unlike me, was something he'd known about while growing up.

Taking a settling breath we exited his truck as I prepared to brace. I had no idea how it was going to go, but part of me was really excited.

He grabbed my hand as I pressed the buzzer, my mom having installed one that had a camera so I knew we were being watched. She would have noticed that gesture for sure.

"Quinn." She opened the door, her blond hair peppered with more grays than I remembered. "Such a wonderful surprise."

I gave her my usual hug, dwarfing her which wasn't hard because she was only five two, and then stepped back to let her look at me. She liked to do a once over, reassure herself that I was fine and whole and happy. It was her thing, and honestly wasn't a big price to pay considering.

"Mom, this is Riley North." Our fingers locked again. "We're seeing each other. And Riley, this is my mom, Lori Rhodes."

My mom's brow cocked, her smile widening. "Well it's lovely to meet you, Riley." She held out her hand. "Why don't we go inside and let me interrogate—I mean—get to know you. And please, call me Lori." She chuckled, pretending like her word choice and the slip hadn't been intentional.

"Sounds great, Lori. And it's a pleasure to meet you too." Riley grinned, leaning in to whisper as we walked in. "I see where you get it from."

The interior was like it had always been—neat but lived in. Tasteful grays, blues and whites of the living room showcasing my dad's black and white photos that were still mounted on the walls. He'd been an amazing photographer and saw beauty in everything.

"Sit," my mom gestured to the love seat. "Coffee, tea?"

Riley squeezed my hand, leaning forward. "Actually I'd love some Darjeeling if you have it."

I was going to kill him.

It had been a mistake telling him that story on the way over, still not much I could do about it now.

My mother's brows popped in surprise, flicking her gaze to me before laughing. "Oh she told you about that, did she? Well, then she must really like you."

And like some freak ass magic, whatever tension that might have been there, disappeared. Riley admitted that he actually hated tea so would prefer coffee, and mom made us two double shot cappuccinos with the new espresso machine I'd given her last Christmas.

We sipped our drinks while Mom asked questions that were masquerading as small talk but designed to garner information. She was skilled at inquiry, which had made her a highly successful and popular paralegal. And like my dad's evening walks, had given me more valuable life skills than could ever have been achieved in a classroom.

"So you're a fire fighter. Was that your childhood dream?" My mother leaned forward with genuine interest.

"Actually, no." Riley looked at me and smiled. "Had no plan, to be honest. I didn't exactly have a conventional upbringing."

My body froze, apology filling my eyes as I opened my mouth. I hadn't even thought about it. The questions he might get asked about his family, and how that might make him feel, not even entering my mind.

"I sent him panties." I blurted out, hoping to deflect some of the attention. "I mailed him a pair of red lace panties with a time and place to meet me."

Confessing it to my mother hadn't been the plan, but I'd sooner throw myself under a bus than subject Riley to possibly uncomfortable interrogation.

"What?" My mother's brow barely rose "Is that the new thing? I thought it was all about online profiles now and dating apps."

Riley interlaced his fingers in mine, bringing my hand to his lips as he shook his head. "Your daughter has a habit of doing things for other people even at her own expense. She was trying to help a friend. A little misguided, but help nonetheless. Like she is now." He turned to my mother. "Both my parents were drug addicts with criminal records. They died when I was eighteen. It's not the sort of thing parents like to hear about the guy their daughter brings home, but I'm not ashamed of who I am and what kind of man I've become. So whatever you want to ask is fine, because I intend to stick around. Hopefully that means her days of sending panties are over, because I think we can all probably agree that's for the best." He shot me a wink.

Riley didn't falter, taking it completely in stride, exuding the charismatic confidence that he'd always had. Meanwhile, my heart had swollen to three times the size and felt like it was going to burst.

My mother looked on silently, which never was a good sign. She lowered her cup, regarding us both carefully before opening her mouth. "Whatever were you hoping to achieve with panties? And please for God's sake tell me they were clean, Quinn."

And just like that, the conversation returned to the ease it had been moments before. Of course, I elaborated, telling her my detailed plan to play matchmaker for Karli and Brad, my effort foiled by the misaddress. Not that I had any regrets, the mistake working out in my favor.

And despite not being prompted to do so, Riley volunteered information about Mack and his stationhouse family. My mother—still very much a woman—was wowed by his recent heroics, winning her over completely.

If I wasn't already dating him, she probably would have demanded it, her eyes filled with joy as the three of us laughed in her living room.

"It was so great to see you, sweetheart." She gave me a tight hug before offering one to Riley. "And you too, Riley."

As much as my mom would have loved for us to stay for Sunday dinner—Carrie and her family descending on the house in a matter of hours—I wanted some more alone time with Riley. Especially after everything he'd shared.

Plus, we still hadn't decided where we were going on our trip and I had some loose ends to tie up for work, so heading back to New York made sense. Not to mention I wanted to go to my apartment and check on Karli, and I hadn't really packed enough clothes for more than a few days.

He'd barely closed the driver's side door when I reached across the console and kissed him before he could start the ignition.

"Feeling nostalgic?" He chuckled. "Nice neighborhood or not, I'm sure sixteen-year-old Quinn didn't give a fuck what the neighbors thought."

I rolled my eyes, his assessment being accurate as usual. I hadn't cared what they'd thought, but it wasn't nostalgia that was responsible for my loved up feelings. "Thank you for coming here with me. I know this stuff probably isn't easy for you."

"Quinn, I meant what I said in there. I'm not ashamed of who I am and getting the third degree is something I'm kind of used to. And no matter what the outcome was, it would have been worth it for you. Besides, it was my idea to come here, remember? And I knew your mom would love me, how could she not? I'm irresistible."

I playfully pushed against his chest, conceding that while he wasn't wrong, I wasn't willing to admit it. "Well, maybe it's my family that's amazing. They're well accustomed to loving unconditionally. In fact, I'd like to take some of the credit. I've more than tested the theory over the years, and yet . . . they don't waver."

Riley smirked, putting the truck into gear as he pulled away from the curb, "Not buying it, Quinn. I think your mom is great, and I loved meeting her. Hopefully some time soon I get to meet the rest of your family as well. But this was totally on me. Did you see the way your mom looked at me? She was charmed."

"Just drive, wiseass. See if you can charm your way back through afternoon traffic." I hid my grin as I pointed to the road.

We chatted the entire drive home about everything and nothing, laughing as we crossed back into New York. First, we went to his apartment, where we picked up my overnight bag and packed another for him, then continued on to mine.

It seemed to make sense for us to base ourselves in Brooklyn. I still had work that needed to be done, and my computer, cameras and software was all there. Not that I hadn't loved his cozy little place in Manhattan, intending to split our time between the two places.

Riley called Mack and organized his vacation time, while I fired up my computer and looked at my schedule.

Monday was intense. I had shoots booked back-to-back starting with an engagement announcement at sunrise. Most couples preferred sunset, but there was something magical about the day's first light. Thankfully it was on my side of town, meeting the happy pair at ridiculous o'clock in the morning at Bridge Park in Brooklyn.

"Hey, you're home." Karli had knocked on the door a little bit before dinner. "How's Riley?"

"Great thanks." He came up behind me and gave me a hug. "How did your date go? Sorry we missed it."

In the turbulence of the last few days, I'd completely forgotten to mention Karli's ill-fated date with Brad. Honestly, I'd have thought it would have been the last thing on his mind. But as usual, he surprised me, paying more attention than most guys and genuinely seeming to care.

Karli shook her head, hiding a shy smile. "Not great. We could have probably used y'alls help to be honest. I had no idea it was a date."

Deciding he needed to hear the whole sorry tale first hand, we invited Karli to stay for dinner. Her sister Josie was predictably out again—I was beginning to suspect she had moved out and was using Karli's apartment for storage—and we were happy to have the company. Besides, as much as I loved having Riley to myself, I was kind of enjoying sharing him too. Letting a man into other parts of my life was a novel idea, and I was really glad to be doing it with him.

We laughed and ate pizza—Karli's with vegan cheese—as I heard the story for the second time. "I couldn't understand why he kept asking me which one I liked better? I mean, it was *his* cat, why should it matter which one I liked?"

"Why didn't you just ask him?" Riley chuckled, his arm around me while taking another slice. "You didn't think it was an odd thing to ask for input?"

She sighed, wistfully. "We're friends. Beginning to think that's all we'll ever be, to be honest. But we hang out from time to time. I helped him pick out his couch from Pottery Barn, so I thought he just wanted a woman's opinion."

"Yeah, he might be too far gone," I chuckled, giving a small shrug. "I tried to tell him it was a bad idea. A pet's a big commitment. You can't decide to pick one up like a pizza." I pointed to the box our dinner had come out of.

Karli sighed again—the theme for the night when it came to talking about Brad. "I know, kind of disappointed though. Josie is gone so much, might have been nice to have the company."

"Wait." I held up my hand. "We talking about the cat or Brad?"

She chuckled, shaking her head. "Honestly, I'd have taken either."

It was late when Karli retreated back to her place, and I had yawned a few too many times by the time Riley and I had crawled into bed.

"How are you feeling?" I asked in the dark, the warmth of his naked skin tingling against mine. "Any shortness of breath, mucus, pain? It can take up to thirty-six hours for more symptoms to show."

"Someone's been Googling," he laughed. "And *mucus* is such a great word, so sexy. Not sure why you haven't said it before."

"Just answer the question, wiseass." I elbowed him gently.

I could feel him grinning against my skin. "Fine, *Web M.D.* No notable changes, no wheezing, no additional hoarseness, no difficulty breathing or feelings of pressure or obstruction. What's the diagnosis? Do I get my gold star?"

"Sounds promising, but your attitude needs work. We can't blame the fire for that though, the patient was troublesome to begin with."

"Troublesome?" He scoffed. "I think you said *awesome* wrong."

I was so far gone.

Had no idea what I was doing but I knew I wanted to be doing it with him.

I lifted my chin, his lips finding mind. "Shut up and kiss me."

"Um, Doc, fairly sure there are a few laws against it, but lucky for you, I'm a rule breaker."

Then he did.

Kiss me.

The rule breaking was sure to follow.

It was early.

I'd hoped to crawl out of bed without waking Riley but he was an annoyingly light sleeper. I'd literally moved two inches when his eyes had opened and he'd kissed me. There'd be no chances in the future of me slinking out of bed and making him a surprise breakfast in bed. Something I told him that he'd only ruined for himself.

Still with him awake it meant I was able to say goodbye before I snuck out of my apartment. He kissed me again before I got into the shower and when I got out of it, threatening to make me late. But it wasn't like I could ask the sun to hold off coming over the horizon while I made out with my boyfriend, celestial bodies weren't accommodating like that.

So reluctantly I left him, telling him we'd meet up around lunchtime and that he could snoop through my medicine cabinet to even up the score. Who knows, maybe I could rope him into being my assistant later. Nothing like a tall, good looking man holding a reflective board to make the day go quicker.

"Okay, let's go through positions now in the dark so you know what we're doing when the lighting is right." The morning air was still cool, my blazer doing its best to keep me warm. "And you need to stand here." I dropped a green-colored square onto the grass, giving them their mark. "The light will reflect off the buildings and the bridge, and we'll get to see the Manhattan skyline."

The fiancée was shivering in a full-length gold evening dress. It was strapless, fitted to mid thigh where it flared out like a flamenco dancer. Pretty, would look amazing on camera, but not very practical for early morning NYC in springtime.

"I get down on one knee, right?" the fiancé asked, adjusting his jacket. Guess it hadn't occurred to him to give it to her until we were ready. "Does it matter which one?"

"Most guys go down on the left, ring box in left hand and you open with the right," I offered, setting up my tripod.

"No, I don't care which one most guys use," the gold-dress diva spat out. Shivering, lip wobbling and shivering again. "Which one is going to look better? That whore, Madeline, had her photos taken at a lake house in Maine and everyone went crazy over them. I need to have more likes than her."

"Babe, isn't Madeline your maid of honor?"

"Of course she is, she's my best friend, Jerry. Why would you even ask that?" She shot him a heated look before turning to me. "Do both knees okay? And I want a dip. Where he kisses me and I'm almost all the way back, I had my extensions redone yesterday."

Sigh.

Their marriage was going to be so much fun.

Not all couples were like that, some didn't care how they were positioned, what they were wearing, or how many likes they were going to get. They just wanted me there, capturing the moment forever so they could relive it later. It was just a shame we had such a stunning location, something as wonderful as promising to marry someone you loved, and they were more worried about which knee looked better. Still, they didn't pay me for judgment, and it was none of my business.

"We'll do both knees, a dip, the kiss, a spin, and a few staged shots in case you want to use them on invitations," I smiled at them both as the sky started to give us a hint of light. "But don't worry, I'll keep snapping. Sometimes the best shots are the ones we don't plan."

"Make sure I look thin." She gave me one last warning before settling into position. "I haven't eaten in almost a week to fit into this dress and I'll just die if I look fat."

I nodded, promising to capture them both from the best angles as the sun slowly started to rise.

It was stunning, the rays of light catching the glass of the towering New York skyline just right across the river. He got down on one knee, opened the box and presented the ring. She faked surprise and excitement, holding her hands to her face as she nodded while he slipped it on the forth finger of her left hand.

All of it was manufactured, curated to look spontaneous, repeated in different positions, with a different knee, from a different angle two to three more times until I was positive they were both happy.

There was no doubt in my mind that the photos were beautiful and the client was happy. They "looked" happy, in love, bursting with joy. And maybe they had been when he'd initially asked. Maybe that huge look of surprise was exactly how it had been. But it made me realize I'd never want that for myself.

If a man was ever crazy enough to propose to me I hoped it was nothing like that. Not sunset, or sunrise, not on a beach or a lake house or in front of a famous monument. No balloons, no flowers, no foil hearts. And how fucking ironic was that?

Just me and him.

Promising to love each other forever, our private moment locked away in my memory and heart with no filter.

"I'll send you the proofs in a day or two, and you can let me know if you want to make any changes." I packed away my camera and equipment. "And congratulations."

"Thanks," she grinned, looking at the ring on her finger instead of the guy standing beside her. "I'm so lucky. It's four carats."

It was going to be a long day.

Chapter 19

Riley

WHEN QUINN SAID her Monday was going to be busy, she wasn't kidding. I didn't even hear from her until lunchtime, telling her not to worry and I'd see her later that night. And as amazing as her apartment was—we were going to have sex in that amazing shower of hers if it was the last thing I did—it wasn't much fun hanging around without her in it.

So instead I headed back to my place, telling her to come find me when she was done. Besides, the Tuesday appointment with the doc was in Manhattan, and I'd rather deal with my inferior bathroom than fight morning traffic.

She didn't walk in the door until nine fifteen.

"Did you make dinner?" She sniffed the air, practically falling into my arms when I'd opened the door. "Oh my god, I've literally only had a bagel since breakfast."

"We take turns cooking at the station. Kiss me and I'll show you exactly how talented I am." I didn't bother letting her decide, taking her mouth as she lowered her bags of equipment and let me lead her to the couch.

There I fed her pasta, carrying her off to bed when she'd had enough and held her all night. There hadn't even been sex, Quinn falling asleep mid kiss.

God, she was beautiful, so utterly peaceful while her thoughts became dreams and she slipped from consciousness. It made me puff out my chest, feeling like a rock star she was with me, in my fucking bed and I didn't care how conceited that made me sound.

Tuesday was exactly as I'd promised Quinn.

"Well, Riley. Films look good. Lung function is normal, nothing here that raises any concern." Doc looked down at his file scribbling some notes while Quinn sat white knuckling the armchair she was sitting in beside me. "No reason why you can't return to active duty. I'll be sure to send the report to the station and the chief."

"You're sure he's ready to go back?" Quinn asked, leaning forward in her seat. "Isn't there a chance of light scarring, don't you think you should scope him one last time? What are his chances of developing asthma? There was also a good chance there was lead paint on those walls, maybe he needs another blood toxicology report."

I'd tried not to laugh.

Mainly because I knew her concern was genuine, and it was kind of sweet. But there weren't a lot of people who'd have the balls to question the doc. The man had so many degrees they lined the wall behind him, he was also one of the best pulmonary specialists in the state. Not that it seemed to matter to Quinn, asking her questions regardless of the man's expertise.

"Obviously with every exposure comes a greater risk, but there is no medical indication at the current time to warrant anymore testing or give me any concerns. Trust me," he respectfully directed all his attention at Quinn. "If there was even the slightest doubt, I wouldn't be signing this paper."

He was surprisingly patient, but then I guessed she wasn't the first freaked out significant other he'd had to reassure. "But I will say she does bring up a very valid point." He turned his attention to me. "SCBA on at *all* times. I don't want to see you back here."

So after giving me an earful about being more careful, and a printout on lung health, we were dismissed. I was fucking fine, and it wasn't anything I hadn't heard before. But given the circumstances again, there wasn't anything I'd have done different. Not that I'd have admitted that to the doc or to Quinn. Please, that little baby was staying tucked away just for me. Besides, she'd looked so fucking relieved when she'd heard I was okay, last thing I wanted was to have her worrying about probabilities and hypotheticals.

And to just further prove how *fine* I was, we spent the day in my apartment where I administered my own tests. They involved a *lot* of strenuous activity and heavy breathing, both of us passing with flying colors. Not to say we wouldn't need to reevaluate frequently; testing and training was important when you were in my line of work. And I was really dedicated to the fucking cause.

It was well before dawn when Quinn woke up on Wednesday.

"Another dawn shoot?" I pulled her body against mine, taking whatever lingering minutes I had with her before she left. "One more day and I get you all to myself."

"Are you going into the station today," she asked, slightly uneasy. Doc had emailed his report but usually we went and touched base with Cap. I'd mentioned the night before that I was anxious to get back into my turnouts as soon as we returned. And I didn't want to risk being left off rotation an extra day due to paperwork.

My finger ran down her arm, loving the feeling of her warm skin. "Yep, I'll head there a little after nine. Give me a chance to say goodbye to the guys before we head off tomorrow. And there's a few other things I needed to take care of too."

"For work?"

"For our trip, silly." I leaned forward and kissed her. "Just go do whatever you need to do today, and leave the rest up to me. Okay?"

She nodded, agreeing and leaving me in bed before walking out the door.

It was late by the time she got back, her smile and eyes lacking their usual shine but I assumed it was fatigue. If ever there was someone who needed four uninterrupted days with me doing nothing but sleeping, eating and fucking, it was Quinn. Okay, maybe the *fucking* wasn't going to help the situation, but regardless, we were leaving in the morning to go on our vacation. She hadn't even asked where we were going, letting me plan the whole thing.

The next morning was D-Day, and it was the first time in forever I'd been so excited not to go to work.

"Are we heading to the airport?" Quinn asked as I loaded luggage into the back of my truck. "What time's our flight? TSA is a nightmare if you aren't pre-approved."

It had been tempting to fly her off somewhere exotic that would make good photos, and I entertained the idea for about a second before I turfed it. Last thing I wanted was to deal with airports and lines and fucking hotel check ins. She could do all of that when she was traveling with models and people who had no last name. We were doing something else.

"No airport, Quinn. I didn't trust you not to smuggle a dime bag into my suitcase. Didn't feel like a cavity search."

"God," she rolled her eyes, trying to hide her grin. "It wasn't a dime bag, like I would do something like that. It was a vibrator. A big one. You're welcome."

I opened the door, chuckling as I shook my head. "You're such a giver, Quinn. Not sure how the hell I got so lucky."

We climbed into the truck, started the engine and got the hell out of the city. It was only when we were on the 87 heading north that she asked our destination.

"Tibbs owed me a favor, and his uncle has a place not far from Lake Placid. It's not in the main part of town, and not all that fancy, but there's electricity and running water. I think it might even have wi-fi. We'll grab groceries on our way through town."

My eyes flicked across to her, making sure she wasn't disappointed. There weren't going to be couple massages at a spa, or room service, and I was almost positive almost no one in the area delivered. It would just be us, left to fend for ourselves and maybe that wasn't what she'd want.

"Lake Placid?" The breath hitched in her throat, her eyes tore from mine, focusing on her hands knotted in her lap. "I've wanted to go for the longest time and just never got around to it. My dad loved the Adirondacks."

I pulled her hand away from her lap, kissing it while keeping my eyes on the road. "Then I'm really glad I get to be the one who takes you."

She gave me a smile that made my heart grow two sizes larger, settling into her seat. "It's going to be a while then. I hope you have some interesting way to entertain me on this long-ass drive. Last trip I went on was to Paris, in Martja's private jet."

My fingers squeezed around hers, not ready to relinquish it. "Ah yes, the private jet with the naked Jacuzzi. Well, state troopers don't really have much of a sense of humor, so we'll have to keep the clothes on at least until we get to the cabin. But I do have an awesome playlist and a bag full of snacks."

Her eyes widened, reaching over to the backseat to where I'd stashed a cooler and the food, and pulled out a bag of Twizzlers. "Oh my God," she moaned, clasping the bag to her chest. "I know these have no nutritional value at all but I love them." She opened the bag, stuffing a couple of the red laces into her mouth before shoving a couple in mine. "If I'm getting fat, you are coming with me."

I coughed, pulling out the Twizzlers and then taking a bite. "A little warning before you shove something in my mouth, Quinn."

"Got it!" She nodded, pretending like she was making an invisible note. "Warn Riley before shoving dildo in his mouth."

"Thought you said it was a vibrator?"

She laughed. "That was in *your* luggage, silly, I packed the dildo in mine. Didn't want you to have all the fun."

We laughed, ate, drank soda and talked the whole six hours. Not even needing the playlist I'd created as we pulled into the main part of town and stopped to get groceries. I even offered to buy her dinner at one of the restaurants or resorts but she turned me down saying she'd wait.

It didn't take us long to get to our final destination. And as much as I'd enjoyed the drive, I was ready to be done with it for a while. Tibbs had told me not to expect much but the wood cabin in Keene Valley couldn't have been more perfect. We'd passed a lodge and a few small town stores on the way, but we were pretty much off the beaten track. I smiled at Quinn, grabbing her hand as I cut the ignition. "Honey, we're home."

Grinning, she jumped out of the truck not bothering to wait for me and racing to the front porch. She tried the door, looking back over her shoulder to my hand jingling the key.

"You're so impatient." I left the luggage in the back but grabbed the groceries and joined her on the threshold. "I bet you're a nightmare Christmas Eve."

"Please, I peek at the gifts long before Christmas Eve. The minute they're under the tree, it's fair game." She rolled her eyes, grinning as I pushed open the old wooden door.

It was a little musty, having not been used for a couple of weeks but other than that it was clean. Not much furniture to speak of, but we had what we needed. I took the food to the kitchen and shoved things away while Quinn explored.

"This place is cool," I heard her yell from the other room. "And it just sits here empty? Would make a great location for shoots."

"Tibbs says his uncle has it listed on AirBnB. They get hikers and campers, that kind of thing. There's great trout fishing not far and hiking trails," I answered, checking the connection to the gas near the stove. I'd checked the outside propane tank when I got the rest of the stuff out the car. I might not be working but old habits died hard.

"There's a fireplace!" Quinn came around the corner, her eyes as wide as dinner plates. "Can we start one? Oh, wait, you know how, right?" She pulled her face into a grimace. "Building one isn't the same skill set as putting one out, I don't want to assume."

I put my arms around her, tucking her up close to my chest as I dropped my mouth to kiss her. "You're a fucking comedian. And yes, I know how."

My kiss was answered with one of her own, the interest in the fire forgotten as I ran my hands down her body. I loved touching her, watching her arch into me and moan as my fingers roamed.

It would have been easy to have stripped her down and taken her right there. And fuck knows, I wanted to. There wasn't a soul around for miles and I bet she would've let me. But we'd been driving for hours and I didn't want to rush. Wanting to feed her, bathe her in the huge antique tub she hadn't discovered yet, and then lay her out on the bed and do it properly.

My hands pulled her gently away from my mouth, her little moan of protest making me smile. "I should go build that fire before you annihilate any more of my reputation."

She groaned, dropping her head to my chest. "Sometimes I hate my mouth."

"Good thing I like it enough for the both of us."

We ate steak on the floor in front of the fireplace. I'd not only impressed her with my fire building abilities, but my cooking ones too, her eyes rolling back into her head and moaning as she ate, making my dick hard.

And while she cleaned the dishes from dinner, I moved our bags into the bedroom and ran the water for the bath.

The old pipes groaned, the water heater taking a little while to heat up but it wasn't long before the old claw-footed tub was starting to fill. I hadn't even thought to bring stuff to put in it, a quick look around the bathroom cabinets not revealing anything more than a bar of soap. Still, I could work with that, my balls clenching just at the thought of lathering her up.

I grabbed some towels, planting them in arms reach as I stripped off and dumped my clothes on the floor. Then one leg at a time I climbed in, switching off the faucet and sliding under the water's surface.

"Having fun?" Quinn appeared at the door, a dishrag still draped over shoulder as she leant against the jamb.

"Can think of a way to make it more interesting." My head tipped in the direction of the tub. "Want to get in and let me show you?"

She pulled the dishrag from her shoulder more seductively than should probably be allowed, taking her time to strip. My eyes stayed glued to her body as her hands peeled layers off slowly, the rod between my legs getting harder with each passing second. She liked to make me wait, but I didn't care, letting her put on a show as she slid off her bra and panties.

"Mmmmm." I licked my lips, my hand disappearing under the water and giving myself a tug. "Am I just looking tonight? Or do I get to touch too?"

With no sense of urgency, her beautiful body strode to the tub and sat on the edge furthest from me. Her long legs swung around, keeping her knees together as she slid them into the water and shot me a barely there smile. I knew she was teasing me, prolonging it and trying to drive me crazy, and I wasn't sure if I wanted her to stop or keep going.

I was mesmerized, my eyes following her hands as they dipped into the water, getting them wet before moving to her tits. She gently massaged each one, pinching the nipples, letting me see them get hard.

They weren't the only things hard, my dick throbbing as she parted her thighs, and then slid a hand down between her legs.

I was going to stroke out.

Not willing to wait any longer, I rose out of the water and pitched forward. Water splashed, my hands gripping her knees as my mouth went to her pussy and did some teasing of my own. Her hands dropped, clamping down on the edge of the tub for balance as I lapped and sucked her, circling her clit before fucking her with my tongue.

She was wet, coating me with her juices as I added first one finger and then two. "Riley." Her eyes closed, her hips tilting to give me better access.

"You wanting something, Quinn?" I rumbled against her core, feeling her tighten around my fingers. She was close, but not there yet and I was feeling greedy.

I continued to play, my mouth and fingers taking turns as her breaths got more uneven, her perfect tits heaving as she writhed on my hand. And then I felt it, the moment she tipped over the edge, screaming out my name as she pulsed against me. Her eyes flashed open, raw heat burning those baby blues as her foot pushed against my chest and backed me away.

She slid into the space she'd created, slipping into the water and wrapping her hand around my cock. "Condoms aren't reliable in the water," she groaned against my neck, the slight sting of her teeth making me hiss.

"Quinn," I tried to concentrate, forming words almost impossible as her fingers gripped my balls. "I know, they're in the bedroom for later." *Jesus, what the hell was she doing with her hands?* "And I just proved I can make you come with more than just my dick."

Her hands worked my length, gliding up and down and twisting toward the tip. It felt amazing, my whole body hypersensitive as everything got tight.

Our hungry mouths found each other, the water splashing over the edge as shit got critical. I wasn't done touching her but the space made it difficult, the uncoordinated grabs making her fall forward onto my chest. Her legs planted either side of me, teasing herself with my length as her back arched.

"Fuck me," she begged, the desperation in her voice almost making me come. "I can't wait and I'm on the pill."

Would have been a good time for some common sense to kick in but unfortunately I was all out. Not giving a second thought to the repercussions as I gripped myself around the base and thrust into her.

"Fuck, Quinn." Her name tore from my throat as I slid in and she sunk down. Everything was wet and tight, and felt so amazing I needed a minute to try to remember how to breathe.

But keeping still didn't last long, my hips rocking whether I wanted them to or not, Quinn matching me with some of her own.

"Hold on to me." A voice more animal than human growled as I locked my hands on her hips. "I need to get in deeper."

My ass lifted off the tub, thrusting into her harder and faster, chasing the high as my balls drew up tight. I wasn't going to be able to last much longer. Between the strip tease she'd treated me to at the start, the taste of her still on my tongue and how good she felt bare, it was a miracle I hadn't already blown my load.

"Quinn, you want me to pull out?" I asked, knowing there wasn't much point but needing to say it anyway. "Because—"

"No." Her response punctuated by impaling herself deeper. "Riley, I'm going to come."

It was all it took, feeling her detonate around me and I was right there with her. My mouth attacked hers, demanding access as our hot, slippery and wet bodies pulsed together until she'd milked me dry. I wasn't sure we hadn't flooded the bathroom, and I didn't care, the waves lapping against our skin as the last tremor vibrated against my shaft.

"I feel like I should apologize but I wouldn't mean it." My lips moved to her neck. "And I won't lie to you."

"Don't be sorry, I'm not." She gripped my arm. "I trust you, and you trust me, right?"

It was a little late to ask the question, but she was right. I *did* trust her, and I'd set myself on fire before I'd do anything to hurt her. "With everything," I answered, not wanting to stop kissing her.

"Good, because I don't do regrets."

Which was good news because neither did I, especially not with her. Giving her one last long kiss, I gently pulled out and reached for the bar of soap. I turned the faucet back on, refilling the tub before washing her slowly and then letting her do the same to me. We rinsed off, wrapping ourselves in towels before finding our way to the bedroom. The fresh sheets were still sitting on the mattress, both of us making quick work of putting them on the bed before slipping inside.

Then I kissed her, made love to her slowly and let her drift off in my arms. It was heaven, and I didn't want to close my eyes.

"Go to sleep." Quinn slid one eye open, dragging my lips to hers. "And then pretend in the morning not to wake up so I can make you breakfast. You're making me look bad."

I pulled her tight against me, her body molding to mine as I laughed. "You couldn't look bad if you tried, Quinn. But I would love for you to make me breakfast."

"Sleeeeeeeeeeep," she mumbled, nuzzling against me and nothing had ever felt as good.

I shook my head, thinking I was fucking delusional if I didn't admit I was in love with her.

I was gone.

Done for.

Totally at her mercy.

And there wasn't a damn thing I wanted to do to change it.

Chapter 20

Quinn

RILEY WAS TERRIBLE at pretending to be asleep. I'd seen preschoolers put on better performances and they'd had their eyes open. So deciding there was no point torturing the poor man—I'd save that for later—I let him get up, ordering him to sit at the table while I made breakfast.

I wasn't a great cook but I could get by. Bacon, eggs, toast—all in my repertoire, managing to even make coffee with one of those Moka pots and not give myself second degree burns.

Mismatched plates and cups were placed on the round kitchen table, the disharmony of colors and patterns making it somehow seem more beautiful.

The itching feeling to take a photo nagged at me, but I'd always made fun of those people. Still, it wasn't a Starbuck's cup or a random cookie and I wasn't going to post it.

"Hey, will you promise not to judge me if I take a photo of our breakfast?" My hand stopped Riley from reaching for his fork.

He raised a brow and gave me a smirk. "Are you asking because *you* usually judge?"

"*Yes*," I groaned. "I judge. I'm a terrible person; I admit it. Just give me a second to grab my camera and then you can mock me."

Scooting off to the bedroom, I grabbed my old messenger bag and dug out my dad's old Pentax SLR. It was such a pain to develop the film and find somewhere to print the photos, but I loved using it all the same. The prints felt more authentic, the skill needed in the execution rather than the post-shot editing, and it kept me sharp.

When I got back to the kitchen Riley had stepped away from the table, patiently waiting while the not-so-surprise breakfast I'd made him was getting cold. He was going to get a blowjob for sure, my smile making his brow arch even higher as if asking what I was up to.

I moved plates and cups and positioned the silverware, stupidly feeling excited about capturing something as boring as breakfast, but I didn't care. Out of the corner of my eye I spotted a newspaper, folding it in half and adding it to the table.

"Are you taking the breakfast's photo or sending proof of life?" Riley chuckled behind me, his hands resting on my hips.

"Yes, yes," I mock laughed. "The black and white of the print plays off the yellow, red and blues of the crockery. Look." I angled the SLR toward him encouraging him to look through the viewfinder. With no digital display or instant replay, it was the only way to see. Like my dad had done when he taught me, I positioned Riley where I'd been standing, bending his body so he'd have a similar perspective. "Is it in focus? You can change the depth of field with the aperture right here," I twisted the front of the lens. "It lets you choose your focal point."

Riley smiled, planting a kiss on my lips before handing the camera back. "Take all the photos you want, Quinn. I was being a jerk."

"No, you were right. It's kind of douchey but still makes for a good photo." I turned my attention back to my camera and captured the shot.

The shutter snapped, my thumb winding on the next frame before snapping it again. And with the two photos taken, I lowered the camera, repositioned the plates, and gestured to the table. "You may eat."

"Only two photos?" Riley asked, sitting down and taking a sip of his coffee.

I nodded, joining him as I bit into some toast. "Yep, only two. If I haven't got it by the second shot, it wasn't meant to be. Besides, old school film is a pain in the ass to develop and process."

"Maybe we can go out today and you can take some more photos," he suggested, not complaining as he forked his lukewarm scrambled eggs. "We can stay local, drive back to Placid—whatever you want."

And nothing sounded more perfect. We ate quickly, Riley packing a backpack with important things like snacks and water, while I grabbed my camera and phone.

Deciding to check out the trails first, we spent most of the day walking, talking, laughing, and capturing stolen moments in the frame. We found a quiet spot and stopped for lunch, taking our time to make our way back as we kissed and held hands like a couple of teenagers.

"Why don't we get changed and go somewhere nice for dinner," he said stripping out of his jeans. "Eyes up here, Quinn." He grinned, pointing to his face. "You look at me like that and we'll never get out of here. And I'm determined to take you on at least one regular date."

"I thought you said you didn't like the word *regular*?" Or was it normal? Not that either of those applied to us so he needn't worry.

His thumbs hesitated at the waistband of his boxer briefs. "I figured since we were doing this vacation thing we might try that too. So are you going to leave so I can shower *without* a hard-on? It's been a while." He winked.

"Fine, have your boring shower." I threw my hands up dramatically. "I'll look up some places to eat."

Riley showered and then changed, leaving the bathroom free for me to do the same. Not knowing where Riley's mystery trip was going to take us I'd packed a couple of nice outfits, and I was really glad I did when I walked out.

My cobalt blue dress skimmed my shoulders, exposing my décolletage but not my cleavage. It was fitted, playing off my curves with a hemline that was short enough to be sexy but not show my vagina. It was a fine line, and I was all about dancing on it.

He swallowed, his Adam's apple moving up and down his throat as I sauntered toward him. Dressed in a pair of dark denim jeans, a button down and smart black blazer, I was having my own moment. Maybe dinner wasn't such a good idea? We had food here, and I hadn't even shown him how good my pancakes were.

Capturing my chin with his hands he kissed me slowly, taking his time to give both of my lips equal attention before sliding in his tongue. "You're so beautiful, Quinn."

"And your body is freaking ridiculous." My fingers trailed down his chest. "Seriously, how can you be so hot?"

"Okay, we're leaving, or this date isn't happening." Grabbing my hand, he pulled me to the doorway and then helped me into his Explorer. Of course I almost twisted my ankle navigating the path in heels but at least I looked good doing it.

He started the truck and we took the short drive, ending up at a gorgeous restaurant with stunning views of Whiteface Mountain. We didn't have a reservation but they managed to accommodate us, enjoying wine and a delicious dinner from local ingredients. It wasn't just the food that was beautiful, the inside of the restaurant almost more stunning than the meal. Furnished with pieces from local artisans, the intimate and fire-lit setting with its exposed wood and brick made it almost feel like a fairytale.

"Take a photo, Quinn." Riley rolled the stem of his wineglass in his hand. "I know you want to."

My hands fisted on the table, tempted to reach for my phone. "You know, what? No. I don't think a photo would ever do it justice and I don't want to waste this amazing night trying. Besides," I reached across touching his hand. "It's not like I'm ever going to forget it."

I was sure there'd be other nights or other moments that would be equally special if not more so than our night. But at that point in time, I just couldn't imagine it, feeling so happy my heart might burst.

After we finished dinner and Riley paid the check we walked back to the truck. The night air was cool making me shiver, Riley taking off his jacket and draping it over my shoulders as he pulled me into a hug. "I love this dress on you, but I don't want you getting cold."

Oh.

Hell.

I was going to cry.

My throat got tight, forcing myself to blink rapidly so I didn't mess up my mascara as I nodded a thank you instead of verbalizing one. And if he noticed, he didn't say anything, opening the door for me and helping me back into the truck.

He was soooooo getting laid.

I felt the zap of excitement in the air as he drove. The stereo was low, playing some local station while I contemplated all the wonderful things—all of them dirty—I would do to him the minute we got back.

My mental fantasy was just getting good when we saw a car driving fast and erratically toward us.

Uh-oh, things did not look good, especially since they were barreling in our direction with no hint of slowing down.

Riley laid on his horn, wrenching the truck to the side as I braced, the car narrowly missing us as the driver corrected at the last minute.

It was a man, and a woman, and she looked terrified.

"Shit." I gripped my chest, my heart still beating a million miles a minute. "What the hell was that?"

"An accident waiting to happen." Riley gritted his teeth, slamming on the brakes and executing a tight U-Turn on the narrow road. "Hold on."

Hold on weren't bad words, in fact I was sure that he'd said them to me while screwing me senseless. But never had I been worried that they might be the last ones he'd ever say.

He punished the Explorer catching up to the erratic Mazda sedan and pulling up alongside. "Pull over." He screamed as his driver's side window lowered. "You're going to get someone killed."

The female passenger was visibly shaking, holding onto her seatbelt while she screamed. Not that I blamed her, I was having a hard time keeping steady too and the guy piloting our ride had probably driven a freaking fire truck through Manhattan at speed. Knew who my money was on.

The driver's face was white, practically passing out himself as he turned toward us and lowered the passenger's window. "My wife is in labor and the baby is coming out."

FUCK.

So it wasn't a kidnapping, or a drunk driver or even a garden-variety road rage psychopath. Instead it was two people about to become parents and scared out of their ever loving minds.

"Pull over, I'm a firefighter." Riley gestured to the shoulder. "If she's already crowning you're not going to make it to the emergency room."

He was calm, but forceful, and exuding so much control I had to remind myself how inappropriate it was to be turned on. It was an emergency for Christ's sake, not a porno. And yet, as his knuckles fisted the steering wheel and his jaw tightened with determination, I was absolutely wet and ready.

I was probably going to hell.

The driver must have realized he had no choice—determined, controlled Riley didn't look like the guy who backed down—and slowed, pulling the car as far over onto the side as he could. Riley followed suit, skidding behind him and using his truck as a barrier against oncoming traffic. He engaged the emergency brake, leaving the engine idling with the headlights on.

"Call 9-1-1." He looked at me, reaching behind my seat and pulling out a first aid kit. "Give them our location, if you don't know, hit the maps ap and let the GPS find you and give them the coordinates."

And without waiting for my reply, he jumped out of the truck, and bolted to the Mazda. She was screaming, "He's coming, he's coming," while I frantically dialed, giving the dispatcher our location and letting them know their population numbers were about to be increased by one. And with a promise they were on the way, I joined Riley and the soon-to-be parents.

He'd already pulled on a pair of latex gloves, crouched beside the passenger side door, not batting an eye that the top of an infant's head was sticking out a vagina.

Oh.

My.

God.

She wasn't kidding when she said the baby was coming.

"You're going to be okay," Riley said calmly, wedging himself into the space between the seat and the door. The room was limited but it didn't seem to matter. "Move the seat all the way back, and use the dashboard if you need to brace. You're going to have to push."

"Shouldn't we wait for the ambulance?" I asked, fairly sure delivering a kid on a badly paved road near a national forest wasn't a good idea.

Riley shook his head. "This little guy isn't the patient type so we're going to help him along. I'm Riley, and this here is Quinn, she's impatient too," he said with a slight chuckle.

He was making jokes? How could he be making fucking jokes when all hell was breaking loose?

"AMANDA," she yelled, gripping Riley's arm so tight it's a wonder his bone didn't snap. "Pete, oh my God!" Her other bone cruncher doing its worst on her husband's wrist.

"Contraction?" Riley asked, her furiously nodding confirming the baby was responsible and not demonic possession. "Okay Amanda, you're going to push through it."

He placed a hand on her swollen belly, directing her how to bear down and breathe through the contraction while his eyes were locked between another woman's legs. And no, I wasn't jealous. Jesus. I was both terrified, and strangely impressed *he* knew what the hell to do considering I had the anatomy and didn't have a clue.

"Is she okay? Oh my God, Mandy, baby, are you okay?" Pete's eyes flashed between Riley and his wife whose face had gone red and was summoning demons to open the gates of hell.

Meanwhile it looked like her entire insides had decided to eject, unidentifiable bodily fluids oozing around half a head that looked to be the size of a melon. It couldn't be a newborn. Those were cuddly, pink and small—I'd seen newborns, held my nieces in fluffy blankets—and they looked nothing like what I was witnessing.

My sister went through *that* three fucking times? God, I was going to have to be nicer to her in the future, maybe buy her a present or something. Like a never-ending supply of spa vouchers, or a freaking island.

"You're doing great, Amanda." Riley smiled before nodding to Pete. "You're both doing great. We need one more big push and the head will be out. First big hurdle."

"The first?" I asked before I could stop myself. I knew I wasn't contributing anything helpful to the situation so freaking out would have to do.

"First the head, and then the shoulders," Riley answered without taking his attention from the task at hand. And when I say at hand, I mean literally. His hands were cradling the child's head while she pushed him out.

"OoOoHHagGHhhheeerrrrrAggHHh!" An indescribable howl broke from Amanda's throat as she planted her feet on the dashboard and pushed.

"Almost there, Amanda. You're so close. You're a complete rock star at this." Riley's voice didn't waver, completely steady.

Pete not so much.

He was praying to five different Gods and trying to not hyperventilate, reaching for his phone. "She made me promise I'd record this."

Finally something I could do.

Whether it was Pete's prayers, my own need to be useful, or the universe throwing me a bone, my purpose for being there presented itself as I grabbed Pete's phone. "I've got this, just tell me if you want it PG or full frontal. Your choice." And like Riley had done, with a dedicated task to perform, I'd found my own calm. I'd opened up his camera, switching into video mode waiting for his directive before hitting the red button.

"PG, so we can show the family," he said, not bothering to confirm with Amanda who was rearing back, another contraction imminent.

Positioning myself at her side toward her shoulder, I hit record and witnessed what had to be the shoulders coming out. Her head sagged for a breath, lifting again and pushing again, the baby delivered into Riley's waiting hands.

Oh.

My.

God.

With steady capable hands, Riley grabbed the emergency blanket he'd prepared earlier, wrapping the baby up like a little foil burrito as the kid let out an ear-piercing wail. Never had there been a sweeter sound, Amanda and Pete crying as Riley laid the baby on her chest, and my eyes starting to leak too.

"Congrats mom and dad, you got a beautiful little boy. Amanda, you couldn't have done a more perfect job. You should be very proud."

My emotions were all over the place, wanting to laugh and cry all at the same time. I was elated, and terrified, and marveling at the beauty of it all, muscle memory keeping my body locked out of habit so the still-running camera in my hand wouldn't shake. I could have my little breakdown later, but not until I hit stop.

Lights and sirens broke through the night air, the paramedics finally arriving. It probably hadn't been more than a few minutes, but it felt like an eternity since I'd made the call, a whole new person joining us while we waited.

Paramedics descended on Amanda, Riley briefing them of the situation while they checked the little guy and brought over a stretcher. I was thinking they might need an extra for Pete who was having a hard time standing when I handed him back his phone.

"Thanks, thanks so much. I don't know what I would have done." His gratitude misplaced as he swayed on his feet. "I need to go thank Riley."

"Out of the two of us, he's the *only* one you need to thank. I'm just glad I could do something other than be decorative," I laughed, adrenaline still coursing through my veins. "And I snapped a couple of photos too, as well as the video. Thought you might want them."

His lip trembled, nodding his head. "Thanks. I really appreciate it."

I honestly felt guilty for accepting the man's gratitude, saved from feeling even more like a fraud by Riley making his way over to us. Pete threw himself at the man, overwhelmed and indebted as he broke down. Riley patted Pete's back, congratulating him again and leaving him to go be with his wife and child. Then calmly—like he hadn't just delivered a baby on the side of the road—turned to me and asked me if I was okay.

Asked *me* if I was okay.

"Quinn, we need to go to the emergency room for you too?" He chuckled, his gloveless hands making their way around my waist. "Minor shock isn't unheard of, especially witnessing your first birth."

"How did you know? And more importantly, it wasn't yours?" My eyes opened in surprise. "How many babies have you delivered?"

"Including that little guy," his head tipped over his shoulder to the mom/son combo getting lifted into the back of the ambulance. "Five. First one was day three as a rookie. I had help though, and still thought I was going to pee my pants until it was over."

I blew out a breath. "Jesus, Riley, can you stop being so goddamn perfect? You are literally a big deal and I can't even pretend you're not."

He chuckled, bringing me closer to his chest. "I did try and warn you, can't blame me when you didn't listen."

God I loved him.

Loved him.

And that was something else I couldn't pretend.

But I wouldn't say it first.

Not yet.

"Take me to bed, Riley," I whispered against his lips. "I need to see more of your *big* deal."

He laughed, wincing. "That was terrible, Quinn. But I'm not stupid enough to turn down the offer. Let's go."

Tucked under his arm, with my heart about to explode, he led me back to the truck.

Chapter 21

Riley

THE THREE DAYS away with Quinn in the Adirondacks were amazing. Apart from our little adventure—helping a couple deliver a baby—it was just the two of us in our own little world.

Neither of us were worried about work, or anything else—devoting all of our time to relaxing. And I had her more *relaxed* than I'd ever had before. And it genuinely sucked when we had to pack up and leave.

She had shoots on Monday and I was back on rotation, not realizing how much I'd missed the guys until we'd arrived back in the city. We'd spent the night at my place since I started earlier, giving her lazy kisses after she'd been my wake-up alarm with a blowjob. I was attempting to pretend to be sleeping longer than I had been, but it was so damn sweet feeling myself get hard in her mouth, the ruse wasn't kept long.

It was going to be twenty-four hours before I saw her again, and I honestly couldn't wait.

"Look who decided to show up." Mack welcomed me with a clap on the shoulder. "Thought you'd be too busy making headlines to worry about coming back. I saw something about you on Twitter. Pretty sure you were trending."

I barked out a laugh, missing him the past few days as both my friend and my boss. "Chief, stop pretending you know what *trending* is. You can't string a couple of buzzwords together and hope to sound cool, old man. You got to understand them as well."

"How about you *understand* how my boot will wind up your ass if you don't help Tibbs do inventory? Or would you prefer me to tweet it?" He grinned, rolling back on his feet. "And by the way, your new BFFs, Amanda and Pete, sent you a thank you card. Local units gave them your company number so it came here."

He handed me an envelope, a small photo and handwritten note falling out when I opened it. It had been one of the shots Quinn had taken, ridiculously well framed considering the circumstances. "They're naming him after me." My grin widened, feeling they were taking the gratitude a little far but appreciating it all the same. "Going to have to send the little guy a T-shirt or something, make sure my namesake's taken care of."

Mack groaned, shaking his head. "Poor kid. Let's hope the name is where the similarities stop."

"Heyyyyyyyyyy!" Leighton strolled through the bay, backpack strapped to one shoulder like a school kid. His grin widened. "North is back! Someone better tell Tibbs to stop using his deodorant."

I rolled my eyes. "How hard can it be to bring your own, seriously? If he's that hard up, I'll pay the four ninety-five."

"Nah, he just wants to smell like you. Hoping to catch a break with the ladies." His eyebrows danced suggestively, no more subtle than when I left.

"He can have all the ladies he wants. I've got the one I wanted." I wasn't saying something they didn't already know, but declaring it was a big move. All the guys had seen women come and go from my life over the years, and not once had I given a shit one way or the other if they liked her. But I did with Quinn. And not because I wanted their approval—because I'd have been with her even without it—but because these guys were my family and I wanted her in every part of my life.

"Sounds serious." Leighton smirked. "Shame too because I was planning to ask Quinn out myself."

"Try it." I shrugged, knowing he was kidding. "It's been a while since I practiced a tracheotomy, seems like a crushed windpipe might be something that would need it."

The bastard laughed, raising his hands in surrender. "Steady, North. You know I'm kidding. I wouldn't even dream of it. But if she has any single sisters or friends, feel free to slip them my number."

"Sister is married, but she has a friend who's single." The idea of setting up Karli with one of my friends not occurring to me before his suggestion. "Let me suss out the situation, and I'll see what I can do." It was a half-hearted commitment, knowing Leighton was a decent enough guy but not wanting to rock the boat. As far as I knew, things with Karli and Brad were *complicated*, not sure I wanted to involve myself in that mess.

After allowing everyone their turn to either give me shit about being away or my assist on the roadside delivery, we settled into work. It didn't take long for the first alarm, one engine responding to a collision. It felt good to have my turnouts on again, working with the crew as we went out to calls. And even though I thought about Quinn, it made the shift easier knowing she'd be waiting for me at the end of it.

Unless you counted Mack—and I wasn't—I'd never had that. And I liked the way it felt. There was a residential fire at noon, and then a gas leak right after. If I'd hoped for a slow alarm day to ease myself back in, I was shit out of luck. Not that it mattered though, I could have been gone for a year and sliding back into the team would have been effortless. It was why I loved these guys, and why I could never give it up.

The busy schedule meant my texts to Quinn had been minimal, not getting a real chance to check my phone until dinner. She had her own full plate to deal with, telling me she wasn't anticipating crawling into bed until eleven. I asked her to keep a side warm for me, promising to be there for wake-up sex after my shift ended the next morning at eight.

"North!" Chief barked from the doorway, his hand curled around a slice of pizza. "Stop playing with your phone and come join us for dinner. Your girlfriend bought again."

My head snapped to the side, eyes narrowed on the slice in his hand. "Gino's?" I'd just messaged her and she hadn't mentioned it, not to say it wasn't possible. Quinn was rarely predictable, and buying me dinner and not saying anything wasn't that far of a stretch.

"Yeah, Gino's. Where else? But you don't need to leave this time." He took a big bite, chewing around his words. "Because she delivered it herself."

It was like my feet had their own mind, my ass lifting from the couch and double-timing to the dining area. If she'd delivered, maybe she'd stuck around and I'd take a few minutes if that was all that was on offer.

The whole company had squeezed into the room. There was Tibbs, Leighton, Cap and Rev but also the guys from the other engine and ladder as well. And every single one of those bastards had a slice in their hand, and a smug grin on their face—Quinn the center of attention.

"Nice of you to join us," she said with an innocent smile, dishing up a slice and handing it to me casually. "You know, gentlemen, this is how it starts. First, they're too good to eat with you and then they want an assistant. Pretty soon you'll only be able to contact him through his publicist. #HotFireman." Her eyelashes batting coyly as I walked toward her.

"It's not like I started that hashtag, and you're the one on the photo credit. You could have cropped me out entirely and I wouldn't have cared." I accepted the plate with the pizza, tossed it onto the table and promptly wrapped her in my arms instead. The fact we had an audience didn't bother me, so I hoped she'd thought it through.

She lifted her hand to her mouth feigning shock. "And deprive the world of your glory. Please, have you seen the growth in my numbers? I've gotten more fan mail from that one photo than I have in weeks. They love me." She huffed on her fingernails brushing them on her cute but incredibly flimsy blouse. "Only regret I have is I didn't ask you to take your shirt off." She leaned in further, her lips just barely out of reach. "Along with asking if I have any other photos, it's been the number one request."

I captured her lips, kissing her right there to the hollering of my buddies. Again, I didn't mind, giving her mouth the attention it deserved while she gripped the front of my uniform. She'd mentioned in passing that my blues turned her on, and I was planning on using that to my advantage.

"North, let the girl breathe for Christ's sake," Chief barked from behind us.

She giggled, grinning at me as her hands stretched around my chest. "I had a break in my schedule and my next shoot is in Times Square, figured I'd surprise you."

"It was a good surprise." I kissed the tip of her nose. "Now let me introduce you to these losers before they eat all my pizza."

I went down the line introducing Quinn to all the guys, letting each of them have a chance to chat.

Like she was in a room filled with a bunch of puppies, every single one of them wanted her attention and her praise. It was funny to watch, even more so from those who hadn't met her yet, Tibbs mouthing *"I think I'm in love,"* more times than I would have liked.

We all sat together and ate, Quinn joining us and managing to have her dinner while she was perched in my lap. Not enough chairs, and all that, and that was just the chivalrous guy I was. And when we were done, I gave her a quick tour, showing her where we slept and worked out, and finally down to the trucks.

"No hose jokes?" I shook my head, hiding my grin. "Quinn, you disappoint me."

Her brow arched, the mischievous glint in her eye returning. "Well Riley, if you must know. I was going to pitch the idea of rolling one out and doing an impromptu shoot. Wouldn't want to disappoint all my loyal followers."

"*Your* followers? Why are you getting all the adulation when I'm the subject?" I pulled her bottom lip with my teeth making her moan. "Low blow using me to bolster your popularity, sweetheart. The Twitter-sphere would be appalled."

"I'm appalled," she groaned, her head rolling against my chest. "I've met all your lovely friends and yet can't think of anything else but getting you out of this uniform. Is it wrong I want to go up to your bunk and defile it."

Her words went right to my cock, making me cough out a laugh as I reminded myself that we were standing in front of huge glass bay doors. Not to mention the surveillance cameras. That would be a little hard to explain to the chief.

"Easy, Quinn, I'll let you do whatever you want when we get home." I dropped a soft kiss on her forehead, tempting fate to do more. "Oh, and by the way." I pulled the photo and note from my pocket. "Pete and Amanda named the little guy Riley."

Her eyes lit up, studying the photo she'd not only seen before but taken, as her fingertips played against it. "I love that, it's such a good name. If I had a kid—"

She stopped midsentence, her eyes flashing wide like she said something she wasn't supposed to. Which was unlike Quinn because she meant what she said.

"If you had a kid . . ." I waved my hand, prompting her to continue.

She shook her head, dismissing it. "Nothing. It's a great name. I'm glad he's named after you."

Yeah, nice try but no dice.

"You're avoiding. That was not what you were going to say."

She swore under her breath, planting a hand to her hip and shooting me a *you asked for it* glare. "No, but talking about babies when we've been dating for like two weeks is relationship kryptonite. It's supposed be hot sex and sneaky hook ups. You really want to hear about my hypothetical children?"

"I see." I arched my brow, pressing my lips into a line.

God, I fucking loved her.

And the only thing more insane than how *much* I loved her, was the thought that talking about kids was going to scare me off.

"You see what?" she asked with a bite to her tone. "Let's just go back, redact whatever it was you *thought* you heard, and talk about defiling your bunk."

I folded my arms across my chest, not willing to concede. "No."

"No?" She snapped back in irritation.

"No, Quinn. I don't want to go back to talking about my bunk. And yeah, I *do* want to hear about your hypothetical children, because I'm hoping they'll be mine."

She blinked back in surprise. "What?"

"I love you, Quinn. I love everything that comes out of your mouth. I love your mind, your unapologetic strength. And I want to hear your thoughts and dreams. And I want them *without* the filter. That means if you want to have kids, then I need to know. Because you know what? You're even crazier than I thought if you'd think they'd be anyone's but mine."

It sounded like a proposal, and maybe in a way it was. I absolutely wanted to marry her, to grow old with her, to never let her go. But I knew we weren't ready for me to get down on one knee yet. Regardless, my intentions would be clear.

Her.

Me.

The long haul.

"How's that for relationship kryptonite?" I brushed the hair away from her face, only the second time I'd rendered her speechless. It was a talent for sure, and something I enjoyed. "I love you, Quinn. Need me to say it again?"

"I love you too." Her eyes welled, grabbing the front of my shirt. "I wanted to tell you over the weekend but it felt too soon."

"Too soon for who? We don't do regular, remember? And I need to say it. And to be honest, I really love hearing it." Her head tilted back, the tears making her eyes look like stained glass. "This is the part where you tell me again," I laughed, lowering my lips to hers.

She took what I'd offered and demanded more, her hands around my back as our mouths did a different kind of talking. If not for the alarm, I might have forgotten where I was.

"Shit." I pulled away from her, giving her one last kiss. "I need to go."

Her hands stayed locked around me, stopping me. "Be careful, Riley. I've gotten attached."

"Always, Quinn."

And with my promise she let go.

Chapter 22

Quinn

THERE'D BEEN NO romantic dinner, no convoluted preamble, no post-sex haze.

He'd said the words—*I love you*—as we stood between two fire engines, crash bang in the middle of our crazy schedules. And then he needed to go, leaving me with those words in my heart as he went back to work.

It was so simple, uncomplicated—and one of the most romantic things I'd ever heard.

God, I think I floated out of that station. The alarm ringing, the light flashing and men pulling on their turnouts while I waved goodbye to the most amazing man I'd ever met and went to my next shoot.

Nothing could spoil my mood.

And when he finally came home—using a key I'd left him for my apartment—he crawled into bed with me and we made love until it was my turn to leave.

It was crazy, trying to balance seeing him and being together with his schedule and mine. But he was everything. And saying I was happy was an understatement of the highest order.

Weeks passed, and I was traveling less. Delaying foreign projects and doing more work on the East Coast. I liked not getting on a plane every other week and enjoyed not living out of a suitcase. And even though declining some of the high profile clients had me working more hours, I was happy.

We were happy.

Dividing our time between Brooklyn and Manhattan, and for the first time ever, I could see a real future.

"Quinn!" Karli came racing into my apartment, her curls pulled back with a terrycloth headband and some crazy mask on her face. "We need to talk. Like. RIGHT NOW!"

Riley was on duty, meaning he'd be gone all night, and I'd finished shooting at six. So I'd done what any self-respecting twenty-eight-year-old who was utterly and desperately in love— put on pajamas and call your best friend for a girl's night.

"You started your mask without me?" I frowned, snapping on my terrycloth headband. "And while you have the burning need to talk I want the gossip on Josie. Did she move in with that guy? The only time I see her at your place is to change or pick up more of her stuff. If she screws you with the rent, I'm going to have some serious words with her."

Karli shook her head, waving her hands in excitement. "Hush, we'll get to Josie later. We have more important things to discuss." She squeezed my hands and squealed. "Brad asked me out! And for a *real* date this time, not some *let's go to the animal shelter and look at cats*. He took my hands in his, looked me in the eyes and told me he couldn't stop thinking about me, and that he'd been an idiot for waiting so long. And would I do him the honor of going out with him. *Honor*, Quinn, the man said honor like me agreeing to dinner was the equivalent of hanging a medal on his chest. It was so romantic. So intense. Exactly like a Jane Austin novel. I can barely breathe." She petered out, her chest heaving while she tried to suck in air.

"Wait. What?" I asked confused, wondering when Brad's magical transformation had taken place. Last I'd heard they were still having polite but very platonic conversations. My earlier intervention hadn't done squat. Brad even regressed a little, acting more aloof than normal at work. I was all but sure that any romantic connection between the two of them was dead, and since I no longer gave a shit about Miss Lillian and her psycho bullshit, I really wasn't worried. I know, I know, I was a horrible friend. And I should have been attentive to Karli and the guy she was prepared to die waiting for, but alas, I was too blissfully happy.

"Karli, hold on." My front door that had been left open during Karli's excited rampage was closed as I considered the information. "He said all that at work? Today? Before you left?"

"Noooooooo," she groaned. "You think I would have held on to it until now? He *just* left. He came to my apartment and declared he couldn't wait another second."

Wowza.

"Wow," I coughed out, wondering if we should be checking for the end of the world or something. Who knew poor old Brad had it in him? Months of sitting on his hands without so much as a flirty hug and a failed dating attempt weeks ago had me assuming he was out for the count. But no, the guy pulls out the big guns. Talk about your grand gesture.

"Right?!" Karli grabbed my hands. "I honestly can't believe it."

I nodded, feeling uncharacteristically uneasy about the good news. "It's pretty awesome." *It* was *awesome, why the hell wasn't I happy for my friend?* "Why don't we settle in, I can get my mask on and then you can tell me all about it."

Shaking off whatever the hell was wrong with me—maybe I'd eaten something bad at lunch or was coming down with something—I guided a giddy Karli to my couch. She proceeded to tell me all about her rather ordinary day, with Brad acting no more or less attentive than usual, and then coming home from work feeling despondent.

"And I know I should have waited for you to put on the mask, but I was just feeling kind of icky. So I thought what the heck, and decided to try this new one out. Sorry."

Dismissing her apology, I waved my hands not really giving a shit about the mask. "And he came to the door as soon as you put it on? This totally sounds like an adorable rom-com." My earlier lack of enthusiasm decided to finally show up. "You didn't even need my panties, you've got your own comedy."

Karli laughed, seeing the humor. "Well, first I got the phone call. It was Lorraine, and while she still isn't fully healed, she's well enough to come back in a limited capacity. Which means my little run at being the boss is over. At least for the time being." Her excitement deflated. "I know I should be happy, and I feel totally terrible that I'm not, considering I only got the opportunity because she got hurt but—"

"Hold on!" I raised my hands, my heart racing as I began to sweat. "Lorraine is coming back? You got demoted?"

"Geez, Quinn, way to make me feel better." Karli laughed, punching me lightly in the arm. "I'm not demoted, I am just back to my original position. No one had said it was permanent."

My throat constricted while my skin started to heat. She was right, no one had ever said it was a permanent change. In fact, back when I had been convinced Miss Lillian's *vision* for me had me hooking up with Mack, I'd been championing that very exact narrative. Trying to prove the point.

"Right. I'm sorry, I'm an asshole." I continued telling her what a wonderful experience it had been, and should the situation change again in the future, she'd be back in there without a doubt. All the things I should have said if I hadn't been caught up in my own stupidity.

"So anyway, I guess Brad got the same call and decided that since I wasn't his boss anymore, he was going to make it count. And raced right over. Didn't even freak that I look like an extra from a circus." She touched her green cheek and laughed. "He told me how beautiful I was, and no amount of gunk on my face was going to ever hide that, or stop him from telling me how he feels."

"Wow, Karli. Wow." Words failed me, feeling slightly light headed. "That's so great."

It *was* great.

Everything was great.

And just because some shady asshole—Miss Lillian had a lot to answer for—had gotten it wrong with her, it didn't mean Riley wasn't my soul mate. And who cared what she thought anyway. As long as we both felt the way we did, that was all that was important.

I loved Riley, and Riley loved me, and I'd been happier than I ever had. So nothing else mattered.

"Quinn, you look weird. Are you okay?" The back of her hand felt my forehead, taking my temperature. "Is something wrong?"

"I-I . . ." My mouth went dry as the room spun. "I don't feel so well."

Black.

"Oh thank God!" I woke up to Karli's scared brown eyes, phone in her hand. "I just about passed out myself, you scared me half to death. I was just about to call 9-1-1."

My head hurt and I still felt woozy but I was awake, and aware that I'd obviously fainted. "Do not call 9-1-1," I tried to sit back up, my slump on the couch saving me from hitting the floor. "It's nothing."

"Nothing? Nothing? Quinn, I watched you go pale and pass out. Don't tell me it's nothing." She pointed wildly to me as I shuffled myself vertical. "So either you have a good explanation or I'm taking you to the emergency room and I don't care what you say."

Ugh.

Where to even start?

"I think I had a panic attack." I rubbed my chest, the tightness starting to ebb. "And apart from confirming I'm an idiot, the emergency room isn't going to do much."

Reassuring her I was stable, and in no danger of going lights-out again, she went into my bathroom, rinsed off her face and brought back a damp washcloth. I was feeling even more stupid saying the words out loud, but knew either I came clean or she absolutely would drag me to the hospital.

"I panicked, hearing about the job and Brad and figured that all that stuff with Miss Lillian had been nothing but a con. It's ridiculous," I tried to laugh, shaking my head at my own stupidity. "I actually believed that if everything she'd said about you wasn't true then maybe the stuff about Riley being my soul mate wasn't true either. It's okay, you can laugh at me now."

She didn't, instead wrapping her arms around me and pulling me into a huge hug. "Ah Quinn, it's natural to be scared. This is the first guy I've ever seen you crazy about. But just because all that stuff she said wasn't true, doesn't mean this isn't. I've seen the way he looks at you, and you two are just so perfect together. If he *isn't* your soul mate, honey, then I'm not sure they even exist."

"It's sooooooo dumb," I groaned, letting my head fall into my hands. "You know I don't believe in any of this shit. I don't read horoscopes, and when was the last time you even saw me bother with a fortune cookie? Clearly, I've lost my goddamn mind."

"Or, you are really, really in love with him and can't imagine your life without him. Quinn, I think you might be more normal than you gave yourself credit for. I think you just got scared like we all do." She gave me a beaming smile as she patted my shoulder like a proud parent.

Great.

"You mean I'm *supposed* to feel like this?" I asked, the panic starting to come back. "Why? How is this normal? And why are you so happy about it?"

I didn't do normal.

Prided myself on dancing to the beat of my own drum and all of that, and was happy to be on the weird side of the street. Things were more interesting there. So it was a hell of a time to find out I was just as "regular" as the folks I made fun of, inflicted with fear over losing my boyfriend.

I swear if I started to cry—

"Aww, Quinn." Karli's eyes misted. "Honey, it's okay."

Goddamn it.

I was leaking, tears rolling down my cheeks like I was a defective faucet. "I'm normal." I sucked in a rattling breath. "This wasn't supposed to happen to me."

Being in love with Riley wasn't the revelation.

No, I'd known that for weeks.

But the thought that somehow I might lose him—now that I couldn't see my life without him—was terrifying. Like I couldn't imagine what that might look like.

Me.

The strong independent woman who didn't need a man, or security, or a regular job. Who took uncertainty like a daily dose of vitamin D, was freaking the hell out.

"Y'all are going to be fine. You know, what? I bet if you talk to him, you'll feel better about it," she suggested.

"Talk to him? Are you insane? So I look like a needy stage-five clinger? No, he likes that I'm crazy. I can't be throwing normal in now. It will change the dynamics."

No.

I needed to work through whatever the hell freak out I was going through and get back to having hot sex and being in love with the man of my dreams.

That was productive.

And Miss Lillian could go fuck herself.

Hard.

With a cactus.

"Okay, well I've known you long enough not to bother trying to change your mind when you get it set. But I'm telling you, as your friend, you should talk to him."

"Noted." I nodded, taking her advice and storing it under not going to happen. "Now let's try and salvage the rest of girl's night and pick your wedding colors for when you marry Brad. And I better be in the wedding, Karli, I'm too invested in this to sit in the stalls."

She laughed, the worry leaving her eyes as she gave me another hug. "Let's not get ahead of ourselves. But if that wedding happens, you will absolutely be my maid of honor. Lord knows Josie would flake."

And that was what we did.

Talk about her flighty sister, her budding new relationship, and the fall wedding they were going to eventually have.

Pretty much everything except the possibility of me losing Riley.

Because I couldn't even think about that happening.

Chapter 23

Riley

"GOOD MORNING." MY lips hit her neck as I crawled into bed beside a still sleeping Quinn. It was unlike her to not already be awake, but I could never keep up with her shooting schedule. So instead of questioning why my amazing girlfriend was still in bed, I was thanking my good fortune and planned to capitalize on it.

Never was a man to squander an opportunity, so wasn't about to start.

"Riley?" Her eyes shot open in panic as they took me in. "Oh hey!"

"Hey? All I get is *oh, hey*? What the hell is that about? And who else were you expecting? Did you get your days confused and figure it was your *other* boyfriend?" My lips didn't stop, peppering kisses across her collarbone as my hands went to her tits.

Man, I was lucky. Quinn wasn't only the hottest woman I'd ever met, but the smartest and most talented as well. Not that my dick cared about any of that, the rod in between my legs getting rock hard the minute her nipple hardened in my hand.

"No one. I was expecting no one." She tried to laugh, a worry line creasing her brow as she pressed her lips back shut.

Excuse me?

I needed a minute to make sure I hadn't fallen into bed and was already asleep. Check it wasn't some crazy-ass dream. Because if it was real life and A. she wasn't expecting me, or B. didn't have some witty and hilarious comeback about having additional boyfriends, something was very wrong.

"Quinn?" I leaned in closer, sniffing for the telltales of a hangover. She'd spent the evening with Karli so it was in the realm of possibility. "Are you high?"

She scoffed, looking legitimately shocked. "Noooooo, why would you even say that? I'm not high."

Whatever suspicion I'd previously held was confirmed as she wiggled out of my grip. "I just overslept. Guess I didn't realize the time."

I looked down at my hand—the boob that was incased between my fingers no longer there—as the woman who usually begged for my cock increased the distance between us.

Something was definitely wrong.

Weird was par for the course with Quinn, hell I got off on it.

But she wasn't acting weird.

No, instead I was in bed with someone else—a Quinn imposter—who was trying to fool me into thinking she was the real deal.

Not a chance.

"Who are you, and what have you done with Quinn?" My eyes narrowed, managing to trap her underneath me before she could leave the bed entirely.

"Riley, stop." She raised her arms, circling my neck. "It's me, I promise it's me."

It felt like Quinn.

Smelled like Quinn.

But . . .

"Nope, I don't believe you. So either you tell me where she is and what your agenda is here, or I'll get the answer another way. And don't think for a second I'll go easy on you because you're a woman."

She laughed, the sound warming my chest as she arched into me.

That was more like it.

"What do I have to do to convince you?" she asked, huskily.

I shook my head, unable to stop myself from kissing her. "I don't negotiate with terrorists."

Our lips met, and whatever doubts I had that it was *my* Quinn were left on the sideline. There was only one woman who could make me feel like that, and she was currently underneath me, moaning into my mouth.

"You had me worried for a second." My hand slid up her thigh. "I wasn't going to enjoy torturing you, but I would have done it."

Actually, that was a lie.

I absolutely would have enjoyed it.

My fingers skimmed her panties when I felt her flinch, and all jokes aside, I didn't touch anyone without their permission.

We didn't move, my hand frozen where it was as our eyes locked, and I blew out a long breath. "I love you, Quinn. And I'm still going to love you even if we don't have sex. You want to cuddle, or hell, you don't want me to touch you right now—I'll deal with it. But you need to tell me if there's something going on."

She swallowed, her mouth opening then closing, stuffing down whatever she was going to say. "Nothing."

"You don't honestly expect me to believe that, do you?" I asked, getting slightly irritated she was not only lying to me, but thinking I'd be dumb enough to believe it. "Because I'm a lot of things, Quinn, but sucker isn't one of them."

Her eyes closed and when they flipped open they were blue pools of confliction. And fuck me if it didn't make me want to hit something. "Quinn, come on. Whatever it is, it can't be that bad."

"I love you, please trust me there's nothing wrong."

And suddenly there were two people conflicted in the bed. Because as much as I wanted to trust her, it was the first time I couldn't.

But I wouldn't push her either.

Not yet.

"Okay, well if you change your mind and you want to talk, let me know." I pushed off the covers, irritation crawling up my spine. "I'm going to grab another shower."

Her hand grabbed my arm trying to stop me from leaving the bed, but staying wouldn't solve anything. I was tired, and it was clear she wasn't volunteering the truth and I didn't want to say something I didn't mean. So I gave her a quick kiss and then went and sulked in the shower like an asshole, because that was smart.

By the time I'd got out she'd made breakfast, a peace offering of pancakes and orange juice, and it kind of irritated me even more.

That she thought it was needed.

Her arms circled my chest but they were tentative, tilting her chin to kiss me. "I have a shoot in an hour, so I need to go get ready. But I made you breakfast, and I might be late tonight."

I nodded, pretending like I didn't have a million things I wanted to say and let her leave. Last thing I wanted was to sit in her kitchen and eat breakfast, but I didn't want to fight either.

"Hey, Quinn," I called from the kitchen, dumping the pancakes into the trash before putting the plate in the sink. "If you have a shoot, I might head back to my place."

Her head poked out from the doorway, pulling on her blouse. "Really? Okay, I'll call you later when I'm in between shoots."

"Sure." I shrugged, not really enthused to continue the dance we were apparently doing. You know the one, where we both pretend like everything is fine and know it's not.

Maybe I'd been pushing her too hard? Things had happened pretty fast, but we'd seemed to be on the same page. Not that I had ever outright asked her what she wanted. I just assumed, expecting because I wanted to spend every free night I had with her that she felt the same way. But maybe she didn't. And maybe the girl who'd been doing her own thing for so long needed a time out.

Determined not to be a pussy and beg her to talk to me, I grabbed my phone and my keys, kissed her one last time and walked out. I was in a situation well above my pay grade, and I needed help.

And for better or worse, I went to the one person I always did when I'd gotten into trouble.

Mack.

"Kid, shit must be seriously messed up if you're coming to me for advice." Mack shook his head handing me a coffee. "Okay, tell me what's going on and let's see where you screwed up."

Like a bad comedy sketch, we sat at his kitchen counter, drinking shitty-ass coffee while he tried to impart some words of wisdom.

I rolled my eyes, not at all surprised Mack had assumed I'd been the one responsible. "I didn't screw up. Not sure what's going on, but I didn't do it."

"Oh, buddy. See there's your first mistake." He laughed, finding the whole thing amusing. "I might not know a lot about women, but I can tell you that nine out of ten times we've absolutely fucked up. We have no idea what it is, and to be honest it doesn't matter. Just say sorry."

"Why would I say sorry for something when I don't even know why? No wonder you're divorced, man, this is terrible advice." I spit the coffee back into the mug. "And if your solution to this is to put me out of my misery by killing me with this coffee, then well done. What the hell is this shit?"

Mack shrugged, not concurring with my assessment as he took another leisurely sip. "Some nice lady at the supermarket recommended it, I don't think it's that bad."

"Jesus, *some nice lady*?" I was reeling from the shock. Hell, if my love life wasn't doing so hot, Mack's was on life support. "When was the last fucking time you got laid? Have you checked your dick still works? And for fuck's sake don't take coffee advice from strangers in the supermarket. My parents sucked but they still managed to teach me that."

He popped his brow, shooting me a grin. "Do you want to continue to discuss my shopping habits or you want to talk about what you did to fuck up with Quinn?"

"I did *not* fuck up."

"Okay." Smug ass motherfucker took another sip.

And to think I came to him for help.

"Fine, let's assume I fucked up. And I apologize." I was willing to play along if he thought it might help. "How does that help me in the future if I don't know what the hell I did?"

"It doesn't, that's life. You just keep saying sorry."

I blinked back at Mack, having real fear for both of us if that was the best course of action. "I just can't do it, Chief. If I've hurt her or pissed her off, then I have to know and make sure I never fucking do it again. This isn't just some girl; it's Quinn. But she won't fucking talk to me."

"Buddy, listen." He put down his coffee and cupped my shoulder. "I don't tell you enough because I worry your head is already too huge to fit through the doors, but you're a good man. There isn't anyone else I'd prefer to have beside me either fighting a fire, or as a friend. I love you, Kid." He raised his hands, stopping me from interjecting so he could continue. "But this thing with Quinn, it's pretty intense. Not to mention you're both impulsive and hot headed. Maybe just slow down a little, okay. Give her some space, trust me, everything is going to be fine."

"Yeah, I guess." I shrugged.

So much for not turning into a pussy.

Fuck.

Doing the right thing had never been my strong point but I guess there was some merit. Maybe we did just need some space. Give us some time to miss each other a little. Or if not, give me time to convince her to tell me what the hell was wrong.

"Hey, you up for a night out?" I asked, thinking I should probably start practicing sooner than later. "And no fucking card games, old man. We're going to go to a bar and maybe find you someone who doesn't drink shitty coffee or is ready to file for their pension."

"And you're going to tell Quinn what, exactly?" he asked, wondering if I was trying to bait her.

"Well, in order for me to tell her *anything*, she'd have to actually call. But if she does, I'll tell her the truth. That I thought we could use a night off and that I'm with you. I'm not trying to make her jealous, Chief, and I sure as hell am not interested in anyone else."

"Fine. I'll go. But I swear to God, kid, if you take me to one of those places that only serves overpriced cocktails, we're having words." He gave me a pointed look. "And you're driving."

"I'll drive, Chief. And it will be a decent bar. Just leave it to me." And hopefully if we couldn't get the chief some female company, I could at least improve my mood.

It couldn't get any worse.

Quinn had texted around four that she was shooting until midnight. As promised, I told her I was going to a bar with Mack and a few of the other guys and she told me to have a good time.

That was it.

Didn't ask questions so I didn't offer anything else. So it was a fairly safe assumption that I was going to be sleeping alone in my own bed.

Fine.

It was one night, and not like I didn't sleep alone when I was at the stationhouse. Or couldn't spend a night or two by myself at my own place.

We were giving each other space.

All good things.

What I couldn't understand was why if it was such a good thing, why it felt so horrible.

Still, contemplating didn't serve me much purpose and Quinn had a history of being distant and radio silent when she was sorting things out. It hadn't been that long ago she'd avoided my call because she'd apparently liked me, but had been worried about Mack being her soul mate. She'd eventually come to her senses and things had turned out just fine. So maybe it was her process, needing a step back before going forward.

"Dude, you are seriously killing my buzz," Tibbs hollered over the music, fisting a bunch of beers before handing one to Leighton and the chief. "If I knew this was going to be so depressing, I'd have turned you down."

"Girl trouble. Has to be. No other reason he'd be out with us when he's dating anyone that hot. I sure as hell wouldn't be," Leighton volunteered, the asshole taking a mouthful of beer.

I flipped him off, taking a sip of my own beer. "Quinn's working, dumbass."

"Really? Isn't it late?" Tibbs screwed his brow in confusion. "You wouldn't think there'd be a lot of opportunity at night."

Mack laughed, thoroughly enjoying the floorshow of dumb and dumber that Leighton and Tibbs were providing. "And to think I thought I was going to be bored tonight. I'm so glad I let North talk me into this."

I was just about to point out that night photography was a thing, or that there were studios with lights, when Leighton stopped me. "Dude, are you *not* following her on Instagram? She does all these cool shoots down by the water. There was one in Battery Park, spooky as shit." He pulled out his phone, flipping it to Tibbs to check out. "I've actually been thinking of getting some photos done myself."

I eyed Leighton hard, reminding myself we were in a decent place and hitting him wouldn't solve anything. "I don't know what's more disturbing. That you follow my girlfriend on social media or that you are considering hiring her. What the hell do you need photos of?"

"Jesus, North. You going full caveman on us?" He laughed. "Nothing shady, just some decent pics at the station to give my mom for her birthday. She keeps ragging at me to give her some in my uniform, but I don't want to look like a tool."

Tibbs, who apparently wasn't content with just seeing Quinn's page on Leighton's phone, had taken his own out and was flicking through her photos. "Wow, she's really good. Not sure I'd feel comfortable with my chick being around so many hot looking dudes though. Who's this guy? Isn't he from that cologne commercial where he strips naked on the beach?"

I knew the guy he was talking about, the model she'd worked with last week. And while it didn't fill me with excitement that she was sometimes around men who liked to have their junk hanging out, I couldn't exactly tell her to stop. She was a professional, and it was her job. And she'd had nothing to do with that commercial, the photos she'd taken, he'd been completely clothed.

"You done yet? Because you're starting to piss me off."

"Easy, North." Tibbs rolled his eyes. "I'm just saying that a girl like Quinn has options. You screw that up and there'd be a line around the neighborhood to take your place, buddy. I mean, she's smokin'. So hot—"

Chief put his hand on my chest, stopping me from grabbing Tibbs and wringing his fucking neck. "North knows exactly how hot his girlfriend is, Tibbs. Probably more so on account he's the one going home with her. So let's keep it respectful."

Tibbs might have been an asshole, but he wasn't wrong. Quinn was gorgeous, and I didn't doubt that if she wasn't with me, there'd be hundreds of guys who'd kill for the opportunity. And not just because she was hot, as Tibbs was helpful in pointing out. It's because she was fun, and so goddamn infectious, and she was so fucking smart. She didn't rely on anyone for shit. And I loved that about her.

I slammed my beer down on the table, annoyed at how his stupid little remark was working its way under my skin. "Fuck."

Chapter 24

Riley

I WAS GOING to kill Tibbs.

Ever since he'd put that stupid idea in my head about Quinn and other men, it was all I could think about.

Not that I thought she'd cheat—that just wasn't her style—but she'd mentioned more than once that she bored easily. And who knew that all you needed to keep your ego in check was to be in love with an amazing woman.

Yep, that was where I was at.

And because my head was still churning, and seeing her would probably not be smart, I went home after the bar and spent the night alone. If Quinn was upset by my plans to sleep alone, she didn't mention it. Which of course just made things worse.

So rather than just leave things the way they were, I suggested meeting her for lunch. And call me an asshole but if she was hoping to avoid me, I wasn't going to make it easy for her. Surprisingly, she agreed, even suggesting a place in Brooklyn. And since she had work throughout the day, I agreed to meet her wherever she wanted, hoping we might get a chance to talk.

Pity, it hadn't worked out that way.

Her lunch break was barely an hour, Quinn spending more time picking at her salad and asking me about my night with the guys than looking at me. And her line about the long hours getting to her wasn't one I was swallowing.

But being the supportive, good boyfriend that I was, I let her go about her day, promising to see her for dinner. She had the night off, and I wasn't wasting the opportunity regardless of my commitment to give us both *space*.

I'd barely made it through the front door when she grabbed me, pulling me inside and kissing me so hard I had to wonder if she'd been possessed. Maybe that bullshit about absence making the heart grow fonder had some substance to it, Quinn tearing at my shirt as I pinned her against the wall.

Sex had not been my intention.

Talking—and hopefully dinner—had been the aim, but the minute her lips hit my skin, I could not say no. We'd undressed and fucked like a pair of starved sex addicts, barely saying two words to each other as we moaned each other's names.

And you'd have thought it would have solved the problem, but it didn't. The divide still being there, her refusing to give me anything concrete really making me consider maybe we really were heading for Splitsville.

I couldn't stand it.

The idea of saying goodbye to Quinn so fucking painful that I shut my mouth, stuffed down my feelings and held her for as long as she'd let me. We ate cold cereal for dinner, neither of us wanting to go out, and made love slowly through the night.

If she wanted me to leave, she was going to have to tell me, kissing her one last time before I had to go to work.

"You should come by the stationhouse for dinner." I brushed the hair out of her face. "Not sure if I mentioned it but a couple of the guys are fans of yours. Leighton wants to hire you to do photos for his mom."

"Really? Ha! Tell him I'd love to." A smile that didn't quite reach her eyes spread across her lips. She snuggled down into the covers, her first shoot not for a few more hours. "Not sure I can make dinner though. My afternoon is sort of crazy."

"Quinn." I closed my eyes, needing a minute so the words came out right. "You've been working a lot lately, and I know you love your job. But do you think maybe you're burning the candle at both ends?"

It couldn't be healthy, her hours so erratic I had no idea when she started and when she finished. And if we had any chance of making it work, something had to give.

"I don't travel anymore." Her eyes flashed up to mine, huffing out a breath. "It means I have to do more locally. It's not ideal but at least I'm here."

"Here? Quinn, you haven't been *here* for days." It was harsher than I'd wanted it to be, frustrated and annoyed and more at myself than anyone else.

And there it was.

I *was* the problem.

Not because she wanted to be with another guy, but because she thought to be with me she had to give up what she'd had before. I was the compromise, and fuck if that didn't hurt.

"Do me a favor, okay? Don't turn down work on my account. You get offered a job somewhere, then go."

Her head snapped up, looking at me like I'd told her to go fuck someone else. "Why are you acting like this? You think if I start getting on planes and heading off like I did before, that you aren't going to get sick of it and then start complaining I'm never around? Go find someone else more accessible? You think I don't know how it works? I'm here, Riley, and yes I'm moody and tired, but do you know how much harder I have to work to maintain my income?"

"Who the fuck cares, Quinn! You think I'm happy that you're just *around*? That I like having a girlfriend who's going to end up resenting me two months from now? Don't fucking do me any favors because that is shit I never asked for." My mouth was on autopilot, the seal completely broken. "And I knew exactly who you were when we started dating, if I wanted an easy lay, I would've kept walking."

It was a shitty thing to say, hurtful and so fucking wrong but it was out of my mouth before I'd had a chance to stop it.

I'd assumed at that point she was either going to call me a heartless bastard—justified—or punch me right in the face—again, valid. But she didn't, her face flushing red as she pushed off the sheet and launched herself off the bed.

"Well, maybe you'd be better off finding an *easy lay* so you won't have to worry about me being so tired anymore. Then on your time off you can have a beck and call girl, ready for your every whim. You know, I'm not the only one who has a shitty schedule. Not exactly a picnic trying to keep track of when you're home and when you're not."

I should have walked out.

Let calmer heads prevail and had the conversation when at least one of us was thinking straight. But she was *finally* having a conversation and I didn't fucking care it wasn't the one I wanted to hear. So I wasn't leaving, and we were going to say whatever the hell needed to be said.

"Please, like *I'm* the problem." I barked out a laugh. "Come on, Quinn. You can do better than that."

And if I'd wanted a fight, I sure as hell gotten it. Quinn pushed back on my chest, raising her voice as she stared me down. "Maybe you are the fucking problem. And it's not just the hours; I have to worry whether you come home at all. At least I'm home every night."

Enraged, and still not thinking clearly, I opened my mouth. "WELL AT LEAST I'M DOING SOMETHING IMPORTANT AND WORTH A DAMN."

Ah.

FUCK.

I'd regretted it the minute I'd said it, her face rearing back like I'd slapped her.

"Quinn." I reached for her, her fists deflecting my arms as she took a step back. "Quinn, I didn't mean that. I was just angry and frustrated and—"

"Get the fuck out of my apartment." She pointed to the door, refusing to let me anywhere near her. "Now, Riley, that is not a request."

She was so mad.

So hurt.

So fucking destroyed and all because of me.

"Quinn."

She shook her head, not willing to hear another fucking word. "Leave. Now."

My feet refused to budge, rooted in their spot knowing if I walked out the door it might be for the last time. But my head knew I didn't have a choice. Either I left willingly, or my buddies in dispatch were going to send a friendly NYPD unit to remove me. And wouldn't that do wonders for everyone involved.

Fuck.

"Okay, I'll go." I held up my hands in surrender and took a step back. I'd been ready to leave for work anyway so my bag and keys were already sitting by the door. Convenient, meant I could make my exit still eye locked with Quinn, who looked like she wanted to kill me with her bare hands.

And then the door shut.

Both figuratively and literally as I closed it behind me and stepped out into the hall. The door next to Quinn's opened, Karli storming out and getting caught in surprise when she saw me.

"You are an asshole," she sneered at me in case I wasn't already aware, opening the door I'd just shut and disappearing inside.

So with no other choices, and no hope of making it better, I did the only thing I could and left.

Work was going to be so much fun.

Fuck.

Turned out I didn't have time to obsess about Quinn or whether or not we'd broken up. Mack was riding us hard, not giving us a minute to fucking scratch and that didn't even take into account the call outs. Ironically, it was exactly what I needed, doing something useful and productive and feeling like I had a purpose. There were no doubts when it came to my job, no question whether I was good enough, fast enough, strong enough. It was something I intrinsically knew. And cocky or not, that's how I'd used to feel about Quinn.

Pity that was no longer true.

I had no fucking idea where we were going or whether I was enough for her. And in my line of work the minute you question your ability to perform, that's when you need to hang up your turnouts and go the fuck home.

So, following the logic . . . you'd think it would be self explanatory on what I needed to do. Just like a has-been who could no longer cut it on the line, or in an engine—hang up my heart, and move the fuck on. Ha! Like I could ever convince myself that would be a viable option, or that it would be even possible.

Man, I loved her.

I really fucking did.

And even though I had my doubts, I wasn't sure I could ever walk away.

"North," Mack barked from his office. "Are you done with those radios yet? I know it doesn't take an hour to change batteries."

"On the last one, Chief," I yelled back, shaking my head as I slipped on the back cover.

Leighton grimaced, handing me a coffee as he took a seat opposite. "Jesus, who shit in his Wheaties this morning?"

"End of the month, full equipment check and stocktake." I took a sip from the cup, putting the radio back on its base. I really didn't care how bad a mood the chief was in, if anything it was a distraction. And I'd rather have Mack yelling at me every day of the week than thinking about how I'd left things with Quinn.

"So, I'm going to call Quinn. Book in those photos."

Annnnnnnnnd it was good while it lasted.

Like a floodgate had opened, all the anger, pain and confusion rushed back and cut me in thirty-five different directions. My chest hurt, my heart feeling like it had been taken in a vise and squeezed within an inch of its life. And then I remembered her face. The look she'd given me, and the motherfucking disgust I'd had in myself for putting it there.

My eyes pinned Leighton with a glare that had the guy visibly take a step back. It wasn't his fault, not knowing that just hearing her name was enough to mess with my head. And now that he'd said it, there wasn't a chance I'd stop thinking about her.

"Wow, dude, I told you." He held his hands up. "Nothing shady I promise, the photos are for my *mother*. You think I'm going to pull my dick out or something? Even if she wasn't your girl, not the kind of photos I'm interested in."

My girl? Not. Fucking. Likely.

Not only was I sure she was no longer *my girl*, but she probably hated my guts. Any happiness we'd shared together had been torched because we couldn't leave well enough alone. How did the fucking argument even start? Escalating out of control before I could even get a handle on it. And even though I was fucking bewildered, and feeling baited, I'd been way out of line. I never should have said that to her, and they weren't the kind of words that were easy to take back.

"Do whatever you want." I planted my feet on the floor, lifting my ass out of my seat, ready to get the hell out of the room. I was positive Chief needed toilets cleaned or his nuts waxed, or some other bullshit that'd stop me from wanting to rip out Leighton's spleen.

Leighton unwisely got between me and the door, his palms hitting my chest as he stopped me from leaving. "What's going on, North?"

"We don't have time to chat," I bit back, shoving his hands off me. I needed out of there. Out of the room and into some fresh air where I could catch my breath. Or maybe I'd get lucky and that damn alarm would ring like it had been all day. I wanted nothing more than to get into my turnouts and hit a burning building at a dead run.

But it seemed I wasn't the only person that day who didn't walk away when he should, Leighton grabbing my shoulder instead of letting it slide. "North, I fucking swear. I'm not trying to mess with you."

I snapped, swinging a fist that narrowly missed his jaw when he ducked. He let out a shout, his arm flying out, deflecting my other fist as I failed to make any contact. I'd wanted to hit the bastard and hoped he'd hit me too, knowing anything would feel better than the pain I already had.

"What the fuck is going on here?" Chief appeared at the door, eyeing us both hard. "North, Leighton, in my office now."

"Fuck." I curled my fists, pissed the fight had been stopped before it had even started and annoyed I needed it at all. I hadn't been Chief's problem child in a long ass time. So apart from the ass chewing we were both going to get for fighting in the stationhouse, he was going to save an extra special heaping of misery just for me.

Leighton's eyes were huge, straining to capacity, still not believing I'd taken a swing. He didn't say a word though, walking past Mack and stepping into his office while Chief thinned his lips. "Now, North. Get your ass in here."

A few of the other guys had heard the commotion and were straining their necks to see. Not that they wouldn't hear it firsthand, Mack could yell like no one's business.

I shoved my hands into my pockets and stormed past my boss and my friend and readied myself for the double-barreled assault I was no doubt going to receive. Truth was, I welcomed it, needing someone to fucking tell me what the hell went wrong.

"Either of you assholes want to explain why you two apparently don't have enough to do?" He walked around to his desk, sinking into his chair as he pointed for us to do the same. "Because I can give you a list of shit to do that'll last you until next century if you're fucking bored."

Neither of us spoke, Leighton looking at me and probably trying to find out himself why I'd flown off the handle. It wasn't like me, so he was justified in his curiosity.

"Nothing?" Chief barked before turning to me. "So I suppose I hallucinated seeing you trying to land a fist on Leighton's face? Maybe you can fucking explain that."

"He wasn't trying to hit me, Chief. We were just screwing around," Leighton interjected before I'd gotten a chance, flicking his gaze to me. "North and I were just roughhousing. No harm done."

My mouth slammed shut, reeling from the shock.

No idea why the hell Leighton was covering for me. All he had to do was tell Mack I'd attempted to punch him—unprovoked unless you counted stupidity—and Chief would have no choice but to suspend me. Zero tolerance on violence in the workplace, and regardless of his feelings toward me, his hands would be tied.

"No harm done? I'm not running a fucking kindergarten. That shit might fly elsewhere but not in *my* house," he yelled, the vein from the side of his neck bulging at the side.

"Understood, sir. We're sorry, and it won't happen again." Leighton bowed his head, elbowing me in the ribs. "Right, North."

"Ah yeah," I coughed, my voice strangled by my throat. "Sorry, Chief."

He blew out a hard breath, pounding a fist onto his desk. "This is the first and the last time we're having this conversation, we clear?"

"Yes, Chief," we answered in unison.

"Fine, then get back to work." His words hard as he spat them out. "Not you, North. You stay right there."

Leighton nodded, getting to his feet and shooting me an apologetic look. Not sure why he was sorry, I was the one who was responsible. In fact, I owed *him* the apology, trying to hit my friend for no good reason, not my proudest moment.

Chief waited until Leighton had closed the door behind him, giving me the same look of disappointment he did when I was eighteen and fucking up. I'd hated it then, stung even worse now.

"If you think I believe that horseshit about you two rough housing, then I misjudged your intelligence." His voice was surprisingly calm. "Now tell me what the fuck happened, Riley. And I want the fucking truth."

He was beyond pissed off, but could rein it in like no other. It's what made him an amazing leader, and an even better man.

"I had a fight with Quinn. Was a complete prick and fairly sure she never wants to see me again. Leighton mentioned Quinn taking photos for him and . . .you do the math."

"Jesus," he cursed under his breath. "Why the hell didn't you come to me?"

"Because, Chief, I'd already pissed off one of the people I loved, I didn't want to try and make it two." I shoved my head into my fists, a rush of air pushing past my lips. "Look, I know I fucked up and what I did to Leighton was totally on me." I met his eyes, giving him the respect he'd more than earned. "He wasn't even riding me; it was completely unprovoked. I deserve to be suspended. Probably deserve a lot more than that too. But the truth is, nothing you do is going to hurt more than I already do."

"Shit, kid, I'm sorry."

Yet another person who didn't owe me an apology was giving me one. And it just made things ten times worse.

"Maybe after you both sleep on it, you can speak to her tomorrow. I know stuff can be said in the heat of the moment, but I bet if you give her time, she'll come around. And then for God's sake grovel. Hands and knees, North. You want her back, the second you get that chance you leave nothing on the table."

"Great advice, Chief, and I hope I get that shot, but it's doubtful," I coughed out, my chest feeling heavy. "Right now I think I'd settle just to have her not hate me."

Mack shook his head, "You want to go home? I can call around, get the rest of your shift covered?"

"Thanks Chief, but I'd rather stay. Actually, if I have to, I'll beg you to stay. This is about the only thing that makes sense right now."

He nodded, understanding, and probably having been there a couple of times himself. "Take a minute and get your shit together." He stood, cupping my shoulder as he walked past. "You're not alone, kid. We've got you, okay?"

I can't remember ever wanting to cry.

Not even when my parents died.

But as he left me alone in that room, giving me my privacy, a sob choked up my throat I had no chance of stopping.

Because I'd been given a family, when mine was taken, counting some of the best men I knew as brothers.

And as I blinked back tears I wasn't sure if it was because I'd been given that amazing, second chance, or because it probably meant I didn't have the right to ask for another.

Losing someone like Quinn wasn't something you'd ever get over.

Best you could do was just hope you survived.

Chapter 25

Quinn

'D BEEN ENTIRELY convinced that I cried for days. But as it turned out, it had just been a few hours. Not that it mattered, I couldn't see myself stopping anytime soon, not unless I dehydrated or cried myself to sleep.

Both of those possibilities having an equal chance of happening.

Riley and I hadn't exactly been quiet during our spectacular finale, Karli overhearing from her apartment. Actually I was surprised, it had only been her at my door, and not the entire neighborhood. Though the lack of people showing up or calling the cops was probably from New York desensitization to drama, rather a lack of them hearing. Guess that was a small victory.

Karli let me cry—not like she had much choice—then helped me clear my schedule. She called in sick to her own job, acting as my assistant to rebook clients and cancel all my shoots. I couldn't have done it, too emotional to even talk to her, let alone try to act professional.

She didn't even ask what I needed, just forced me to open my laptop and grabbed my phone. And when the last call was done, she curled up on the couch beside me and held me while I sobbed. I didn't even remember her getting up, blinking down in surprise at the bowl of soup in my hands.

"I know you probably prefer chicken, but I can't do that." She winced, handing me a spoon. "It's vegetable, and if you eat it, you get a brownie."

"I'm not really hungry, Karli." I tried to laugh, thankful for Karli's effort even if she was drawing the line at poultry. But it wasn't in me. My spoon swirled around the liquid, not having the energy to bring it to my mouth. I knew I should probably try, but the idea of eating just made me want to gag.

Her head shook, sitting beside me and tucking into her own bowl of soup. "You don't have to be hungry for soup, you can just drink it. It's good, trust me and it will make you feel better."

Yeah, it was going to take a lot more than soup to make me feel better but I wasn't going to hurt her feelings by saying that. Especially when she was being so considerate and caring. So begrudgingly I brought the spoon to my lips, forcing the liquid down until it was all gone. And she was sort of right, it did make me feel better.

It was hours and a box of tissues later before she finally asked, her worried eyes making me even sadder. "You want to talk about it, Quinn? We don't have to, but I'm here to listen if you want."

I sighed, my body aching, my head hurting and my eyes burning. I hadn't looked in a mirror recently but could imagine my reflection. It was probably accurate considering I felt like death that I looked like it too, my eyes closing as I let out another breath. "I'm fairly sure I picked a fight. He wanted to know why I'd been acting so weird, then I got scared and defensive. I'm not taking responsibility for what he said, but I am one hundred percent the one who started it."

Karli's eyes widened, shaking her head no doubt to tell me I'd been wrong. But I stopped her, because having someone defend my own stupid behavior wasn't something I needed. "Every time he walks out the door, I worry I'm going to get another call from Mack. Worried that it's going to be a boring afternoon, and I'll be doing something completely unimportant and he'll be gone, Karli. Just like my dad."

I shook my head, swallowing hard as I tried to get the words out. "I didn't fall in love with an accountant, or a school teacher or some guy who washes cars. He's a fireman, and will without question put his life on the line. And the only other man I loved was taken from me for much less of a reason."

I needed to get it out, to hear it out loud if only to make sense of it myself.

"And I tried to reason with myself, reason that it would be okay but deep down I knew I was holding on too tight. That I'd lose him one way or another. So I stopped traveling. He never asked me to, it was my choice. But I'd always thought that when I found someone worth giving my heart to, that I needed to stop."

It sounded so ridiculous hearing my own thought process, but at the time it had made so much sense. "It was logical, but he'd never asked that of me. And part of me—and I hate even admitting this—wished by me giving up some of my job, he'd give up his. He'd be safe, we'd be together and everything would be okay."

Like a scared little girl, I sat still. My body unmoving, feeling wounded as I hiccupped a breath. My hands knotted in my lap, Karli rubbing small circles in my back as she listened.

God, what must she think?

"But I think deep down I knew he never would. It's a part of him. So I rationalized that at least if I was around, then I would be *here* if something did go wrong. But staying local meant more hours and it didn't give us more time, and I worried that maybe he'd get sick of it and find someone else. Someone less complicated. Someone less scared. Someone who would've been stronger. So I blamed him for that. Blamed him for my insecurity, blamed him for the extra hours I needed to do, and blamed him for being so tired. I even blamed him for me being petrified when he went out on a call. Making him feel like it was somehow his fault. I don't think I'll ever get over seeing him in that hospital bed. But it was easier to lie, easier to throw it in his face that even though I'd made all those changes and sacrifices for him that he still wasn't happy. Because if I admitted the truth, and we didn't make it anyway, I don't think my heart would have been able to take it."

There was so much going on in my heart and my head, but mostly I just felt so overwhelmed. I'd been happy with my life, had loved my job, but it had started to feel like I'd been working on a factory production line. I loved taking photos, but my work hadn't been about memories for a while. It was about bragging rights, it was about likes, it was about who got the most attention on social media. I was just a cog in a machine, no longer capturing life moments, instead creating manufactured cells for a graphic novel of someone's life. And I knew that if my dad were still alive, he would have hated it.

"It was only after I'd fallen in love with Riley that I saw how much I didn't love everything else. Every day he went to work and put his life on the line, and I did what? I was worried about losing everything. Worried about not only losing him because of his job, but also because of mine. That he'd see how shallow what I did really was." I laughed at the irony. "I hate that he was right, what I do *doesn't* matter. God, I'd wanted it to. I wanted to love the travel and the lifestyle and the money, but I haven't loved any of it for weeks. And if I went away, there'd be some other person taking my place. The only photo I've taken recently that I honestly gave a shit about was that baby Riley delivered in Lake Placid. No filters, no editing—I shot it on the guy's superseded iPhone and then handed it right back. But I felt like I was part of something. Like I had a purpose."

I took a breath, Karli probably getting more than she bargained for. Instead of the heartbreak, I'd hit her with a full life crisis and we were probably going to need more soup. "You see, deep down, I felt like I wasn't good enough. Me," I chuckled, clearly losing my grip on reality. "The person who thought she was bulletproof was scared the man she loved would see exactly how much of a fraud she was. Because he isn't, Karli. God, he is as authentic as they come. And the idea of him not loving me back . . . it was easier to blame him."

Oh, I know he had said some really hurtful shit.

And despite my crumbling self esteem, I hadn't deserved that. But I knew he'd been desperate, backed into a corner and unable to understand why his girlfriend was acting like a fruit loop. Hell, I didn't even understand it myself. So as I finished explaining to Karli all the ways it had gone wrong, I knew the end had been sort of inevitable. I'd have found a way to sabotage it, whether it was Miss Lillian's prophecy, me being afraid for his safety, or my work schedule.

Anything other than admitting I wasn't good enough.

Because as much as I wanted to believe it, I wasn't totally convinced.

"I should have just gotten a dog like I wanted. Man, if only I'd gone to the pet adoption day with you and Brad. I could be cuddling some poor little mutt instead of being such a screw up."

"Ahhhh Quinn, you remember why you couldn't go on that "date" with us?" She eyed me carefully, reminding me exactly why I'd had to cancel.

My heart ached in my chest, that call and the trip to the hospital a blur. I couldn't even think straight until I'd known he was okay, praying so hard I promised I'd never ask for anything else. "Because Riley was hurt."

"Because he *needed* you," she corrected me. "Yeah, I can only imagine how scary that call would have been, and yes what he does is terrifying. Girl, I can't tell you I'd be any better at dealing with it. But when something went wrong, you were there. By his side, helping him get better. That's not a screw up, and I bet if we asked him, he'd say that he'd have preferred no one else."

"But I—"

"But it's okay to be scared, Quinn. No one is fearless all the time. And he's a pretty good reason to take the risk. I know losing your daddy was hard, especially because he was so young. But it's not the same thing. And saying he would've hated what you do is just not true. He would have been so proud. So proud that his daughter was not only creative and business savvy but had such a big heart. You're not a fraud, Quinn. We've all seen exactly who you are, and guess what? We love every part."

Great.

And I thought the tears had stopped.

"I'm such a mess." I sniffed, my heart feeling like it was too big for my chest. "I need to find a way to get him back."

Riley didn't call and I hated how disappointed I was. Given how it ended he probably assumed I didn't want to hear from him, and I hadn't exactly picked up that phone either. It was complicated and I needed to get some things straight in my own mind before I could even attempt to repair things with him.

There were things I couldn't change.

Riley's job and the danger level attached to it was one of them.

But what I did and how I reacted, or just basically went through life—were all things I had control over.

The next morning I spent hours reassessing jobs, and palming off all the ones that didn't excite me. I'd worked hard and saved so afforded myself a little cushion to be choosey. So rather than doing social media posts, I changed my focus looking to do more feel good stuff. I'd even contacted that animal shelter I was supposed to go to with Karli and Brad and struck a deal to do portraits for their dogs and cats. It could only increase their opportunity for adoption, and I'd seen the success rate rise in other shelters that did a similar thing.

It was lunchtime when my phone buzzed with an incoming message from Riley asking me to call him.

I knew it was his day off, my finger hovering over his name as I debated whether or not to call, my heart begging me to stop being an idiot and just do it.

And I was just about to give in when a wave of nausea overtook me, barely making it to the bathroom before I threw up.

Huh.

My head was still down the toilet as my brain started its own calculation.

Tiredness.

Irritability.

Moodiness.

Lightheaded.

Nausea.

"OH MY FUCKING GOD!" I was pretty sure I screamed, my fingers fumbling with my phone to check when I'd had my last period. I was terrible at remembering, using an app in my phone to track it so I wouldn't forget. And there it was, its happy little animated picture, showing me I was two weeks late.

Fuck.

Fuck.

Fuck.

Testing to see if my stomach would hold, I rinsed off my mouth and scrambled to my living room to grab my keys and my purse. Assuring Karli I didn't need a babysitter, she'd returned to work and thus leaving me solo as I left my apartment in search of a pregnancy test.

Thankfully I didn't have to go too far, the small convenience store in walking distance as I grabbed a test, paid for it and then ran the entire way home. Probably wasn't the smartest decision, my stomach rolling as I sucked down a huge glass of water after my little sprint.

My hands were literally shaking as I unboxed the wand, not bothering to read the instructions. It was peeing on a stick, if I couldn't work it without a step-by-step then there really wasn't much help for me.

It was only after I'd peed on said stick and washed my hands that I felt myself take a full breath. We didn't always use condoms, stupidly getting caught in the moment and assuming the pill would make do. But with erratic work hours and weird sleeping cycles, I wasn't "regular" in taking it, which translated into—you're probably pregnant, dumbass.

Shit.

Shit.

Shit.

It was going to be a few minutes, my heart racing as I watched those little square windows like NASA looking for life on Mars. And then I took another breath.

And another.

Annnnnnnnd another.

And by the fourth one, a weird sensation spread across my body. Either I was settling into some weird acceptance or I'd lost my mind, and I didn't feel qualified to guess which.

What if I *was* pregnant? Would it really be so bad? Sure, I was not currently with the father or in a relationship, and had spent the morning restructuring my business, so work was going to be insane for a while. And considering I'd wanted a pet for years and hadn't been able to find time to make the commitment it probably didn't speak volumes of my readiness.

Fine, not the best examples.

But I was twenty-eight, healthy, self-sufficient, and as Karli had so eloquently pointed out last night, I was loved. And even if I had to do it all by myself—because hello complications—I would never be alone.

And before his or her existence had even been confirmed, I'd already decided I wanted the baby. Because he or she was made in love, and hopefully would have the best of each of us.

My tear-filled eyes glanced over to the test, the plus sign telling me what I already knew. The whole time I'd been thinking I was acting moody, having feelings like a normal person who was in love and scared. But I needn't have worried, there wasn't a chance I was normal. I was pregnant instead.

Chapter 26

Riley

THREE MESSAGES AND nothing in return, and I had to accept the very real possibility that she wasn't going to respond.

I probably should have waited.

Given it another day or two, and then tried.

But I couldn't, not willing to let her believe that I didn't give a shit or worse, that I was just going to give up.

So rather than get in my car, sit outside her apartment and beg her to talk to me, I spent the time in my own apartment, avoiding a stalking charge.

She'd eventually have to talk to me.

Even if it was to file the restraining order so that I stopped calling, she'd have to face me one last time. And when that time finally arrived I was planning on doing exactly what Mack had said.

Making it count.

It was late in the evening when I had an idea—probably not a very good one—and called Leighton.

"Hey, man," he shouted into the phone, the sound of club music making it hard to hear him. "You want to come join us? Tibbs says he'll buy."

"Thanks but that's a hard pass." I shook my head, preferring to get a root canal than go join them at a club. "But I need a favor if you're up for it."

"Sure, dude. Anything you need. Shoot."

Leighton had gone above and beyond since our little *incident*. Not only had his fabricated version of events saved my ass, but had been more than understanding regarding Quinn. He'd offered not only his support, but was willing to drag my sorry ass out if it looked like I was getting too depressed. And while I appreciated the offer, I was looking for help of a different kind.

"Your mom still want those photos of you?"

He chuckled nervously. "Yeah, but no offense, I kind of wanted professional ones. Tibbs took the last ones and I looked like I had a pole up my ass."

"Not me, moron. Quinn."

"Ummm, okay." He paused, his voice turning serious. "Did she call you? You guys back on?"

"Nope, still nothing. Which is why I need *you* to call her. Book in those photos at the station, tell her you're desperate and will pay double. I'll cover the cost."

It was shady as all hell.

Not only was I involving Leighton—the poor bastard genuinely wanting photos for his mom—but putting her in a position where she either turned down work or had to face me. And while I knew there was no guarantee she'd even accept the gig, I had to at least try.

Not to say I'd thought the whole thing through, or even knew what I was going to say or do. But even if I had to make a fool of myself in front of my whole crew, it was worth it just for the chance.

"Dude, you sure that's a good idea?" Leighton tried to reason with me, too bad he was way too late.

"It's a terrible idea and will probably blow up in my face, but I need to see her. I figure getting her to the station of her own free will is less threatening than showing up at her doorstep. And Leighton, I've spent the last two days trying to talk myself out of the latter."

"Fine. I'll call her and ask. But it's short notice so don't freak out if she says no. And brother, if she does turn it down, no going back to the doorstep plan, okay? I want your word we're not going to hear your name on dispatch when they come to lock your ass up."

I laughed, feeling hopeful for the first time in the last twenty or so hours. "My word, Leighton. She says no, I'll figure out another way, but I won't go to her apartment."

"And you're buying Gino's for dinner," he added, knowing he could probably ask for a kidney at that point and I'd still agree. Desperate men did desperate things, and they didn't get any more desperate than where I was at.

"Extortion isn't a good look, Leighton. Not sure your mother would approve. But fine, whatever, I'll buy Gino's."

"My mom loves me, dude, why you think she wants the photos? She's going to mount me on her wall with all the other saints and angels." He chuckled. "Better go set up this photo shoot with your girlfriend. Talk soon."

I didn't bother correcting him on the *girlfriend* part because clearly I liked to live in delusion. Instead I said goodbye and waited for him to give me the thumbs up or down.

Didn't have to wait too long, a message coming about ten minutes later with a confirmation that although he'd had to beg, and pay double her usual rate, she'd managed to squeeze him in for seven tomorrow night.

Perfect.

I could work with that.

All I had to do was wait.

The rest of the night crawled at a snail's pace. I think I set a record for time spent staring at the ceiling and was considering drugging myself with Tylenol PM or some shit when I finally fell asleep. And when the alarm went off the next morning, I was up and ready to get out of the door in record time.

There were no promises she'd even look at me, let alone talk to me, but just knowing I was going to see her was enough to put me on cloud nine.

"Leighton mentioned we're expecting a visitor." Mack stopped me just after the morning briefing. "You sure this is smart?"

"Not the first person to point it out, Chief. But I'm ready to go down in a blaze of glory. I won't push the issue, but the fact she's even agreed to come here speaks volumes." I couldn't wipe the smile off my face.

Again, nothing had even happened yet. But she could have turned down Leighton, or demanded a change in venue. She had to know I'd be around, so it had to be a good sign, right? Even if the only reason she turned up was to look me in the eye and tell me to go to hell, it was better than the silence.

He cursed under his breath, shaking his head before heading to his office and leaving me to it. We still had a whole day to get through before Quinn arrived, and I prayed an alarm didn't sound right when she turned up. Always a risk, again, one I was willing to take.

By six thirty I'd lost the ability to keep still. I was pacing in the rec room, having already done four sets in the weight room and run five miles on the treadmill. It hadn't helped that Manhattan was having a lower than average alarm day, something we usually cheered for—today, not so much.

"How do I look?" Leighton walked in sporting full turnouts and lounging an ax on his shoulder. "Pretty badass, right? My mom's friends all have daughters my age, and some of those chicks are hella hot."

"You are a disturbed individual, Leighton. Using your mother to procure dates is seriously messed up." I shook my head, but agreeing he looked pretty good.

"Hey, we want to talk about messed up, North?" He raised an eyebrow. "Exactly what are you doing here about to crash my photo sesh?"

I flipped him off because he had a point, and more importantly I didn't care. Messed up or not, it got me where I needed to be.

"Leighton. Photographer is here." Tibbs strolled in, sporting a grin I didn't like. "By the way," he leaned in, lowering his voice, "Not that I noticed or anything, but she is looking extra hot tonight."

I pinned him with a look that said he better not try anything and he laughed it off. He—like everyone else in the stationhouse—knew Quinn had me by the balls.

"Okay, best not keep her waiting." Leighton shot me a two-finger salute and walked out to meet her. I hung back, listening as her voice floated through the wall as she said hello. She sounded excited—happy even—and her laugh was a double-edged sword that went straight through my heart.

"You going to stand there like an idiot?" Mack poked his head through the door. "Or you going to go get her back?"

I didn't bother with the response, tipping my chin in thanks before heading out to where the action was.

Tibbs wasn't wrong.

It was a one-two punch when I saw her.

Her body was wrapped in a simple black dress that clung to her curves like it was its life's mission while her blond hair cascaded down her shoulders. She was understated but fucking beautiful, the natural warmth of her smile lighting up her blue eyes like fireworks on New Year's Eve.

"Okay, so probably best if we do this in the bays?" She looked Leighton over, not realizing I'd entered the room. My eyes were restless, taking in every single part of her like it was the first time and somehow found her a hundred times more attractive.

Leighton nodded, turning and leading the way. "Just don't make me look like a tool, Quinn. This is for the saints and angels wall, stakes are high."

She laughed, the noise making my blood vibrate as I moved, whether I wanted to or not. If she hadn't noticed me, she soon would, following the two of them into the bay like a stray dog.

Her eyes flashed to me, giving only the slightest register of surprise before she gained composure. She gave me absolutely nothing, no indication if she wanted me or not, grabbing her camera out of her messenger bag like I wasn't even there.

Fuck.

She didn't seem mad—which was promising—but wasn't going to make it easy. Not that I expected anything less, she chose to ignore me while I leaned against the back wall as I bided my time.

"You want to climb onto the side for me?" She turned her attention to Leighton. "Hold on with one hand and open the front of your jacket."

He complied, doing whatever she said as she positioned him before taking some photos. He shot me a sly wink, grinning from ear to ear as she physically moved him, her hands on his arm as they alternated for another shot.

"Okay, maybe take the jacket off. And can you rest that axe along your shoulders, kind of hang your hands over the edges like you're taking a break," she called out, giving Leighton her full attention while she continued to pretend I wasn't there.

"This isn't going to look like a porno, is it?" He snickered, shucking his turnout coat and doing as she directed. "You know these photos are for my mom."

"Not sure what kind of porn you're watching, Leighton. But I'd say it's the wrong kind if there's an axe involved." Quinn rolled her eyes, doing her best to hide her smile.

It was killing me.

Every inch of my body burning with the need to touch her, and having to keep my hands to myself.

"Swing to your right."

More photos.

"Drop your chin."

More photos.

Every second I breathed her in and knew there was no way I could ever let her go. Whatever it took, whatever she needed— she owned me.

So I stood there, watching her touch Leighton, shooting Leighton and wanting one tenth of that attention.

"Now throw the axe, aim for that back right corner."

Leighton coughed, staring at me like a deer in headlights because Quinn's latest directive had him tossing his axe in my immediate direction.

She didn't even look up, snapping photos and ignoring the fact she'd just asked one of my friends to attempt to maim me. And fuck me if I wasn't thirty ways of screwed up because it actually made me hard.

Not because she wanted to hurt me—although I'd accept that too—but try as she might, she couldn't ignore me either.

"Against regulations." My voice stayed calm, doing my best not to tell her if she wanted to toss an axe at me, I'd probably let her. "Leads to a lot of paperwork."

"Well, that's a shame." She shrugged, positioning Leighton against the front of the engine while I watched. "Okay, just a couple more and I think we're done here."

I waited, letting her finish with her subject but couldn't stop myself getting closer. It was too much to ask, and considering I hadn't backed her into a corner and kissed her the minute she'd walked in, I'd say I was doing pretty fucking good.

"Thanks, Leighton." She lowered her camera, giving him a smile. "I think we have everything we need."

The bastard grinned, giving her a hug that was too familiar for my liking, but I'd deal with him later. Currently I had only one thing on my mind, and it wasn't his hug.

"Quinn."

Her name cursed out on a breath. Both her name and the air with equal amounts of need because I couldn't live without either of them.

She didn't turn, keeping her back to me but stilled. "This probably isn't a good idea to do this here, Riley."

Ha! I fought the urge to tell her she hadn't been all that original. I'd been told how *unsmart* it was or some other variation no less than three times, and it didn't change shit.

"Well I'm all out of good ideas, Quinn, so I only have bad ones left." And wasn't that the truth.

I got closer, standing just inches behind her as she continued to face the opposite direction. "What I said to you was not only wrong but so untrue. What you do, *matters*. And it matters a whole lot more than you think."

She spun around, eyes blazing and her mouth opened. "Riley, I—"

"Wait." I lifted a finger, daring to rest it on her lips. She didn't stop me, the brief connection killing me thirty times because it wasn't enough. "Let me just say what I need to say. If you listen to me and then want to walk away, I won't stop you. If you never want to see me again, I'll disappear. And if you still want to throw that axe, I'll kneel in front of you to make it easier. But please just hear me out."

She took a breath, nodding her head but staying silent. Her struggle not to say anything forced her to bite her lip, making me want to laugh

"What I do is important, Quinn, because I save lives. And I love my job. I love making a difference. But you make people happy. You capture that moment, let people live in it a little longer. You give them something to remember when they're having a shitty day. You're letting people be *seen*. Giving them a chance to step out of the noise and to feel important. And it matters, Quinn. Nothing hurts more than being invisible, so you're saving lives too. And you save mine, Quinn. You save it every single day that you're in it, just by loving me and giving me a safe place to land. I need you, Quinn. I do. So if you need to get on a plane and be gone for a while or if working around the clock makes you happy, I'll wait for you. I'll do whatever it takes. There's no one else, there won't be anyone else and I'm sor—"

"No, I'm sorry," she blurted out, her attempt to let me finish falling short. "I was a freaking idiot. I was pushing you away because I was insecure and scared. I felt like *I* wasn't enough, because for a while I've been compromising. And I couldn't do that with you. Riley, I am so terrified of something happening to you. I thought I was fearless, until I met you. And then I saw what it really looked like. And I love it and hate it all at the same time. Because that one thing that makes my heart beat faster, is the same thing that could take you away."

"Quinn." My hands were around her chin, unable to stop the contact. I was primed, every muscle wound tight while our bodies stood inches apart, my lips burning with the need to kiss her. "I love you, and nothing could ever take me away. I'd fight my way back to you until my last breath."

Our mouths crashed, my arms wrapping around her so tight that I worried I was crushing her. But I couldn't stop—tasting her, feeling her, drinking her in—our mouths devouring each other like they couldn't get enough.

I didn't care what the reasons were—if it was something I did or said, or something with her—it would never be enough to convince me that what we had wasn't perfect.

"Marry me, Quinn." I breathed against her neck, needing to make her my fucking forever more than anything in the world. "I haven't got a ring, and this is the shittiest proposal ever, but please just say yes."

I wasn't even down on one knee, too busy making up for lost time as I kissed her mouth and her jaw, letting my hands get reacquainted with her body.

"Marry you?" She pulled away, taking her delicious mouth away as she looked at me confused. "Are you crazy? We're just getting back together, isn't that a little backward to get engaged before we're even a couple?"

I laughed, the thought that we'd do anything like two regular people being absolutely hilarious. "Come on, Quinn. Don't pretend like you're not just as crazy as I am. That ship has sailed, beautiful."

And even though there was a risk she would say no, I had to ask again. "I know it is wrong to ask, and I can't tell you it's going to be easy. And I know you're scared. But I promise you I'll make it worth it. I promise you I'll be careful. Marry me, Quinn. Say yes. I don't care if it's tomorrow, next month or five years from now. The way I feel about you is never going to change."

"Yes." She grinned, gripping my shirt and kissing me. "Wait. No." Her face changed, her smile slipping as her eyes filled with uncertainty.

"No?" My heart stopped, part of me hoping it was a joke but not being encouraged by her demeanor. "You're turning me down?"

She took a breath, nailing me with a stare that could knock a man on his ass and said. "I need you to know something first."

Chapter 27

Quinn

LEIGHTON'S DESPERATE NEED for photos wasn't a coincidence.

I hadn't returned any of Riley's messages and ducked his calls, so I assumed he was willing to get creative. And had I not been pregnant with his child, needing a medical professional to confirm it before speaking with him, I might have appreciated the effort. But I was too busy freaking out, wondering what the hell he was going to say.

Not that anything he said or didn't say would change my mind. I was having our baby and I wouldn't accept it as anything but a good thing.

So when I accepted the shoot, I was going to use it as an opportunity to test the water. Talk to Riley in a crowd where I didn't think it would get too emotional before I met with him by myself.

In short, I was a coward.

Sure, I pretended like it was no big deal, walking in and saying hi to his friends while secretly looking for him. I was a professional, used to shooting in difficult situations. But professional or not, it was by the grace of God that I didn't attack him when he finally walked in.

Lord, that uniform.

There was something about that navy blue that lit my core on fire, and it took everything I had not to launch myself at him, lips first.

But I continued, wondering if it was pregnancy hormones or I'd always been that crazy, taking photos of Leighton while my mind was on dirty things with my baby's daddy.

Seriously, I was a hot mess.

Not that he seemed to notice, casually standing around and spectating, oblivious to the inferno. Hell, I was only half joking about Leighton throwing the axe. Not because I wanted Riley hurt—not a freaking chance—but because I needed the distraction. Willing to do almost anything to have a reprieve from feeling his eyes on me.

It was going to be a long nine months, my brain making a mental note to pick up some batteries for my vibrator on the way home.

But when he started talking—saying all those nice things—it was no longer lust I felt.

God, I loved him.

Loved him so completely, and I needed him to know how much. To really tell him what had been on my mind, and why I'd been acting like a fruitcake. Well, *mostly* why. I didn't want to scare the poor guy when he was saying such nice things.

Never in a million years did I expect him to propose.

Well, I thought maybe he might out of some warped sense of duty after he found out I was with child. Assuming he didn't die from the shock. But I'd already decided that if he did, I'd turn him down, not wanting a marriage out of obligation. But when he proposed *before* I'd told him, my ability to stop myself from saying yes only lasting about a minute.

So much for my grand plans.

"I don't want to turn you down." My heart pounded, feeling like it was going to explode in my chest. "But I was supposed to. If you asked. But you don't know, so it doesn't count, right?"

WOW.

Even I didn't understand myself and I was the one talking.

"You thought I might propose and already decided to turn me down?" His brow scrunched in confusion. "Quinn, if you thought I was going to propose, why were you so surprised? And why the hell would you say no? Because I can assure you, I've been tortured enough the last few days. Just tell me what else I need to do and I'll do it."

"I was surprised because you're asking to marry *me*, just me." My throat got tight, the urge to cry overwhelming. *Jesus, kid, let me get through an hour without turning into a puddle.* "It couldn't have been out of obligation."

He took my face in his hands, kissing my lips as he grinned. "You know when you act crazy it's a huge turn on, Quinn. But you're not making any sense. Of course I'm asking *you* to marry me, who else would I ask? In case you couldn't tell, there's no one else around. And why the hell would it be out of obligation?"

"There is someone else." I grabbed his hand and laid it on my flat-for-now stomach. "I'm pregnant. Surprise," I added with jazz hands.

As far as testing the water and easing into the situation, I seriously sucked. Not only did I tell him I was knocked up, but announced it like a bonus set of steak knives. I should never be trusted with important news.

His eyes widened, looking at my stomach before lifting them back to my face, only a second passing before he took my mouth.

"Jesus, Quinn," he mumbled between kisses. "We're having a baby? When did you find out?" His arms wrapped around me tightly, pressing me against him as he whispered against my mouth. "And you can forget about turning me down. You already said yes, and there are no take backs."

It was hard to answer, my lips wanting to keep kissing him while my brain was trying to make words happen. Mostly I just groaned, unable to form sentences when he was holding me like he was.

"I did a test the day after . . . well the day after I was acting crazy. But I went to the doctor yesterday. I needed to be sure before I told you, because regardless of what your feelings were, I wanted to have the baby."

His lips brushed against mine softly, teasing me before smiling. "Don't you remember me telling you that any babies you had were going to be mine? I'm nothing if not a man of my word."

I poked him playfully in the chest, shaking my head. "That was hypothetical, like some time down the line in the future. I wasn't going to hold you to something you said when we were sex-drunk from vacation."

"Then look at me now." He tilted my chin, forcing me to look in his eyes. "I want you, this baby, and every other one that comes after it. That clear enough for you?"

"Yes." I laughed. "Yes, yes, yes. I'll marry you. But steady with the baby talk, Riley. We might not survive this one. It's half me and half you, dangerous combination."

"Hello?" He leaned in, chuckling. "Did you forget how awesome we both are? We're going to rock this gig."

And then I was lost.

His hands.

His mouth.

His body.

Consuming me as I burned inside and out, so happy it didn't seem fair.

"*Relations* in the bays are frowned upon." Mack cleared his throat. "If it's not one of you giving me a headache, it's the both of you."

Riley lifted his head, spinning me around so we could both face a smiling Mack. "Chief, got some good news."

"Yeah, can kind of see you're back together, North. Your tongue down her throat was the giveaway." Mack rolled his eyes.

Riley laughed, dropping a soft kiss on the top of my head. "Ha! True, but that wasn't what I was going to say. I was going to ask you if you wanted to be grandpa or pop? We can try them out around the station and see which you prefer, it's a big decision."

Mack's eyes widened, clearly only catching some of our emotional display. "You're pregnant?" he choked out.

"Not me personally, Mack. Doesn't work that way, we can have the talk later though. But Quinn is." His hands rested on my stomach, patting it gently. "We're having a baby."

Mack swallowed, walking up to Riley and cupping his shoulder and smiling. "Good work, kid. Now please, for all our sakes. Do not fuck it up."

Riley looked down at me, his grin bigger than the most perfect sunrise—and I should know because I've seen a few. "Not a chance."

If it had been an Instagram story, Riley would have gotten down on one knee between those two fire engines, their bright shiny paint providing the perfect contrast to his navy blue uniform. In his left hand would have been a huge diamond, the sparkle that would've rivaled the chrome from the engines, to which I would have shakily nodded yes. There would've been an embrace, dipping me carefully into a long passionate kiss, where heart eye emojis would have exploded across the screen before panning around to a wide-angle shot of the whole firehouse applauding our news.

But there was none of that.

And it couldn't have been more perfect.

There was no ring, no bended knee, no fanfare.

No photos, no sparkles or applause.

There was me and him, and the promise of forever.

It was if he saw inside my head and gave me exactly what I'd wanted.

Mack coming in at the end was a nice touch. Apparently after yelling at everyone to stop looking at us on the surveillance screens, he was coming to yell at us. Our baby news kind of took the wind out of his sails a little, which meant he didn't yell.

But that was where the congratulations ended.

The alarm sounded, the light above our heads turning red and before I wanted to, I had to kiss Riley goodbye.

He promised me he'd be safe, his hand lingering on my belly one last time and telling me he'd see me in the morning. And it was a promise I chose to believe.

My full heart took me all the way home, picking up tubs of ice cream—both vegan and regular—and spent the night with Karli who was already scheming a trip to Jersey to visit Hobby Lobby.

Apparently, in my absence, she'd started planning a baby shower, so imagine her surprise when she was going to have to add wedding shower as well. She couldn't have been more pleased, her adorable face giving me a smug grin as she pulled out a wedding magazine from behind her back.

It was her emergency—just in case—subscription she'd claimed. Telling me she'd been collecting them on the off chance Brad came to his senses and she needed to plan her own wedding. I wasn't convinced, but didn't care, happily flicking through the glossy pages and seeing exactly how my wedding *wasn't* going to be.

We ate ice cream and laughed, talking about how much things had changed in a short couple of months. She and Brad were finally going to be dating—my intervention apparently unnecessary, although I still claim partial victory. And I was engaged to an amazing man and pregnant with his child.

To think I'd been worried about committing to a pet. Clearly when I make the choice to jump into things, I did it headfirst.

My shift in focus for work also was on my mind. And while I absolutely wanted to do more feel good stuff and be selective of those shoots I took, Riley's words had stuck with me. Being seen, capturing memories, finding beauty in every day moments, and making people happy was important too. And every job, no matter how frivolous, had value.

Weird I'd needed someone else to point it out to me, and deep down, I know my dad would have felt the same way. My mother on the other hand—that was a challenge. She was ecstatic, assuming her only grandkids would be the three she had from Carrie, so was over the moon to hear my news.

Mother's intuition—and the fact I brought him home to meet her—had told her he was apparently the one. And while marriage and babies had never been a measuring stick she applied to me, all she wanted was for me to be happy. Who knew that those two things would be what it would take.

But it wasn't only that, I was happier in myself. Learning more about who I was and what I wanted, and learning what real fearlessness looked like.

It wasn't about not being scared.

It was about having that fear choking at your throat, and still taking that leap.

So that's what I did.

I felt the covers lift, Riley's warm body snuggling next to mine as his hands went straight to my slowly growing belly.

"Quinn."

His voice saying my name still gave me goosebumps.

"I have something for you." I felt his smile against my back.

I turned in his arms, wiggling my fingers to display the two rings he'd recently given me. Our engagement had been short—I know, there was a surprise—followed by a simple ceremony at the registry office. "Between the last name and the baby growing inside of me, I'd say you've given me enough."

He laughed, kissing me softly and then pulled out the red lacy panties I'd sent him almost an eternity ago. "When I got these and the note, I had known they weren't for me. It was part of the reason why I agreed to let Mack go in my place. But I kept thinking about what kind of woman would have sent them, the note being so adorable I almost felt guilty keeping it. So I figured after we met *her*, and the truth was revealed, I'd give them back."

"So why didn't you?" I asked, not having seen them since Mack shoved them into his pocket that day at the coffee shop.

"Because, after I met you, I was convinced that they *had* been for me." His lips brushed against mine. "That, and I didn't want to take a chance you'd send your crazy to someone else."

I scowled, Riley ignoring my sharp poke at his chest as he laughed before continuing. "I took them back from Mack so quickly, he thought he was getting mugged. And I kept them, for me as they were intended."

"Pretty sure of yourself, weren't you?" I rolled my eyes, still turned on by how cocky he was. "So now what? You're giving them back to me because they probably don't fit? Not very nice, Riley. My growing ass is entirely your fault."

He reached down, grabbing the ass in question. "I love your ass, and every other inch of your body. But that's not why I'm giving them back."

"Then why?" I arched into him, my whole body warming against his touch.

His lips skated across my throat. "Because I know your crazy is all mine, Quinn, and I don't need panties as a reminder."

Great.

So we both were crazy.

Poor kid didn't stand a chance.

"*You* send me crazy," I groaned, my fingers raking through his hair as his mouth did amazing things.

He chuckled, lifting his lips for a second before grinning. "But you sent me crazy first."

Epilogue

Riley

IT WAS LATE, the rain was beating against the bedroom window and I was missing Quinn.

She had a shoot in California and had only been gone since the morning, but I was itching for her to get home. I loved that she'd decided to go back to traveling sometimes, getting to tag along on some of her interesting adventures. No naked hot tubs in private jets just yet, but we'd visited some pretty cool places on her clients' dime.

My smile spread as my phone vibrated, her name lighting up my display. "Quinn," I murmured into the phone, letting my head fall against the pillow. "I was beginning to think you weren't going to call."

"Well, just trying to keep you on your toes." I could hear the smile in her voice. "Wouldn't want you to get bored."

I laughed, trying to keep my voice down. "Boredom and you wouldn't find themselves in the same sentence, beautiful. Tell me about your day."

She blew out a long, happy sounding breath, the rustle of sheets hinting she was getting into bed herself. "It was great.

We did some glamour photos for breast cancer survivors. It was really inspiring, and a little emotional to be honest."

"I'm sure it was great for them too, getting to feel special for the day. And I'm positive those photos would have been beautiful."

My wife was the most amazing woman I'd ever met, and she was talented beyond belief. But more than anything, she had an amazing heart and a smile that could change the world. It sucked being away from her, but I wasn't selfish enough to keep it just for myself.

"Thank you, Riley. It was great but I can't wait to come home."

My eyes glanced down at the sleeping beauty beside me and I felt a small pang of guilt. Before I'd asked Quinn to marry me, we had a small misunderstanding. It was after that that we promised to always tell the truth, for better or for worse.

"Quinn, full disclosure, I'm in bed with a gorgeous blond." My finger gently stroked her golden curls, careful not to wake her.

"You are such a sucker," she laughed. "You know she is more than capable of sleeping in her own bed."

"I can't help myself. She looks at me with those beautiful eyes and I can't tell her no. What was I supposed to do? I'm not a monster."

Hell, there wasn't a thing I'd deny our daughter, fuck knows she already had my heart. Between her and her mother, I was owned on every level, and I couldn't be happier.

"Riley, she hasn't even had her first birthday yet, and she has you wrapped around her little finger."

"Like you can talk?" I scoffed, knowing we were just as bad as each other. "How many unnecessary gifts do you have stuffed in your suitcase, Quinn? Can you say *excessive baggage charges*?"

"Stop it, mother's guilt is a real thing and I won't be shamed!" she chuckled. "How was Ava today? Please tell me she isn't walking yet, I don't think I could take it if I missed it."

"Not a chance, beautiful. I've carried her around the whole time; her feet barely touched the ground. She might be having her first steps soon, but not on my watch."

Quinn laughed, my chest warming at the sound. "You're sooooo bad. You know she's going to eventually grow up, and not only walk, but run."

I shook my head, my beautiful sleeping daughter safe by my side. "I don't know why you say such hurtful things, Quinn. I thought you loved me."

"I do love you, Riley. With every single fiber of my being."

Now that was something I would never get tired of hearing. And it didn't matter she was across the country when she was saying it, it was as real as if she was in the bed with me whispering it in my ear.

She was my person.

The one and only for me.

And we had a great fucking family.

Guess having such a shitty one first round was worth it, meant I hit the jackpot when I finally got my own. I didn't even hate my parents, I think they truly did their best. But what I had with Quinn and Ava was something I never could've imagined. Not something you could put into words either; was something you just had to feel.

"Right back at ya, Quinn. I love you too."

"Oh, before I forget, tomorrow night's Brad's bachelor party."

"I still can't believe he proposed. Who knew Panties Brad had it in him?" I chuckled, knowing I was probably going to have to stop calling him that when he moved in next door.

He was going to be my new neighbor, Karli's mostly absent sister finally biting the bullet and moving in with her boyfriend. Not that I'd seen much of Josie since moving into Quinn's apartment. She'd said hello briefly when I moved from Manhattan to Brooklyn, and I think gave us a baby present when Ava was born. Other than that, she was an enigma, checking in with her sister just enough so no one filed a missing person's report.

"Be nice," Quinn warned. "Besides, it's going to be Ava's first sleep over with my mom tomorrow. Guess who is going to get very lucky?"

Her little taunt went straight to my balls, making me as hard as a rock. We hadn't gotten a lot of alone time since Ava was born but we somehow made it work. Hell knows I'd gotten pretty good at fucking Quinn in the shower, or both of us struggling to keep our voices down during those quickies in the early mornings or late nights.

"You want to be pregnant again?" I half moaned into the phone. "Because I can pretty much guarantee I can make that happen."

"Not just yet so maybe we just practice. A LOT."

Yeah, that was a plan I could get behind.

"I like this plan. Go to sleep, sweetheart. I'll be at the airport in the afternoon to bring you home."

"Okay," she yawned into the phone. "Make sure you're *not* in your uniform. I don't want to get into trouble with airport security again."

The last time I'd met her at the airport was right before I had to go into work, my wife practically mauling me at baggage claim. Can't say I didn't enjoy it, even if it did earn us some sharp words. "How about this, I'll put my uniform on *after* I get home from Brad's party. And then let you get me out of it."

She yawned again, her drowsy voice turning me on more than it should. "And I'll put on your favorite panties."

Fuck.

I was so getting her pregnant.

My chest expanded, my heart feeling like it was too big to fit inside my ribs but knowing it was time to let her go. Just for the time being though, because I was going to get her right back.

"Love you forever, Quinn," I promised.

"Love you forever, Riley."

The End

To keep up to date with all T Gephart's news, appearances and releases, please subscribe to her mailing list (http://eepurl.com/bws5Av).

Also please consider leaving a review on your retailer of choice. They help the author and future readers and we're all eternally grateful.

Acknowledgements

As usual, thanks to my family—Gep, Jenna, Liam and Woodley. I know you don't read my books—or see the acknowledgement—but I honestly couldn't write a book without thanking you. Hopefully you feel my gratitude, and most importantly, know how much you all mean to me.

HUGE thank you to Kelly Elliott, who has the kindest heart and the brightest smile. I adore you. You not only listen to my crazy, but actively support it. This is your book. For appreciating all my hairbrained ideas, and not only *not* judging me but loving me all the same. I hope I still make you laugh twenty years from now.

Thank you to my extended family and friends for all the love, patience and support. My life is better with you in it even if I'm irritable and moody when I'm juggling deadlines.

Thanks to MY Gayle Williams who I haven't managed to freak out just yet. I'm positive many people want to steal you because you're so awesome, but I refuse to give you up. Penny Rudge will hold my earrings while I fight for you because she is that kind of friend. #FYMForever #TellYourFriends

Thanks to Team Brower—Kimberly, Aimee and Caroline. Love you guys!

Thank you to Nichole Strauss from Insight Editing who will one day get a manuscript that isn't crazy. You should probably call someone and let them know I was abducted by the aliens.

LOL Thanks for continuing to work with me and making my words sparkle.

Thank you so much to MK—I LOVE YOUR BETA NOTES. You are without a doubt amazing. Even if we don't agree, I get you, and you get me.

Thanks to Elaine York from Allusion Graphics LLC Publishing and Book Formatting. This is #2…. YAY, look at us. Thanks for making my pages pretty.

HANG LE! LORDY! Is there a word beyond, thanks? Because that's what we need to insert here. Your covers, graphics are amazing—and I couldn't imagine publishing without you—but not as awesome as your friendship. Thanks for everything, most of all, just being YOU.

Thank you to my amazing proofreaders Rosa and Lisa! Thanks for your sharp eyes and laser focus!

Special thanks to my author friends who I see nowhere enough. I'm giddy being able to count you as friends, and love the time I spend with you either between the pages of your work or when we finally see each other. I'll be the one in the Koala suit. #NoShame.

A million thanks, and special hugs to all the bloggers, reviewers, bookgramers, group admins and promoters, who read, promote, review, and share my work. It's getting crowded out there, and you just can literally choose anyone. So incredibly honored and humbled you included me. Thank you xxx

Thank you Liz, MJ and Jillian at 1001 Dark Nights.

THANK YOU TO THE T GEPHART REVIEW CREW AND ENTOURAGE. Love all of you, thanks for your messages and making me laugh. Thanks for the reviews, shares, Skarsgard pics, memes, messages and just general mayhem. How boring would it be if we were just a book group? LMAO

And lastly and no less importantly, thank you to YOU. My readers. You are important, and every single one of you matters.

About the Author

T Gephart is a *USA Today* and International bestselling author from Melbourne, Australia.

With an approach to life that is somewhat unconventional, she prefers to fly by the seat of her pants rather than adhere to some rigid roadmap. Her lack of "plan" has resulted in a rather interesting and eclectic resume, which reads more like the fiction she writes than an actual employment history. She'd tell you all about it, but the statute of limitations hasn't expired yet. But all those crazy twists and turns have led her to a career she loves—writing romantic comedy.

When she isn't filling pages with sassy and sexy characters with attitude, she's living her own reality show in the 'burbs of Melbourne with her American husband, two teenage children, and her fur child—Woodley.

She loves adventure, to laugh, travel, and strives to live her life to the fullest.

Connect with T

tgephart.com
Facebook (https://www.facebook.com/tgephartauthor)
Goodreads
Twitter (https://twitter.com/tinagephart)

Books by this Author
The Lexi Series
Lexi
A Twist of Fate
Twisted Views: Fate's Companion
A Leap of Faith
A Time for Hope

The Power Station Series
High Strung
Crash Ride
Back Stage

The Black Addiction Series
Slide
Sticks
Stand

#1 Series
#1 Crush

#1 Player
#1 Rival
#1 Lie
#1 Muse
#1 Love

Collision Series
Train Wreck
Car Crash

Hot in the City Series
Send Me Crazy

Standalones
The Fall
One-Night Stand-In
Viral

www.ingramcontent.com/pod-product-compliance
Lightning Source LLC
Chambersburg PA
CBHW050142120726
47903CB00002B/458